CHIEF OF SCOUTS

>>>>>>>>>>>>>>>>>>>>>>

DON BENDELL

A SIGNET BOOK

SIGNET
Published by the Penguin Group
Penguin Books USA Inc., 375 Hudson Street,
New York, New York 10014, U.S.A.
Penguin Books Ltd, 27 Wrights Lane,
London W8 5TZ, England
Penguin Books Australia Ltd, Ringwood,
Victoria, Australia
Penguin Books Canada Ltd, 10 Alcorn Avenue,
Toronto, Ontario, Canada M4V 3B2
Penguin Books (N.Z.) Ltd, 182–190 Wairau Road,
Auckland 10, New Zealand

Penguin Books Ltd, Registered Offices:
Harmondsworth, Middlesex, England

First published by Signet, an imprint of Dutton Signet,
a division of Penguin Books USA Inc.

First Printing, September, 1993
10 9 8 7 6 5 4 3 2 1

Chris Colt saw Custer across the river and waved his arms frantically. Both of Chris's wrists bled badly from the tight rawhide bonds he had worked loose. Crazy Horse charged across the river, whooping and hollering, puzzling the camp defenders.

When the warrior was upon Chris Colt, the two men gave out loud yells as Crazy Horse dove headfirst from his horse's back and crashed into Chris Colt, both men rolling over and over. They both jumped up in fighting stances, shaking their heads to clear the cobwebs out. Chris's left eye started swelling, as did Crazy Horse's, where they had slammed their faces into each other during the Oglala war hero's dive. Crazy Horse nodded to men behind Colt, and a group of warriors approached and knocked him to the ground. He was tied, once again, with rawhide thongs, with several guards watching him.

Colt and Crazy Horse stared at each other for a minute, a pleading look on Chris's face. Crazy Horse, followed by hundreds of Sioux and Cheyenne, charged down upon Custer's column.

CHIEF OF SCOUTS

This book is dedicated to Roy Rogers, Gene Autry, Jock O'Mahoney, Lash LaRue, Hopalong Cassidy, Red Ryder, The Three Mesquiteers, Guy Madison, Hugh O'Brian, Clint Walker, James Arness, James Garner, Clayton Moore, John Wayne, Glenn Ford, Jimmy Stewart, Kirk Douglas, Joel McCrea, Henry Fonda, Iron Eyes Cody, Chuck Connors, Duncan Renaldo, and all the other men who served as hero/role models for me as a young boy. Trying to sometimes emulate your characters saw me through a tough war and many tough times. Thanks for all the hours of entertainment. May some more kids be positively affected by future heroes of your ilk and by the true American cowboy.

Listen, Little Children

Now listen, little children, as
  I speak of Father Sun:
He made the mountains and the trees.
  He made the rivers run.

Your fathers climbed on lofty peaks
  To look upon his face,
But you just play Nintendo games
  And dream of flight in space.

The copper-red that's in your blood
  Has faded with the years.
The drumming beat of bisons' hooves
  Don't echo in your ears.

The strength of Brother Eagle, and
  The taste of mountain streams,
Or the bugling of wapiti;
  Are not there in your dreams.

You have not watched the prairie wind
  That's dancing in the grain
Or smelled the misty river fog
  Or tasted summer rain.

You have not fought the mighty bear.
  You have not counted coups.
Now listen, little children, please.
  I'll tell you what to do.

The Keeper of Dreams is crying.
  He wants you to be freed,
Not shackled by the white man's ways.
  Like alcohol or greed.

Please listen, little children, now,
 You heed my iron words:
You cannot soar on eagle's wings
 With hearts like little birds.

Oh, Manitou is watching you,
 So honor Mother Earth,
And walk the warrior's spirit path,
 Like those before your birth.

—Don Bendell
 from *Songs of the Warrior*

Chapter 1

>>>>>>>>>>>>>>>>>>>>>>>

Colt

Sarah Guthrie coughed on thick black smoke and quickly opened her eyes. The smoke passed across her naked body and suddenly rose with the angry wind. With her eyes opened, she couldn't help but notice the bloody corpses of her son and husband on the front porch of the burning cabin, and she vomited again. Sarah closed her eyes again and bit her lip, trying to ignore the grunts of the warrior on top of her, or the cheers of the rest of his war party. He was the third rapist, but Sarah decided she would survive this and not let them hear her cry out. She felt the warm, sticky blood running down the side of her head. They had staked out her arms and ankles near the well, so she couldn't even reach up to the nasty cut in her straw-colored hair.

The brave grunted, and she choked back tears once again.

She looked up at the wild face of Two Bears, as he pulled off his breechcloth and entered her. He seemed the most aggressive of the Crow warriors, and the most muscular. He looked crazy to Sarah, and again she considered the possibility that they would kill her like the rest of her family. One part of her wanted that, but Sarah was a pioneer woman, a woman of the West, and she really wanted to survive.

The mountains far off to the west had a purple tint to them, with patches of green here and there. The prairie in between would seem just a mile or two to a visiting easterner, but it was more than twenty miles to the high ground. The space between the cabin and the war party contained a lot of sand, rocks, sagebrush, cacti, greasewood, mesquite, rattlers, bunch grass, and one lone rider, a white man.

The eight other Crows sat their ponies, laughing and cheering while Two Bears raped the well-built woman. Their graying leader, Thunder Talk, turned his head and spotted the rider approaching in the distance. The other braves looked that way too, and a murmur started among them. Preoccupied, Two Bears didn't notice their noises or the approaching rider.

Even at a distance, they could tell he was a white man. Tall, he rode a large, muscular lineback buckskin gelding. Little puffs of dust flew out to the side every time the cantering horse's feet hit the ground. The man seemed to get much larger with each step. As he rode closer, the Crows saw the chiseled features on the man's face, and the copper hue of his skin from many hours under the sun. He wore jeans and a flop-brimmed leather hat, but his shirt was a porcupine quill-decorated Minniconjou Lakotah war shirt, and he wore Sioux moccasins.

Amazed by the sudden interference of this brazen white man, the braves stood transfixed and open-mouthed in wonder, maybe awe. Finally, a few of their number snapped out of the temporary trance. Several warriors aimed Henry rifles at the white-eyes, but a signal from Thunder Talk made them put the guns down. The old war chief was amazed by this white man's bravado. He just kept coming, seemingly not even noticing them, but he had a great purpose in his bearing.

They didn't know that his mouth was totally parched and dry, and he felt like it was stuffed with cotton every time he attempted to swallow. They didn't know that he could feel his heart pounding in his neck and ears, but just didn't give a damn. If they killed him, he decided, he would just have to die. He was frightened, all right, but he would not let them know it. He was a man with a mission. He had a job to do, and that was to kill Two Bears in hand-to-hand combat. He didn't want to do it to prove he could conquer fear. He didn't want to do it because he wanted to become known as a hero. He simply *had* to do it, because of a code he lived by, a code that was more important than common sense.

They all could see now that the man wore a pearl-handled Colt .44 in a low-slung holster, with a large bowie knife in a beaded sheath on the other hip. The worn stock of a Henry .44 repeater stuck out of the case under his right leg.

In the throes of passion, Two Bears, the current rapist, was totally unaware of the man's approach. He didn't even hear the grunts and gasps from the other warriors, as the white man slid to a stop right in front of Thunder Talk and dismounted without looking at anyone but Two Bears. The white man briefly glanced at Runs

Too Hard, the youngest of the group, as he handed the lad the reins of the sinewy buckskin horse. Shocked like the others at this brazen display, the teenaged warrior accepted the reins and stared, then glared, at the white-eyes.

Finally the white man looked up at Thunder Talk, as he removed his gun belt and tossed it to the old man.

He stuck his razor-sharp Bowie knife in his belt behind him and stormed over to Two Bears, grabbing the hair that hung over the muscular brave's forehead.

He yanked the brave up and back, as the white woman opened her eyes in even greater shock. Seeing the tall white man, a new sense of survival and relief swept over Sarah, and she fainted. She came to in seconds, however, and watched with renewed hope as the white man tore into the rapist.

Thunder Talk just grinned and watched as the gargantuan brave, Two Bears, flew into a complete rage, attacking the white man with a flying head butt and a loud Crow war cry. The white man simply sidestepped and let the six-foot-five-inch brave fall on his face. Two Bears jumped up, lips curling back over his teeth. He groped for his knife, then suddenly noticed that he was naked. His eyes went to the breechcloth and blade that lay near the naked woman.

The white man walked forward, and his right foot suddenly lashed out, the instep smashing the brave's groin. This was followed by a quick left-right combination of punches to the jaw. Two Bears' head snapped quickly with each blow, and the Crow went up on his toes.

Bleeding profusely from the mouth, Two

Bears lunged to his feet, swaying slightly as he faced his deadly foe. He took a step and the cowboy's foot snapped out, cracking against the brave's left kneecap. The white man then smashed a right uppercut into the Indian's solar plexus, then a left-right-left combination into the man's temples, sending the brave unconscious to the ground.

The white man heard several guns cocking, as he approached the prostrate brave. He spit on the man, then walked to the well and retrieved a wooden bucket of water. The rugged but handsome cowboy walked back to the warrior with all the others staring in wonder and poured the bucket on him.

Two Bears sat up quickly and shook his head from side to side. He jumped to his feet and looked at the white man, who simply grinned. Next, the white-eyes did something even more brash, courageous, and totally unexpected. He slowly walked over and retrieved Two Bears' knife, tossing it to him. The cowboy heard several grunts of approval and admiration coming from his foe's buddies. Two Bears didn't care. Nobody could beat him with a knife.

The cowboy was beyond fear now. The shaking legs would come later, when he was alone. He was accomplishing his mission, and thus felt confident of this battle's outcome. After it was over he knew he might have to have another one, but he also knew Indians well enough to know that all tribes greatly respected and admired acts of supreme courage and heroism.

Two Bears faced the white man, while holding his knife firmly, blade up, ready to thrust or slash. The cowboy hadn't reached back for his own knife, but the Crow didn't care. He just wanted to kill this intruder who had made him lose face, and who was frightening him more than he had ever been in his life. This white-eyes had just ridden up into their midst while they were taking a white woman, after killing her braves and burning down her lodge. Either the big man was crazy, or his medicine was very strong.

The worried brave now gave his white-skinned enemy a queer look, as the man pulled little pieces of metal from his leggings. The cowboy held out several twenty-dollar gold pieces and some more change in the palm of his hand, and he smiled at the brave. Then he simply closed his hand and stood his ground as the giant Indian inched forward, the knife looming menacingly large.

The trepidation kept building in Two Bears until he finally lunged, letting out a courage-building war whoop at the same time. Unfortunately for him, however, the cowboy's hand whipped out, throwing all the coins into the brave's face like a mini shotgun blast. Every coin hit him hard in his scarred, copper-colored face, and despite his many years of training he winced with the pain. Two Bears felt a vice-like grip grab around his knife-hand's forearm, and he blinked his eyes open.

The white man yanked the large brave up close, and while his right hand whipped out from behind his back, bowie knife in its firm grip, he thrust the knife, blade up, into the brave's abdomen. Two Bears' mouth made several contortions as the white man pulled him closer still, holding the knife in his belly as he began to slowly twist it.

The white man said, "I am called Wamble Uncha, One Eagle, and I have killed you. My white name is Chris Colt, and I make war on men, not on women and children."

He yanked the knife sideways and out, and the brave's intestines spilled into his own hands. Two Bears, now in shock, looked down at his own insides. His body convulsed several times, then stopped forever. The white-eyes bent over and wiped the blood on his blade onto the dead Indian's bicep, took one last look at Two Bears' corpse, and spit on it.

Then he walked to the woman, who had awakened from her faint, and cut her loose, helping her to her feet. Sarah wavered, but steeled herself and walked beside him to the chief. She couldn't even swallow. The man then took off his quilled war shirt and placed it around the nude woman's shoulders. His shirt was so large that it covered all her exposed private areas adequately.

She and the Crow braves admired the rock-hard sinew and muscles that rippled all over Colt's upper torso, but what amazed them were the numerous scars on his body. Words didn't need to be spoken, for the scars on his body told an entire story, like an Indian's winter count—his calendar—painted on a tanned and stretched-out hide.

On his pectoral muscles, right above the nipples, there were telltales scars of the sundance ceremony, in which a shaman pierces a warrior's breasts with the talons of an eagle and places wooden pegs through the holes. Then, staring up at the sun through the hole in the sundance lodge's roof, the warrior dances in circles, with leather thongs attached to the wooden pegs and going up over a pole in the lodge's ceiling and back down to a number of heavy buffalo skulls on the floor. He dances and dances until he falls in a faint and has a vision. The brave is then lifted up by the thongs and spun in circles, while the flesh and pectoral muscles stretch out grotesquely.

Right above the sundance ceremony scar on Colt's left breast there was a bullet-hole scar, with a larger exit hole in the back of his shoulder. There was another bullet-hole scar low down on the right side of his abdomen, and a small slash scar going horizontally across his washboard stomach, just above the navel.

Finally, there were four long claw-mark scars running down his very large right bicep. They had to have been made by either a bear or a mountain lion.

The white man reached out for his gun and the chief, still overwhelmed, handed it to him. He buckled it on and slipped the knife into the sheath, after further wiping the blade on his leg. He started for his horse, but now was stopped by the other angry warriors. The old chief rode in front of him.

"I am Thunder Talk of the Crow nation!" the man said in a loud, booming voice.

The white man said, "I am Christopher Columbus Colt, Chris Colt, and my work here is finished. I will take this woman and leave."

The chief stopped Chris by pointing his rifle at the brave man and cocking it. Chris felt the blood drain from his face, but tried to hide any fear.

Thunder Talk said, "You killed my best warrior! You will die here, Chris Colt!"

Colt stared at him and said calmly, "Then, old warrior, you and I will sing our death songs here together, and some of your braves will die with us. My fight was with him, but the woman and I will leave, or we will die here with you and your brothers. My knife is a lightning bolt, and my guns talk much thunder. I can go, or we can die; these are my words of death, but they are words of iron. The choice is yours, old man."

Thunder Talk grinned. "You are named well, One Eagle, for you are not meek like the birds who fly in flocks. But why did you kill Two Bears?"

Chris looked away, then back into the war chief's eyes.

He said, "My wife was Lakotah, of the Minniconjou tribe, your enemies, and so was my baby daughter. I scouted for the cavalry, like many of your braves do. That man and three others came to my cabin while I was away. They took my wife and killed her. They killed my baby, too. I tracked each man and killed him. Now I have killed the last man. There is a wolf in my belly and a pain in my heart. I will take this woman and go, find food, and rest. Look into her eyes, old warrior. You have already killed her, and you have taken all the medicine from your enemy here." Chris looked at the bloody, burned corpses of Sarah's husband and son.

The chief looked over and simply nodded at Chris. Then the gray-haired leader spoke. "You speak of scouting for the long-knives. You truly are a strongheart, but why do you scout against your own brothers?"

Chris Colt looked at the far-off "Shining Mountains," as the Indians called them, known to white men as the Big Horn Mountains.

"It is a long story, Thunder Talk," Chris replied, "and better spoken of at a lodge fire while passing a pipe."

Thunder Talk spoke again. "Two Bears was not of our lodges, and so his friends. If they were of my circle you would be screaming now, asking me to shoot you."

"Old Thunder Talk," Chris replied, "I believe you that I would be dying now, but I would not be screaming."

"It is so," the old chief said. "You are indeed a warrior. Take the squaw and go."

Chris said, "She is a woman, not a squaw," making reference to the derisive term *squaw*, which actually described a female's genitalia.

Thunder Talk laughed and said, "Colt, you are like the mighty oak which does not bend even in the strongest wind. Yes, she is a woman. Now take her and go, for I do not know how long I can make cool river water flow through the flesh of these young bucks, instead of the hot rocks and mud that runs through their veins when their ponies tails are tied." His reference was to tying one's horse's tail into a knot while on the warpath.

Chris Colt said, "You are not only a warrior of many years, but very wise. The Great Mystery must surely smile upon you for your wisdom."

The chief straightened his shoulders back a little and puffed his chest out, grunting pride and approval. Chris hoped that his last words would buy them a little more time before the old man finally gave in and let the young bucks go after the pair.

The youngest warrior, Runs Too Hard, now felt he had to strut his stuff, for he had been suckered into holding this enemy's horse while Colt killed his hero. He let out a war whoop, drew back his bow, and fired an arrow into a small hand-carved pot full of flowers on the front porch. This show of bravado was supposed to frighten the white-eyes, but Chris Colt's hand flashed in a blur and the Colt .44 boomed. The arrow and flowerpot disappeared in a shower of splinters and dirt. The braves stared, as a number of colored flower petals swirled to the ground and blew across the bloody porch.

Again humiliated, Runs Too Hard bared his teeth in anger and tried to bring up his bow. This time, he would simply shoot the white-eyes through the breast. How could he know that this enemy's uncle was Samuel Colt, founder of Colt Firearms and inventor of the many famous boomsticks used by the whites? How was he to know that this large white brave had started to shoot pistols and rifles before he'd even attended school back in Ohio?

Runs Too Hard almost grinned, as he knew he would best this enemy with a surprise shot. As a boy growing up, not many winters earlier, he and the other boys in his band had played a game where they walked through the thickets by the river. They had to carry their bows and arrows in the same hand, without having an arrow ready to fire. They would then see who could shoot the most rabbits, if any, when they spooked them from the underbrush. Runs Too Hard always won, several times shooting rabbits that were closer to other boys who couldn't get an arrow flying quickly enough.

He would send an arrow through this man's breast, then take out his heart and carry it in his left hand into their village, the white-eyes' bloody scalp hanging from the end of his powerful bow.

The arrow wasn't even at quarter-draw when the shot boomed and Runs Too Hard felt something slam into his head, and heard the other Crows begin to laugh. He wondered why they would laugh at the sight of him being killed by the enemy, but the young lad was in a daze. He shook his head and began to understand what had happened.

He had tried to draw an arrow against the killer of Two Bears, but the man's boom-stick had flashed out quickly and had spoken with a yell. The bullet from its muzzle had shattered his bow just above the handle, the top limb of the partially drawn bow flying up and smacking him in the head, while the bottom part struck him across the left kneecap. The two bow limbs were still attached together by the bowstring, which now hung across his shoulder.

He looked into the smiling face of Chris Colt, then at the smoke coming from the barrel of his pistol. Runs Too Hard knew the man was not going to shoot again, so he would now be shamed by all the fellow warriors whose approval he wanted so badly. He hated this white man, and he knew that someday he would kill him.

Chris had picked up his gold coins when he'd wiped the blood from his knife, and he now tossed one to Thunder Talk. He lifted Sarah up with little effort and placed her crosswise in front of him on the saddle. Thunder Talk raised his hand and Chris nodded, then wheeled his horse and squeezed his calves against the big gelding's flanks. They took off at a slow trot.

Sarah started to sob, but Chris warned, "Don't cry, ma'am. We're not out of this yet."

She straightened up and stared off at the horizon as he rode away from her homestead. When she started to look back over his shoulder, he stopped her.

"Don't look back, ma'am. You can look forward to the horizon, but don't look back. You'll see nothing but pain."

She whispered, "What about burying my husband and son?"

She started sobbing, but caught herself.

"Ma'am, it won't make any difference to them, now," Chris said softly. "And if we do, you and I will die, too. We might anyway."

"Do you think so?"

"Yes, ma'am," Chris replied. "Thunder Talk won't be able to hold back those bucks. They'll be coming along eventually."

"We're riding double. They'll catch us," she said, a chill in her spine now.

"Maybe not," Colt said. "We're over the rise now. Ma'am, I'm sorry, but if you need to cry, do it now and get it over with. I need you to be tough and clear-headed later, if we're to survive."

She looked up at his chiseled features and gave him a blank stare. Suddenly, she burst into tears and threw her head against his massive chest. Racking sobs came from her in waves. Chris Colt's big right hand came up and softly stroked her hair. She cried harder. Secretly, he had often wanted to do just what she was doing now, and this was one of those times, but Chris hadn't been raised that way. A time or two he did, though, privately shed a tear, but only when he controlled the conditions. Chris realized that it was a natural act, and could even make you feel better at times.

They rode like that for another half-hour, with her still crying, but it finally tapered off.

"I'm sorry, Mr. Colt," she said. "My name is Sarah, by the way. Sarah Guthrie."

"Call me Chris, ma'am. Don't worry. I haven't seen sign of them coming, yet, and I still have a few tricks up my sleeve."

They rode into a narrow gulch that ran crosswise of their path toward the mountains. One quarter-mile down, the gulch widened out and deepened. Sarah could now see the thin ribbon of a stream far down below them, and figured that was where he was headed. Numerous slashes in the ground cut down into the sides of this gulch, and the possibility of ambush lay everywhere. About halfway down to the stream there was a very long dead cottonwood log, which stretched out from the east.

As they approached it Chris said, "See that log down there?"

"Yes."

"When we ride by it, I'm not going to stop," Chris said. "I'm going to swing you down with my left arm, and you need to walk to the end of the log and wait for me."

Sarah whimpered, "I can't, Chris. If they get their hands on me again . . ."

"I know you're scared," he said firmly. "So am I, but there's no other way. I'll come and get you, but I have to throw them off our trail."

"Maybe they won't follow us," she said hopefully.

"Maybe eagle's will start flying backwards," he replied. "Get ready."

They came to the log and Sarah held onto Colt's ax-handle-like forearm while he swung her off the saddle onto the log. He turned his head and nodded at her, as she looked after him with a frightened faraway look in her eyes.

He kicked his heels to the horse as the trail narrowed down and steepened. The big dun's rear end almost slid on the ground as he plunged down the path. Chris figured, with the deep sand in the gulch's bottom, the Crow would have trouble telling that the horse's load had been lightened. He knew they would assume he was heading west toward the relative safety of the mountains, so he would make it look that way. While they headed toward what they thought would be his destination, he would try to put the slip on them and go a different direction. It would take him miles and several days out of the way, but that was a hell of a lot more convenient than closing your eyes and holding your breath forever. Chris Colt had two advantages on this day; one, he was a trained and experienced warrior, and two, he could backtrack the two-day old pheasant's flight trail through the sky after a major storm.

The big horse seemed to sense Colt's desperation, and stepped out with more urgency now. They plunged down as quickly as possible, and within fifteen minutes were in the knee-deep stream. Chris knew that whoever it was who'd said you can lose someone by walking down a stream was either full of bull or a dude. Footprints in a clear stream bottom hold for a while. Besides that, many rocks get turned over and scarred by the horse's hooves. Chris counted on that.

He went west up the stream toward the mountains, but finally climbed out on a grassy area, passing up more obvious spots where tracks could be hidden easier. That was what Colt counted on. The Crow would look more carefully at the most obvious places to leave the stream and would probably pay very little attention to this one.

Leaving his horse ground-reined beyond the grassy area and in a little groove just beyond, an apparent tributary course when the stream overflowed its banks during the rainy season, Chris climbed from the saddle and pulled his extra cotton shirt out of his bedroll. Crawling forward on his hands and knees, he carefully dried the wet grass with his shirt, checking to be sure he had left no threads. He carefully covered each hoofprint in the soft ground with dirt he brought from the depression beyond the grass, then he manipulated the grass back into place. This took Colt a long time to accomplish, but he knew being thorough would save his life, and more importantly, the woman's. If it hadn't been for her he might have just set up an ambush and taken on the braves, but he could not let his ego get in the way of her safety. Satisfied that he had done a thorough job, he moved his horse beyond the depression and covered up those tracks as well.

He kept looking back up the giant slice in the earth they had come through, but he saw no sign of the warriors. He knew that they would be coming. Chris reached into his saddlebags and pulled out four patches of leather with strings around the edges. One at a time, he slipped these over the horse's hooves, laced the thongs through the top of each one as a drawstring, and tied them in place.

He mounted up and rode slowly along a long, flat rock outcropping. He went from this to each new outcropping with as few steps as possible in sand or soft dirt. In each instance where he had to, however, he dropped down off the horse and cleared away the tracks again. Chris passed the area where he had originally entered the stream and kept going up the watercourse.

One quarter-mile along, he found a flat spot, took the horse back, and spurred him toward the far bank. Reaching a ten-foot-high cut in the banks on both sides, he leaned out over the horse's neck and let the buckskin fly. The big horse cleared it with inches to spare and Colt reined him up on the far bank and dismounted, patting the steed on his muscular neck.

"Good boy, Nighthawk," Chris said. "Let me wipe out some more tracks, then you got a bunch of work to do, buddy."

Chris started covering his trail again. He knew how to track as well or better than any of the Crows following them. The best trackers can read a whole story when they follow a man, and he wanted the Crows to think he didn't know as much as he did. He had gotten out of the stream one time, crossed it twice, then reentered it, just to make them laugh at his feeble attempt to hide his trail. Thunder Talk would know better, but Chris figured the old man might keep quiet anyway, mildly amused at the ambitious charging on of his young warriors.

They would assume that the only safe place for him to go would be to the mountains in the west, so Colt would double back and actually hide within sight of Sarah's burned-out home. He would salvage as much as he could there and hide out in the rock outcroppings overlooking her place. It was a crazy idea, but this wasn't the first time he had been pursued, and he still wore his hair. In the meantime the Crows would probably keep pushing on west, after making sure he had headed upstream. Many times when you track someone you only need to get their general direction and figure out where the person is headed. After that, you can just go there, occasionally checking the trail to be sure. Chris figured by the time the Crows checked the trail and couldn't find tracks, they would figure that enough time had passed for the water to have washed out the sign. They'd continue in the creek.

Leather boots still on Nighthawk's black hooves, Chris Colt rode over a steep ridge coming off one of the many chutes running down into the gulch. They scrambled up that, down into and across the chute, and up the other ridge. By the third chute the big horse was sweating and panting heavily. Chris looked back, seeing the little stream far below and behind them, and he gave Nighthawk a pat of encouragement and kept on.

It took over an hour, but he finally made it to the slash where Sarah awaited him. She was now three hundred feet lower than Chris, and didn't even know that he was in the narrow gulch up above her. He spurred the big buckskin downhill, and she finally turned her head and saw him coming. He looked to his right, up at the head of the big gulch, but fortunately they hadn't entered the cut yet. When he was one hundred feet away, he started walking the horse forward while signaling her to walk from one clump of mesquite to some other clumps.

She clambered up the arroyo, and soon he was grabbing her forearms again and swinging her onto the saddle behind him. She wrapped her arms around his neck and clung to him as though there were no tomorrow.

"I was so scared that you weren't coming back!" she said, her eyes shut tightly and her voice full of tension.

He kept tapping Nighthawk's ribs with his heels, encouraging the lathered horse up the cut. The higher they went, the more treacherous the terrain got and the steeper the cut. The dun seemed to sense that his master's life depended on him, or at least Chris Colt liked to *feel* that he did.

Chris felt a twinge of guilt, though, as he thought back to some years before. He had been a young teenager then, and had gone off to fight in the Civil War. Having grown up in Cuyahoga Falls, Ohio, the son of an itinerant shoemaker, Chris had longed for excitement his whole childhood. He desperately wanted to explore the wild lands of the Far West he had read and heard so much about.

His father was poor, and he had leaned heavily on Chris for support after the lad's mother had died of consumption when Chris was ten. The boy had twice been allowed to visit his uncle, Samuel Colt, in Hartford, Connecticut, and he

was taught just about everything a little boy
could learn about firearms. The curious young
lad had won the heart of every gunsmith and
expert working for Colonel Colt. The boy was
like a sponge, absorbing knowledge about the
most important of a cowboy's tools of trade.

When his father's estranged brother, Samuel
Colt, died in 1863, Chris entered the Ohio National Guard on a whim and went off to fight
with Company G of the 171st Regiment in the
Civil War. Although only fourteen years old at
the time, he was able to pass easily.

When the war was over Chris felt decades
older, and he was so anxious to get back to
northeastern Ohio that he killed a horse by riding it too hard. Trying to swim the exhausted
steel-dust mare across the Tuscarawas River in
southern Ohio, the young Chris Colt watched
the animal drown because its intestines had
knotted up while it tried to swim. He swam to
the bank and lay there crying for an hour, he
felt so bad. The young veteran vowed that he
would never, *ever* mistreat an animal again. His
horse would get fed and watered before he did,
and would be treated like a friend instead of a
tool, which was the way so many treated their
animals.

He knew, on the other hand, that Nighthawk
could run many other horses into the ground.
The horse plunged up the narrow cut, stones and
dirt rolling downhill behind his powerful hind
feet. Fifty feet from the top the land narrowed
into a steep slash through rock, with the cut
coming out on top onto prairie, slightly to the
south of where Colt had ridden away from the

Indians. From here, Sarah's ranch lay one half-hour to the east.

Just as they had started to scramble up into the last slot near the top, Chris saw a bunch of little dots entering the big gulch. He was positive he could not be seen by the braves. He was also quite sure that he had created a false trail that would take the crows so many miles away from Sarah and him that eventually they would lose all interest in pursuing them.

They came out of the slot with one final lunge from the sweaty horse, and Chris Colt immediately dismounted and had Sarah do the same. He started walking toward her burned-out ranch, the horse following. Again Sarah started to cry.

"Why?" she asked. "You told me not to look back."

"Ma'am, I'm sorry, but this is the last place on earth that those Crows will look for us," Colt said. "We'll see if we can find any supplies, and some clothes for you."

With that, she looked down at herself and saw that her pubic area was showing where Colt's buckskin shirt separated. Red-faced, she pulled the sides together. She couldn't tell if he had noticed, but Chris paused and walked back to his horse and removed a piggin string from a tie-down on his saddle. He handed the braided leather piggin string to Sarah and walked back to Nighthawk.

While she tied the thong around her waist as a belt and drew the shirt together, he removed his saddle and blanket from the horse. Next, he grabbed some bunch grass and started rubbing the horse's leathered-up chest, belly, thighs, and neck. He also wiped down the sweaty area on the big dun's back where the saddle had been. Sarah came over and helped him wipe the horse down. Following that, Chris led Nighthawk to a small dried-up buffalo wallow and right away the horse started to paw the ground. He didn't have to be told what to do. The buckskin went down on his knees and lay on his side. He then twisted his body and kicked his legs, rolling over in the dust. He rolled three times in the dirt, then stood again to shake his whole body, a cloud of dust whirling away into the prairie wind. Chris led him back to the saddle and re-saddled him, and they continued back toward the ranch.

"Don't we have to hurry?" the worried woman asked.

"No, ma'am," Chris said. "Those young bucks won't find our trail, except by accident maybe. This horse has worked really hard today, and we'll let him rest while we can."

They walked toward the relative safety of the home that, hours before, had become a living hell for the blond-haired woman. The home that had been her safe haven for so long. The home where she had shared love with her man. The home where she had raised and nurtured her innocent son. The home where she would now have to bury her family—and her past.

As Sarah plodded along, one foot in front of the other, she thought back to memories of her home.

One memory stood out, for some reason. Sarah's husband, John, had been a solid man. Not handsome, rich, or even with much of a sparkling personality, but simply a solid man. That was what she had wanted and needed. He was the kind of man the West had been built on. John had never even really proposed to Sarah. They'd met and courted in a backward sort of way.

One night, sitting on the veranda of her parents' house in Cheyenne, Wyoming, Sarah had finally said, "John, I'm wasting away waiting on you to propose to me. When are we going to get married?"

He looked shocked for a few seconds, but finally said, "How about June? The crops will be started good then, and the calving will be over."

John walked over to her mother's flower bush and picked half-a-dozen pink roses and handed them to Sarah. It was such a small gesture, but so sweetly out of character for a man who was more comfortable turning around a breeched calf, plowing a field, or repairing a harness. It brought tears to Sarah's eyes, but she immediately started to act practical again, the way John liked her the best.

"June it is," Sarah replied firmly, and she and her mother started making plans for the wedding.

Sarah and John had been married for five years, and their life had been such a struggle and such a nose-to-the-grindstone existence that even she had forgotten their anniversary. Sarah had made a big supper for her four-year-old boy and her husband. They had baked potatoes, fresh salad, steaks, and beans. They came in from the barn and John was acting funny, and little Johnny kept giggling. Sarah walked outside to get the apple pie she had cooling off on top of the butter churn, and walked back into the cabin to a big surprise. Tears flooded her eyes when she saw a vaseful of pink roses and a store-bought gingham dress lying across the back of her chair.

John arose and said, "Happy Anniversary, Sarah."

Sarah thought of that moment and fell onto the dry prairie, her sides heaving with sobs. The rough-skinned but gentle hands of Chris Colt helped her up, and she buried her face in his chest and cried some more. He held her until she was finished. When she had wiped away her tears, he turned and started for the homestead without a word.

Five minutes later Chris Colt said, "Sarah, the first month especially will be hell, but you have to just get through the trials of each day, one day at a time."

It dawned on her then that he had suffered the same loss and in much the same way. He was such a strong and powerful man, he probably felt tremendous feelings of guilt because he hadn't been able to protect his family.

They topped one more rise and then there it stood in front of them, smoke still streaming from many burning embers. Even at a distance the bloody corpses of her husband and son were visible, and three buzzards were already starting to spiral lazily in the afternoon sun.

Choking back tears, Sarah said, "Mr. Colt, we have to bury my husband and son before anything."

He stopped for a minute and sighed, then said softly, "Ma'am, I'm sorry, but that would be inviting those Crows to look for us, if they showed up back here again."

She said, "But you said this is the last place they would look. And aren't they good enough trackers that they will know if we go around the place anyway?"

He smiled at her and said, "Yes, ma'am. That sure does make good sense. We'll bring them back behind the house, on that hill there. I'll go down first and bury them, then you can come down to the house."

She set her jaw firmly and said, "Like hell you will. You are taking enough of a chance, and I won't have you taking twice as much time digging their graves. We both will dig."

She tilted her chin up and marched forward, firmly set in her mind and the thought showing clearly on her face.

Chris followed meekly with a simple, "Yes, ma'am."

She stalked across the prairie, and Chris looked at her well-formed buttocks as they brushed against the tanned buckskin shirt. He glanced at her legs and long blond hair and started to think thoughts he hadn't thought in a long, long time. Chris's face flushed, and he felt extremely guilty. He tried to convince himself that he felt very sorry for this beautiful woman, that was all. He knew that she was very vulnerable now, and he couldn't allow any feelings to show other than pity.

As if to make matters worse, at that moment she screamed "Ouch!" and sat down in place, lifting her leg up and checking the bottom of her bare foot. Chris ran to her and grabbed her foot. She had brushed against one of the many types of ground-hugging cactus plants and had two long needles in the side of her foot. Sarah had been through so much that she now seemed oblivious to this pain. Chris tried not to look, but as he examined her foot he could clearly see her crotch. He couldn't help but glance a couple of times. The second time, he looked up and her eyes caught his, both of them looking away quickly, their faces beet-red. Sarah shifted her foot and leg, so she wasn't exposing herself to this samaritan anymore. This man had been wonderful so far, and a real savior, but he was also a real man, and she was a lady.

She wondered why it had gone through her mind that he was a *real* man, instead of just thinking he was a man, period. She got very embarrassed again and confused, then developed strong guilt feelings herself. She loved her husband, and they were going to bury him. He had just died trying to save her life, but he hadn't been able to save himself or her son.

Next she got very angry at John. Why hadn't he fought the Indians off and saved their happy family? Why had he been stupid enough to try to talk things over with them? She got very angry, and then started to feel guilty about that, too.

Once more tears streaked down Sarah's cheeks, and when she saw her young son's bloody corpse again she simply broke down and ran forward, throwing herself across his broken little torso. Covered with blood, she stood when she felt Chris's gentle hands lifting her once again.

She wiped her eyes and nose with her arm and sniffled several times, then lifted her chin and steeled herself to the task, saying, "Come on, Mr. Colt, we have graves to dig. There was a shovel out behind the barn in the manure pile, and one in the barn if it hasn't burned up."

She went straightaway to the manure pile and

retrieved the shovel, while Chris tried the still-smoldering barn. He found the metal part of the blackened shovel, but the handle was totally burned away. He did find, however, a pick with just the end of the handle partially burned off, so he grabbed it.

As he dug, Colt turned his thoughts toward his work. After the death of his wife and daughter, he had started working every place he could find a scouting job. He wouldn't sleep, eat, or allow himself the time to stop and think about what had happened. Finally, he shook himself out of it and went off into the mountains to think things through.

Like many westerners, Christopher Columbus Colt was a friendly independent man, a lone wolf, a lobo. He had learned, years before, that whatever life handed him, he could not solve the problem by diving to the bottom of a bottle like so many men did. He knew he couldn't run from whatever was bothering him. He would have to face it and deal with it. The only way Chris could do that was to face himself first, because, most often, the problems that confronted him began inside.

Colt would reach a certain point when he knew it was time to go up into the High Lonesome and get away from mankind. That was how he dealt with the death of his wife and daughter. He could yell, kick bushes, even cry there, hidden from the eyes of all others who might spy on him in his time of weakness. Chris only knew that facing himself and his pain helped him to conquer the problem, no matter how large.

He tried to picture this strong yet very feminine woman packing up above the timberline on some lonely peak and staying there to sort things out, and the mind-picture was totally ludicrous. Chris Colt wondered how Sarah would deal with the brutal death of her family, and her own gang rape. He remembered his own mother, and mused on the incredible quiet strength that so many women seemed to possess.

It was close to dark when the graves were completed and Chris had put two stones in place, side-by-side. He found one vase of Sarah's flowers that hadn't been broken, and he placed that on her husband's grave. Sarah picked it up and placed it on her son's grave.

She explained, "My husband is—was—a man. He could take care of himself, but Johnny was just an innocent little boy."

Chris bowed his head and said a silent prayer. Sarah followed suit. Then she grabbed a handful of dirt and tossed it on each grave. She didn't know what to say, so she finally just recited the Lord's Prayer.

Chris looked at the two graves, then at her, and said, "This is a hard country, Sarah. This is a very hard country, and it can only be tamed by really hard people. I have a feeling your husband was a good man, and your boy, too. Some of us die young and some of us die early, but we all die. We're all part of creating this new country. They didn't die for nothing. May they rest in peace."

He turned and placed his battered hat back on his head and walked away. Sarah lingered a few seconds, then followed.

"I don't think they found our fruit cellar," she said.

"Where is it?"

"Right over there," she said, "come on."

They traveled across the trampled-down garden twenty feet further, and discovered a door leading to an underground bunker of sorts. Chris was impressed when he looked at the notched-log construction of the roof and the shoring up of the walls. John had known how to build for permanence. He was also impressed with how well the location had been camouflaged, primarily by the use of natural land features around it.

Almost as if she could read his mind, Sarah added, "It's ironic, but John said this would be a safe place for Johnny and me to hide in case Indians ever attacked. When it actually did happen this morning, they just appeared out of nowhere."

Chris scrambled down the stairs into the fruit cellar and found numerous jars of canned vegetables and fruit. He also discovered a bag of potatoes and some jerked beef.

"Who jerked this beef for you?"

"I did," she replied. "I learned from an Indian woman I knew in Cheyenne, where I grew up."

"Come on," Chris said. "We need to put some of this in these burlap bags and get back away from here. You load the bags, while I go get us some water and try to find you some clothes."

"I have some trousers, boots, and a shirt over there," she said, walking to a set of old mildewed saddlebags hanging on a post in the center of the room. "My husband wanted to keep some get-away clothes, in case we ever had to hide out here in the middle of the night in our bedclothes."

"That was smart," Chris said.

Sarah said, "He was very practical."

Chris said, "I'll go get some water and see

what I can find for us to take. You get dressed right away, okay?"

He started out the door of the bunker, as she forced a smile and a nod. Chris Colt was amazed at the strength of this woman. This morning she had been viciously gang-raped, had watched her husband and little boy being brutally murdered, had ridden double on a horse for miles with a strange man, while all but naked, all with the fear of the rapists coming after her again, then had dealt with returning to her burned-out little ranch to bury her husband and son. Yet she was functioning. The woman really has sand, Chris thought. Sarah Guthrie was part of what had created the West as the world had come to know it. It was a rough, unforgiving land, and it took men and women of the utmost strength and pioneering spirit to help tame this wild frontier.

Sarah's father ran a mercantile store in Cheyenne, having come out west with his wife in the early days. He and his wife went to plains Indian villages and traded goods for artifacts and weaponry. He spent a long time learning about the tribespeople, and as he traded fairly he was respected by them. He also did not take any of the usual shortcuts of many of the traders by trading liquor or weapons to the Indians. He traded with fur trappers and other traders, and was sought after at mountain men's rendezvous, as he was fair and honest. More importantly, Sarah watched her mother stand by her father through some very scary situations over the years.

Now she reached for the bag with the clothing and pulled it away from the post. There was a rattle, and Sarah looked out of the corner of her eye directly into the face of a five-foot diamondback rattlesnake, coiled up on the shelf by her face. It was like a living spring ready to strike, and Sarah heard a whimper escape her lips, then *boom!*

She screamed and jumped back, watching the body of the snake writhe in circles. She kept screaming as blood poured out of the body where the head had been, and it fell off the shelf onto the hard-packed dirt floor. She stopped screaming as she realized it was dead, and her mind registered the instantaneous realization that Chris had jumped back in the door as soon as the snake had started rattling, drawn and cocked his gun and fired from the hip, blowing the deadly viper's head off.

Sarah ran to Chris, sobbing again, and threw herself against his chest, while he comforted her with his embrace.

"Thank you again, Chris!" she said. "Thank God you are such a good shootist!"

"No, thank God I'm such a good cavalry scout."

She stopped crying and looked up into his eyes with a questioning look. Chris just smiled, as he stepped back and wiped her tears on his war shirt's sleeve.

Chris explained, "We were in the bunker, which was very dark. When I went out into the bright sunlight I closed one eye without thinking, and that saved your life."

He chuckled, as she looked *really* puzzled now.

"What do you mean?" she asked. "I don't understand."

Chris said, "I never look directly at a campfire at night because it destroys my night vision, and it takes several minutes for my eyes to readjust to the darkness. An old Indian trick, though, is to close one eye when you're pouring coffee or looking toward the fire. Then when you face the darkness again and open that eye, it's adjusted to the dark. If I hadn't closed my eye without even thinking about it when I left the fruit cellar, it would have taken a minute anyway for my eyes to get accustomed to the dark again."

She looked up at him and smiled softly, saying, "Mr. Colt, you are a damned good shootist, too."

Chris grinned, turned, and walked out the door. He headed toward the back of the still-smoking barn, as he saw the sun start to slide down below the far blue range of mountains. It had been a long day indeed. He found the well again, and it had a good solid bucket, still intact, attached to the rope-and-pulley system. Chris checked inside the well to ensure the Crows hadn't dropped a dead animal inside to make the water unpotable, a sometimes-used trick. It was fine.

He would be late for his assignment, but he didn't care. He was not looking forward to becoming chief of scouts for the Seventh Cavalry anyway. After his last assignment working in Colorado, out of Arizona, he had been able to put his beautiful wife and daughter out of his mind part of the time, but their images would haunt him for the rest of his days. He knew that the wound would need time to heal, but was getting better all the time. But he also knew that he would never be the same, nor did he want to be.

He thought about how beautiful his wife had been, and how much they had enjoyed being together. She was called Chantapeta, which means "Fireheart," so named because she was so passionate, even as a little girl. Colt had been an independent man, a loner. She had changed all that while they were married. Actually he changed it himself, for he didn't care to be alone anymore, not after he'd met Chantapeta. They had named their own daughter Winona, meaning "First-born," as they had planned to have many more children. Chantapeta was the only woman who had ever tamed his wanderlust. He wanted to be with her and Winona, sharing their lives with each other and let the rest of the world be damned.

His experiences in the war, against the Indians, the visits to his uncle's firearms factory, all of these things had led up to his becoming a chief of scouts for the cavalry. He could track like any brave, fight like any warrior or soldier, figure tactics like any war chief or troop commander, and command respect like the oldest and most experienced first sergeant. What was really good for him, however, was the freedom.

Also he had a job, an important one that made a positive contribution in the settling of the West, and one that put him in a position to watch out for the noble warriors against whom he led the blue-coats. As a cavalry scout he would be there, and Chris Colt knew that the Indians were regarded by many as savages worthy only of extinction. He felt that he could make a difference as a scout by being there and trying to intervene when he could. As a scout, he worked for a cavalry commander; some were good and some were bad, but Colt's jobs never lasted long. It was always off to a different campaign, a different unit.

While ahead of the columns of troops, he was

his own boss. He set the trail and speed of march and advised the commander, if he was a good one, on tactics. He used his growing body of knowledge to read what was going on in the territory, and it sometimes saved lives, both white and Indian. It sometimes cost lives, too, but Chris knew that others would guide if he didn't. He, however, could make at least a small difference in the harsh treatment and decimation of the American Indian.

On top of all that, Christopher Columbus Colt was a warrior, and his job took him into battle. He counted coups. His adrenaline flowed often enough to make him feel really alive. That was important for him. He could never have been a John Guthrie, but he admired the man, for he had been brave, solid, practical, and hardworking, and the West needed both types of men.

With Chris's ability with guns, he could have become a gunfighter of great repute, but he didn't want that. His life's work had to have meaning, purpose. He also could have become a famous lawman, and had worn a badge a couple times, but his heart lay in the lodges of the Lakotah and Cheyenne, the wickiups of the Apache, along the shores of rushing pyrite-shiny mountain streams, the dung-filled trampled grasses behind the great bison herds, and up in the High Lonesome of the Grand Tetons, Wind River Range, Sangré de Cristos, Superstitions, and all the other giant rock sentinels that stood watch over the mighty plains and valleys.

He loved his work but didn't always love his job. He had heard much about Long Hair Custer. The man simply was an egomaniacal son of a bitch, hell-bent on getting elected President of the United States. There were those who hero-worshiped Chris's fellow Ohioan, but Colt knew what the real man was all about, and in his opinion Custer was a low-life bastard. Oddly enough, that made Chris all the more anxious to get to his assignment and try to help safeguard the rights of the red men as much as possible.

He filled the bucket with water and started to winch it up out of the well. Chris knew that before anything else Sarah, after having been gang-raped, would want to bathe for hours. If he had to, Colt would find a trough or something and make a bathtub, heat the water, and let her bathe. The woman's incredible strength and passion reminded him in some ways of Chantapeta.

He suddenly felt guilty again for comparing the two women, and his eyes searched around for more things they might be able to use for their camp. He focused on a patchwork quilt that had fallen to the ground along with Sarah's clothesline, and he retrieved it.

Sarah met him as he was wrapping the quilt into a roll and placing it behind his saddle. She handed him two bags filled with food, which he hung on both sides of the saddle horn. He handed her the bucket of water, and she looked at it as if it contained gold.

"Have you had any yet?" she inquired.

"Yep, go ahead," he said, smiling.

She lifted the dipper and drank cupful after cupful, then splashed water all over her face and head, letting it run down and soak her shirt.

Chris said, "Later, I'll come back and rig up some kind of bathtub for you, and heat up water."

She smiled, "Thanks, but you don't need to. There's a great spring and pool back there in the rocks. I used to bathe there all the time."

"Great," he said, "let's get going. It'll be dark soon."

The spring and little pool were nestled back under a bunch of cottonwood trees and surrounded by an outcropping of rocks. Chris didn't really like it, because from there he couldn't see unwanted guests approaching, but on the other hand nobody would see a fire until they were actually inside the clump of boulders. Another advantage was that the little path that wound its way among the big rocks to get into the little bowl was hard to discern. There were always advantages and disadvantages about every location picked for a campsite, so Chris tried not to worry about it.

He cut boughs off a cedar and a long-needle pine to use to make a mattress for Sarah, while she went to the nearby pool to bathe. She got behind some bushes and removed her shirt, boots, and jeans, then entered the cold but welcome water. Once her body had warmed a little, she rubbed and cleaned herself over and over again, tears streaking down her cheeks as she remembered the horror of the blood-covered, taunting braves as they took turns with her. Sarah knew that she must put off her grief and sorrow until she was in a truly safe place. That was necessary for her very survival, so this time she didn't cry for long. She stayed in the water until her teeth started to chatter, then crawled out, dried off with the burlap bag she had left there, and dressed.

When Sarah walked to the fire, she was pleas-

antly surprised. Chris had the entire campsite
set up. Nighthawk stood picketed on a patch of
grass about twenty feet away, and Colt was
handing her a cup of scalding hot coffee.

"Hope you like cowboy coffee, Sarah," he said.
"What do you want in it?"

"Just black, thank you," she said smiling
warmly. "What do you mean, 'cowboy coffee'?"

He grinned and said, "To test if it's strong
enough, I pour a cup, drop a small rock on it,
and if it bounces off the coffee's surface it's
strong enough to drink."

Sarah chuckled and took a sip. The coffee was
strong and hot and just what she needed. The
fire felt wonderful, too.

Chris went over to remove the picket pin and
line from his horse. The only way into the bowl
of rocks was the path they had taken, so he
would make a gate across it with a fallen branch.
Nighthawk could graze freely, and water if he
wanted, without being held down to the twenty-
foot picket line. Chris liked having him around
the camp, as he was better than a guard dog.
The horse would whinny if he heard or smelled
anyone, and even before that Chris could watch
the horse's ears if they pricked up to see what
direction they were aiming in.

Colt turned and started back toward the campfire. He stopped as he looked at the wet-haired
woman by the fire. Still damp from swimming
in the pool, she had her shirt clinging against
her body and Chris couldn't help but pay attention to it, despite himself. He decided he should
take a bath in the icy-cold water.

As Chris walked up to the fire, Sarah handed
him a cup of coffee. He accepted it and nodded

with a wink, which caused her to notice another slight scar, just below his right eye. He sat down and removed his moccasins.

Sarah pointed and said, "I hadn't noticed that scar. What's that one from?"

He smiled and said, "Comanche arrow."

She shook her head and said, "Tell me, Mr. Colt, is there anybody around who *hasn't* shot or stabbed you?"

He grinned broadly and said, "Well, *you* haven't yet, Sarah."

A serious look came onto her face and she said, "I couldn't, Chris. You've been absolutely wonderful. You saved my life. I just want to tell you thanks."

He said, "I'm going to take a bath myself, ma'am. Even my horse has been holding his nose around me."

Chris went down behind the bushes and removed his war shirt and jeans. He dived into the pool of cold spring water and swam underwater for a full minute before coming to the surface. He was upset with himself for his thoughts about the poor woman who had just lost her husband, son, and home. He stayed in the water, swimming back and forth underwater until his muscles grew fatigued.

When Chris climbed out onto the bank, he lay on the grass a few minutes and replaced his jeans, not wanting to feel the leather shirt against his wet skin. Carrying it, he walked back to the fire just in time for Sarah to hand him a plateful of beans, potatoes, and jerky, along with another steaming cup of coffee.

Again, Sarah couldn't help but notice the muscles that bulged in his shoulders, chest, and arms. She felt angry over these thoughts that she couldn't quite understand. She loved her husband, and he had just been murdered.

The pioneer woman knew what it was. Chris Colt was a big, strong, handsome, and dangerous man. He had saved her life and had risked his, all day long, to keep her safe. He had lost his own wife and daughter in the same way she had lost her family this morning, and this man still loved his wife. She could tell.

She wanted to feel those big arms wrapped around her, to feel protected from the horrors she had endured this day, the horrors she would never get over. She wanted to sleep safely with her head on that big, scarred chest. Sarah wanted something to make the empty feeling inside her go away.

After eating, they shared a tin of peaches.

"Thank you for fixing the bed for me," she said.

"No problem. Let me know if you need any more boughs."

Chris climbed into his bedroll, using his saddle for a pillow as he had done so many nights before. He closed his eyes. Sometimes those nights had been in the mountains, and he had awakened the next morning covered with a blanket of snow. Some nights he had fallen asleep to awaken to a freezing desert wind or a mounting thunderstorm on the lonesome prairie.

There was a noise, and Chris's eyes popped open. He looked up and didn't speak. The firelight shined off the tears running down Sarah's cheeks. She stood over him, completely nude, a look of bewilderment on her face. He looked at her breasts as the dying firelight played on them.

He looked at her flat stomach and rounded hips. Chris looked up into her pleading eyes.

Softly, Sarah said, "I loved my husband."

"I know," he replied just as softly.

"I'm so scared."

Chris Colt didn't speak. He just raised his arm up and held his blanket open. She lay down, and he wrapped her up in his mighty arms. She squeezed tight against his body, and Chris let his lips meet hers.

They kissed long and slowly. Finally their lips parted, and Chris removed his jeans. He pulled her to him again and stared into her green eyes.

Chris spoke softly again, "We both have a deep emptiness that needs to be filled. We have a void that can be filled with love."

Their lips came together again.

The Lakotah, or Sioux, and the Cheyenne called him "Long Hair." The Crow called him "Son of the Morning Star." Lieutenant Colonel George Armstrong Custer wanted the presidency of the United States, and a major victory over the warring tribes would bring the Civil War's "Boy General" even greater fame and glory. More dime novels would be written about him. More children would tell stories about the famous Indian-fighter. Custer had no regard for the American Indian. They were only tools whom he would use to get himself into the top office in Washington.

"General," the sergeant said, using the Civil War title Custer insisted upon, "she's in your tent and fired up."

Custer grinned and said, "Thanks, Sergeant. She's a looker, isn't she?"

"Yes, sir," the old noncom said, "she shore is."

Long Hair entered his tent and looked at the young Cheyenne maiden chained to his cot. She was only fourteen, but she had large breasts and was very pretty. He already had one illegitimate son with a Sioux woman. The Indians suited his needs nicely.

The young girl watched as he removed his clothing, stared at this white man's naked body. She was terrified and ashamed, but she would not scream when he took her innocence. She was a *Chyela,* a Cheyenne, and she would act like one with this enemy. To her, what would happen was what she had wanted to save for the brave who would offer many ponies for her to her father, but this would be torture by an enemy. She would survive the ordeal.

Long Hair Custer lay down with her and caused her pain. She bit her lip and closed her eyes and prayed for a Chyela warrior to strike this man down and cut his heart out someday. She prayed that she would not become pregnant from the seed of this hated enemy. She had heard from the other prisoners that Long Hair would be here on this bivouac two more days. She would have to endure him that long, then maybe she would be allowed to return to her people. He had done it before, but with him, who knew. She only knew that she was Chyela, and she must be true to her blood.

The sky had darkened slightly just after false dawn when Chris felt Sarah rising from their bed on the earth. His senses deemed it safe to sleep a little longer.

For the first time in a long time he smelled the wonderful morning aroma of bacon frying and coffee boiling, being prepared by someone else. He turned on his side and looked at Sarah by the cooking fire, clad only in her oversized shirt, long blond hair dangling down to her buttocks. She looked at him and smiled, but he could tell by her face she had been crying earlier.

"Breakfast is almost ready," she said. "Hungry?"

"Famished," he replied.

Embarrassed, he looked for his jeans and slipped them on, walking off toward some nearby bushes. Out of sight, he relieved himself, and his eyes searched the ground until he had found what he wanted under some trees. He reached down and pulled up some peppermint leaves and chewed on several, carrying the rest back to the fire with him. He handed them to Sarah, and she gave him a smiling but questioning look.

"Peppermint," he said.

"Oh, thank you," she replied, and her face flushed just thinking about the fact that he was thinking about how their breath would smell.

Sarah stopped tending to the bacon for a second and said, "Chris, about last night. I—"

Chris held his hand up, palm out, and smiling, interrupted her. "Sarah, please don't try to explain, just listen. Maybe understanding this will make you feel better. You loved your husband and son very much, but they died yesterday, and you lived. The same thing happened to me, and I loved my wife and daughter very much. You and I are survivors, and must go on living.

"What we did last night and might want to do again, was done to shed a lot of pain and feelings we both had from what happened to our loved ones. I will always love my wife and will never forget her. Now, you will always be an important part of my life, too. The only thing is, you and I have just lost our loved ones, and we must not mistake hurt and pain for love. We are helping each other in a way right now, but soon, when we are in the right and safe place for you, we will say good-bye and that will be it."

He saw two tears running down her cheeks, but she also wore a warm smile of relief and understanding.

"It will be hard to say good-bye," she said.

'It would be harder to try to make the right thing out of the wrong thing," he said.

She replied, "I know."

She poured two cups of coffee, handing one to Chris Colt, and said, "There is always going to be a very special place in my heart for you, Chris. You are an incredible man."

"And you're an incredible woman, but this isn't the time to say good-bye," he replied.

She reached out and touched his hand, and he held hers as their eyes met.

Long Hair walked back to his tent, still drinking a final cup of coffee after a breakfast of flapjacks, bacon, and strawberries with milk.

He stepped into the big canvas structure and whistled.

Custer stepped back outside, laughing heartily, and hollered, "Top! Top!"

His big walrus-mustachioed first sergeant popped out of a tent across the way, quickly buttoning his tunic.

"Sir!" he yelled.

Custer signaled with his hand and said, "Come here! You aren't going to believe this!"

The large-framed noncom ran across and saluted the officer, who just waved it off and turned toward the tent flap and went in, the sergeant right on his shoulder.

"I'll be damned, sir!" he said. "Never seen the likes!"

Custer laughed, "Me either. The little thing hates me so much she decided to imitate a beaver."

He and the first sergeant stared at the naked Cheyenne girl on Custer's bed, as she glared at them with real hatred. Actually, she glared only out of the left eye, as the right was blackened and swollen shut. Then the first sergeant noticed the discoloration on her neck, cheeks, and breasts. Being smart and a survivor of many years in the tough Army, the old soldier humored the Boy General, but he had been happily and faithfully married for twenty-four years to the same woman and could not understand how Custer could be so callous, rotten, and ruthless, or how he could cheat on his lovely wife Elizabeth, let alone be a rapist.

He was sickened by the sight of the girl on the bed. Her left arm was handcuffed to the frame of the metal bed, but a big hunk of the forearm was missing where she had chewed it away, hoping to chew through her arm before Custer returned to his tent. Her mouth, cheeks, and chin were covered with blood from the desperate act. Fortunately for the girl she hadn't severed an artery, and the bleeding was already clotting, but the wound would have to be tended.

"The little girl actually think she's a coyote in a trap! That proves that these damned redskins are animals and not real people," he went on. "Know what I mean, Top?"

"Ah, yes, sir," the senior NCO said.

"Have some men get her out of here and take her back to the other prisoners," Custer said. "And have this mess cleaned up."

"Yes, sir," Top said. "General, what about her arm? Should I have the surgeon look at it?"

"Hell, no!" Long Hair said. "She shouldn't have done it. Would you send a damned coyote to the regimental surgeon?"

"No, sir," the first sergeant said sharply.

He turned and walked briskly from the tent, shouting orders to some men outside.

"Top!" Custer shouted.

The first sergeant appeared in the doorway of the tent again.

"Sir?"

Custer said, "Have someone bring me a fresh cup of coffee, too."

"Yes, sir."

The sun was heating up the land as Chris held his cup out, and Sarah poured him another fresh cup of coffee. He smiled at her and winked.

"What now?" she asked.

Chris replied, "I'm taking you to your folks in Cheyenne."

"Thank you so much, but you had to have been on your way somewhere when you found me," she said.

"I've been contracted to scout for George Custer and the Seventh Cavalry, out east of here," he replied.

"Won't they get angry at you?" she said.

Chris smiled, took a sip of coffee, and said, "To hell with Custer. He's trying to blaze a trail to fame and glory over the bodies of innocent people. He'll just have to wait a little while and be patient if he needs a scout to show him the way. He probably won't listen to me anyway."

Sarah smiled and took another sip of coffee, saying, "He will if he's smart."

Chris grinned and said, "As I said, he probably won't listen."

A little west of Fort Abraham Lincoln, the battle-hardened old first sergeant walked into Custer's tent with a detail of men and had them remove the Cheyenne prisoner. They walked out the door with her struggling feebly against their grip.

One of the men, a corporal, who went up and down in rank according to the fort's liquor supply and the number of willing fighters in the area, said to the first sergeant, "Hey Top, shouldn't we get this poor little girl some bandages and medicine and shit?"

The first sergeant smiled and nodded beyond the group, saying, "Why don't *you* tell him that, O'Hara?"

The detail turned their heads and looked at Custer, two tents away, standing right-side to them, with a mirror in his hand, carefully trimming the hairs on his drooping mustache. He wore spit-shined boots, cavalry trousers, and a specially-made fringed leather jacket, with his official rank and insignia attached as if it were an authorized blue tunic. He also wore a red sash around his middle and twin pearl-handled Colt Peacemaker .45s.

O'Hara laughed and said, "Hell with it. Poor girl. I ain't losing these stripes again over a red nigger."

Sarah and Chris bathed nude in the cold, clear water. Making love at that time didn't seem right to either of them, so they finished and simply got out, dried off, and dressed. Chris started to strike camp, and Sarah looked for things to be done to help out.

"Are you sure you want to risk your life any more for me?" she asked. "You've done far too much already."

Colt gave her a sidelong glance that made her flush with embarrassment, and she figured her question probably was stupid. Within minutes they'd struck camp, and Chris was saddling Nighthawk. The horse had had plenty of graze during the night and seemed ready to go. So did Chris.

They started down the path through the rocks and headed back toward the cabin. There were still a few little tendrils of smoke coming from the burning embers at the house, and a steady column from the smoldering haystack in what had been the barn.

Chris and Sarah went past the ruins of Sarah's dreams and paused briefly at the two graves. Sarah knelt by both graves and prayed, then rose, wiped the tears away, set her jaw, and walked on. As soon as they had walked out of the grove, Chris set a course south.

"Isn't there a well-traveled road not too far away that goes to Cheyenne?" she asked.

"Yes," he replied, "and we'll take it when we get close to the city, but any warriors looking for trouble will watch the road also. It'll be safer going cross-country."

"Oh," she said, and seemed to be satisfied with the answer.

They crossed the prairie, and it seemed to Sarah as if they would never get to Cheyenne. The land looked exactly the same all the way around in every direction for miles. Near dark, they spotted what Chris had been looking for, a homestead ranch. Approaching the little structure, Chris spotted a draw that wound around the house and went on south beyond it. He took Sarah and his horse into the draw and approached that way.

When they were parallel with the ranch buildings, Chris said, "You keep on south in this draw and stay in it. I'll catch up. If you hear any gunshots, you go until the draw turns at all and get out and head east. You'll hit the road to Cheyenne and you just turn to your right, that's south."

"If I hear any gunshots, I'll stay put and wait for you," she replied. "You'll handle it. But why can't we just see if these folks will let us spend the night here?"

Chris said, "Whoever is living out here all alone has to be pretty tough to survive all the war parties coming through the place. I don't want to take a chance on them getting ideas about you."

Fifteen minutes later, he walked up to the house and hollered, "Hello, the house! I'm a friend, and my hands are empty!"

In those days and in that place, that was the

only sensible way to approach somebody's property without getting your head blown off.

Chris was surprised to see a slight old man with a toothless grin walk out the front door and signal Chris to come in.

He said, "Come on in and set yersef down, youngster. Come talk to Ma, she loves comp'ny."

Colt was totally puzzled, as he followed the man inside. His heart just about stopped when he walked into the sod-roofed cabin and looked into the blank, vacant eyes of the drying-out corpse of an old woman.

"Ma, we got a visitor," the old man said, then turned to Chris saying, "This is Sadie. She loves folks. What's yer name, young man?"

"Chris Colt; uh, pleased to meet you, ma'am," Chris replied, feeling sick in his heart. "Sir, I'm in a rush. I have to get to Cheyenne in a hurry. I noticed that you and your lovely wife have several head of horses in the corral. Can I buy one?"

The old man didn't miss a beat. "Yep, the blood bay'll do. Ma, takin' this young man out to look at the blood bay! Gonna sell it to him mebbe, if'n he's got cash and knows horseflesh."

"I only have a little cash," Chris replied, "but I do know horseflesh."

They got to the corral and the old man snaked out a loop on a rope hanging from a cedar corral post. He tossed it and it landed deftly over the neck of the blood bay horse, which looked quite sound, as did the other horses.

The horse did not move once the loop was around his neck. Chris and the old man examined the gelding, and Chris was impressed.

"How much?" Chris asked.

"Yer Henry repeater, and I'll throw in a saddle

and bridle fer the young lady ta use," the man said.

Chris was really taken aback.

"The young lady? My Henry repeater?" Chris queried, dumbstruck.

The old man replied, "Yeah, the Henry repeater ya got in the saddle boot on that nice-lookin' line-back dun the purty young lady's on."

The old man chuckled. "Don't need no money, Colt. Not every Injun that comes 'round here is gonna leave a crazy old man be. Some of 'em might wanna shoot it out."

"How did you know about the woman and the horse, let alone the rifle?" Chris asked.

"Telescope," the oldster replied. "Did ya really think ya was gonna injun up on my place through that draw an' put the sneak on me?"

Chris laughed and replied, "Yeah, I guess I did."

The old man chuckled. "Probably figgered whoever could last out here has to be grizzly-tough or plumb crazy, huh?"

Chris grinned and the man went on. "Guess I'm a little a both, but this is my home, and I'm still here. My wife went under a month back, rest her soul, but she's helping keep me alive. Three war parties been through here in the last two weeks. Lot a Sioux and Cheyenne on the move. Won't mess with a loony bird, figger it's bad medicine. Heerd they's goin' to join old Sittin' Bull up on the Little Big Horn. Ya got the look of a scout, probably awready heerd it, eh?"

"I've heard talk, that's all," Chris said.

"Take the damned horse," the old man said. "She can pay me when ya git to Cheyenne. Her folks can, anyhow. I'll go in fer supplies and such 'fore winter."

"How do you know about her?" Chris asked, really curious.

"I seen her from a distance, time or two," the old one replied. "Need to know who my neighbors are, even if'n they're twenty, thirty miles distant, specially since I used to see her in her folks' store all the time growin' up. She didn't lose her ole man and that cute little 'un, did she?"

Chris looked down and kicked the ground with his toe, saying, "Yeah, but not Lakotah or Cheyenne. A band of Crows raising some hell. What kind of work do you do, mister? Whatever it is, it takes brains."

"Oh, let's jest say that a lot a lawmen in several states liked to keep pitchers of me when I was younger and better-lookin.' I'm retired now, but I'm fer sure they'd still like to find me and discuss them tintypes," the man said.

Chris caught up with Sarah an hour later, and gave her the smooth-riding horse. She was really amazed. He told her about the man and his crazy act while they rode south at a fast mile-eating trot. Ten miles further on, Chris found a small spring and a grove of cottonwoods. They decided to make camp there.

It was well past dark before they fell asleep. They made love again, and afterward she lay with her head on his chest while he stroked her long hair. Every once in a while Chris heard a sob escape her lips, but he really admired the strength she had displayed so far.

The next morning, they took off shortly after daybreak and pushed on toward Cheyenne. Chris still wanted to stay away from the road for a while longer, so they stayed a few miles west of it.

At one point during the day Chris spotted a distant war party, so he and Sarah took refuge in a buffalo wallow. Neither they nor their tracks were spotted, as the group was traveling far to the east.

They made camp that evening in another small grove of cottonwoods, this one running for about a half a mile through a small cut with a spring-fed creek running along its bottom. There were several other groves in the area, so Chris deemed it safe to go ahead and camp near the water. If it had been the only watering spot for miles around, it would have been the last place he would have selected for a campsite, but with others around, it was only a calculated risk that someone would select that particular watering place to watch or to obtain water from.

Again the two lonely people made love, but they were interrupted by Nighthawk's whinnying. Colt was up and dressed in seconds, watching the horse's head the whole time. Both ears were pointed out toward the open end of the draw to the east, and his nostrils were flaring like a hound dog's on a hot coon trail.

"Get dressed and ready to ride," Chris whispered. "Stay here, and shoot anything that moves."

"What if I shoot you?" she asked.

"You won't," he said flatly. After quickly kicking over the fire the big pile of loose dirt he had put there for just such an emergency, he disappeared into the shadows.

Sarah felt her heart pounding wildly in her

chest, and she felt a horrible, panicked feeling. All she could think of was that group of wild-eyed, screaming Crows taking turns with her. She wanted to run, but she couldn't figure out where to run to. Her mind raced as her eyes strained to catch a glimpse of her protector, but he was not within sight or sound of her senses. She thought about climbing a tall tree and hiding in the branches, but finally reminded herself just how good Chris Colt was. He had been doing a good job of protecting her so far, and she would have to listen to what he said. Her breathing slowed a little, and she started to relax her racing thoughts.

Sarah took a couple of deep breaths, then quickly pulled on her clothes and started packing her gear, then his. She kept looking anxiously beyond the horses, but saw nothing. She noticed that the ears of both horses were pricked forward and aimed at the open, but dark, end of the grove. She walked over to the two animals and pulled their picket pins, leading them back to the campsite. She first saddled Colt's horse, then her own. The whole time she kept in her hand the Navy .36 that Chris had given her to carry, and she cocked and pointed it twice at various night sounds. It was a spare from his saddlebags.

She caught her finger in the girth strap and ring of her saddle as she tightened it, letting out a whispered "Ouch!"

Turning, she was face-to-face with Chris, who put his hand over her mouth and stifled her scream, while his other hand grabbed her gun hand.

She grabbed him and pulled him as tight as she could, while he kissed her injured finger.

Chris held her and whispered in her ear, "You did real good, Sarah. There's a small band of Cheyenne moving across the prairie. Even if they find us it will probably be okay, but I'm going to keep an eye on them until they're out of sight. I'll be back shortly. You can put your bedroll back out and lay down, and I'll picket the horses again, but keep your clothes on."

Sarah whispered, "Please hold me close when you come back."

Chris smiled and turned, moving once again into the darkness with the horses in tow. Sarah had already taken her bedroll off the back of her saddle and spread it out on the ground. She lay down and was asleep within seconds.

"Wal, wal, wal, lookee what we got us here, boys!" In Sarah's dream, the voice came from an ugly man about ten feet tall. He was a white man, but he wore Crow warpaint and a breechcloth.

Her mind slapped into a big black wall and she gasped for air, as she awakened and realized suddenly that the voice came from the real world, not the world of dreams.

There were three of them, and they each held the reins to a horse and the lead line to a pack mule. Two were very large and ugly, with dirty, scruffy beards. The third was thin and wiry, and wore two fancy pistols in quick-draw holsters slung low on his hips. His eyes were beady, his nose thin and pointed. Sarah thought he looked like a person who had to have a rat in his ancestry.

Where is Chris? she thought. How long have I been asleep?

Her eyes glanced at her Navy .36, lying two feet from her right hand, when the thin one, the gunfighter, said, "Lady, I don't want to shoot out here with Injuns all around, so don't make me. Just slide away from the gun and start unbuttoning."

Sarah panicked.

The largest of the group grabbed some of the firewood and kindling and began to make a new fire, saying, "Wait, I wanna watch her takin' off her clothes."

The other two chuckled.

Chris watched from the shadows, trying to figure how to make his play. There were three of them. One was carrying a Sharps buffalo gun, something that could make a hole you could drive a wagon and team through. The one he had to watch was Rat-face. He was a gunfighter. The second to the biggest would go next. He was the oldest, and probably hadn't lived so long by being stupid.

As in the Indian fight, Chris was afraid, but he had conditioned himself to let it show only *after* the danger was past. Right now, he had to figure out the best way to handle this situation without getting Sarah hurt.

The flames went up about three feet in the air and both of the larger men removed their coats, the smaller of the two grabbing Sarah's gun.

Rat-face said quietly, "Now, clothes off before I count to ten, or Buck'll take 'em off for ya."

His glance indicated that Buck was the largest man.

"I have a better idea," Chris said, stepping into the firelight. "The three of you take off your clothes, and *we'll* watch."

The three men looked shocked, but the big barrels of the twin Colt .44s helped to make believers out of the two large men. They immediately removed their gun belts and kicked them toward Chris.

Buck said, "We didn't mean nothin', mister. We was just funnin' yer ole lady. I swear, we wasn't gonna do nuthin'."

Chris paid no attention to them, directing it all at Rat-face. The gunfighter wanted to make a try, Chris just knew it.

Sarah was shocked as she saw Chris's rugged face break into a broad grin, as he said, "Go ahead, Rat-face. I love to shoot rodents. Grab some iron, and we'll see how many shots I can pump into you before you clear leather."

He went on, "Sarah, get those clean kerchiefs out of my pack, in case I need any bandages. These gents opened the ball, and in five seconds we all start dancing. I'm going to shoot the one with the rat face first, then these other two. When I start shooting, you get into the woods and find your brothers. One, two, three—"

"We're unarmed!" Buck pleaded.

"So was she," Chris said. "Dangerous game. Don't get into it if you plan to fold."

"Drop your guns, you dumb son of a bitch!" Buck screamed at Rat-face.

"Four—"

"Wait! Wait!" Rat-face yelled. "You win, you bastard."

Rat-face dropped his guns and kicked them toward Chris.

Colt said, "Now your clothes, all of them."

He cocked his left-hand gun, and that was all the prompting the men needed. They stripped down to their birthday suits. Totally naked, they covered themselves with their hands, but Chris had other plans.

"Unsaddle your horses and pack animals," Chris said. "And make it fast, or die."

They ran to the horses and unsaddled them, Rat-face staring daggers at the scout all the while. Chris then had them stand with their backs against a large cottonwood trunk, and he wrapped them tightly with one of their lassos while Sarah covered them with her gun. Next, he and Sarah mounted up.

Rat-face couldn't contain himself any longer and screeched, "Mister, you better kill me right now, 'cause I'm damned shore gonna kill you!"

Chris smiled, doffed his hat, and said, "Name's Chris Colt. I'll be working out of Fort Abraham Lincoln. You're welcome to visit, anytime."

Chris and Sarah rode off into the night, heading due north. He cut to the east after a few minutes and got off his horse, looking closely at the ground.

Sarah finally spoke, saying, "What are you doing?"

"Shh!" he hissed angrily, then stopped dead in his tracks and looked at her more softly. "I'm sorry. I got mad at myself for letting that gunfighter know who I am and where to find me. It was stupid."

Sarah smiled and said, "No. If he goes after you, *that* would be stupid."

He grinned and shook his head, saying, "Found it."

Chris jumped up and pulled out his Bowie knife. He grabbed the front right hoof of Night-hawk and started to pry the horseshoe loose.

"What are you doing?" she asked.

Chris said, "Found the tracks of that Cheyenne war party. I'm going to pull our horse's shoes, and we'll ride along in their tracks for awhile. Indian ponies don't wear shoes. We'll peel off at a good place, and those critters back there won't be able to follow us."

"Do you think they'll try?"

"Rat-face damned sure will."

Chris finished pulling the shoes and tossed them under a large mesquite clump. He mounted up and led Sarah along the same trail taken by the Cheyenne war party. The couple rode along under the moonlit sky for several hours, after a while taking off up a side draw that eventually turned back toward the south, toward Cheyenne once again.

Trotting along, Sarah looked over at Chris and said, "Won't it hurt the horse's feet not to wear shoes?"

Chris replied, "No, not at all. They'll be moving across soft ground for the most part all the way there. How many Indians have you ever heard of with blacksmiths in their tribe?"

Sarah laughed.

The rest of the trip went without event, and a couple of days later they rode into the outskirts of Cheyenne. Colt turned in the saddle to see Sarah's head bowed, tears running down her cheeks.

"You're home," he said.

Sarah's parents were what Chris Colt had expected. One look told him they were true pioneer stock. Sarah's mother wasn't really that old and had no gray in her hair. The woman was obviously the source of Sarah's golden tresses. Her mother's hair looked as if it had been dipped into a large vat of honey and thoroughly soaked with the golden liquid. She was pretty herself, but hardy as well. Sarah's father had a large frame, a twinkle in his eye, and a well-trimmed beard. Colt liked them both immediately.

After quickly explaining the events of five days ago, Chris excused himself and walked out the door of their mercantile with Sarah following.

"Are you leaving now?" she asked, a little desperately.

"No," he replied, "I'm just going to Western Union. I have to send the Seventh Cavalry a telegram and let them know what's happened to me."

"Good, I'll be here when you're done," she said.

Sarah's father looked at his wife and indicated the couple through the window. The mother was still crying about her grandchild and son-in-law, but trying to regain her composure.

He said, "Look at the way they look at each other and touch each other." He sniffled. "They've been together."

The mother got angry and said, "Our daughter came from hardy stock! She came from you and me! She will do whatever she needs to do to survive, and you will never judge her! Do you hear me?"

He looked down, ashamed.

He looked at his wife and winked. "We still have our little girl. Thank God for that."

She said, "I have. And I'll thank God every day the rest of my life, but I'll also thank Chris Colt. He saved her life, and I'll never forget that."

Sarah's parents locked the front door of the mercantile and stood on the plank-board sidewalk in front of it. When Chris came around the corner a smile appeared on Sarah's face, as she gave a little half-wave. Chris walked across the street in his mile-eating stride, when Sarah screamed, a look of horror on her face.

Colt turned to see Rat-face, gun drawn, bearing down on him with a shot. The man's face was crimson-red with rage, and he was about to pull the trigger when Chris dived to the ground directly in front of the oncoming horse. He looked at Rat-face and drew his legs and arms up into a ball. Rat-face leaned around the horse's neck, but then switched to the other side, hoping for a shot. The horse was at full gallop, and was on top of Chris in no time. Colt rose up on all fours and the horse had no choice but to vault over the man's back or slam into him with its forelegs.

The horse leaped over the scout, and Rat-face had to forget shooting and hold the saddle horn to keep from being thrown out of the saddle. As the horse cleared Chris's back, the chief of scouts rolled behind it, drawing his .44 and firing from the hip, then rolling again and firing three more times. The fourth shot finally hit its mark and took Rat-face in the upper chest, spilling him from the saddle. The man's left foot hung up in the stirrup, and he took numerous kicks in the face from the spooked steed as it raced down the street.

As the terrified horse dragged the limp, bloody body behind him, Sarah and her mother ran to Chris's side, as he stood up and dusted off his clothes.

Her mother was in a state of shock, but finally said, "What was *that* all about?"

Sarah said, "He and some other men tried to attack me, Ma. Chris changed their minds."

Her father grinned, through his own tear-stained cheeks, and said, "I'll bet he convinced them pretty good, too. If I ever get in a war, Colt, I want you on my side."

Chris smiled and glanced at Sarah, saying, "I already am, sir."

Sarah said, "I wonder where the rat-man's partners are."

Chris grinned and said, "Mexico, I hope."

Leaving Cheyenne the next morning was one of the hardest things Chris Colt had done for a long time. Sarah's love had helped to fill the horrible void in his life. She couldn't help herself when he pulled out, and started to cry in front of her parents. Her mother put her arms around her and held her protectively. Sarah's father, however, stepped up and hugged her warmly.

"Sarah," he said softly, "Colt did more than save your life. If you hadn't had someone to show you love and kindness in the past few days, you might have gone insane."

"I know, Daddy, I know," she said.

Chris decided to head north to Fort Laramie, then east to Fort Abraham Lincoln at Bismarck. He figured he could catch a patrol at Laramie either returning or going to Lincoln, and could earn some of his wages scouting for them.

Colt spent part of the time on the road and part of the time traveling just to the east of the road, trying to keep out of sight as much as possible. He found one area, however, where the valley narrowed and he had to go back to the road. It took him past a rock outcropping, which Chris eyed closely.

He tried to figure out what to do about the two big men who had ridden with Rat-face. When he told Sarah's dad what they looked like, the man knew them. Buck and Luke Sawyer, two ruthless cutthroats who had gone from hide-hunting to selling really good trade goods and cattle, then using part of their profit to buy inferior goods and Mexican cattle. They also carried letters of introduction from Long Hair Custer himself. The honest trader couldn't figure out what they were up to, but Chris Colt had an idea.

He kept his eyes on the rock outcropping, and as he approached it he caught the glint of sunlight on a rifle barrel. Chris slammed his left knee into Nighthawk's shoulder while pulling up and back to the right on the reins. At the same time he dug his right heel deeply into the gelding's ribs. The well-trained mount did a rollback, in which he reared up immediately and spun to the right on his heels, while twisting his body around to take off back in the other direction.

A look of horror came over Chris Colt's face

as he saw the flash of the muzzle in the rocks, followed by the bullet exploding through Nighthawk's head, splattering bone and blood across its rider. Chris saw a second muzzle flash and felt something slam into his head, and a world of blackness enveloped him. He felt like he was falling backward off a cliff, then felt a jarring thud as he hit the ground hard and went out.

Chapter 2

>>>>>>>>>>>>>>>>>>>>>>

Into the Jaws
of Death

Chantapeta was on a brilliant sorrel-and-white Overo paint gelding, riding him full gallop across the mountain meadow filled with wildflowers. She had a beaded white buckskin dress with a long thin fringe hanging down from the bottom. It was pulled up high while she squeezed the well-muscled horse with her legs, and Chris could only look at her with love and admiration of her beauty.

Chris stood at the edge of the meadow waiting for his gorgeous wife, and she kicked the magnificent horse into a faster lope. Finally she pulled up to a sliding stop in front of him, and a giant cloud of dust enveloped the scout. The dust was so thick, he couldn't see her. In fact, the dust cloud started to choke him.

The cloud finally cleared away and Chantapeta was gone, the horse was gone, nothing was there but the meadow. The dust cloud enveloped him again, but he heard thunder in the distance. He had trouble breathing from the dust cloud, but the storm came like a giant sponge and soaked everything in its path, crushing it all with water. Chris was drenched, totally drenched, so he slipped back into the comfortable envelope of blackness.

Chris saw Chantapeta and Winona, both in flowing chiffon-white buckskin dresses. There was a white light all around them, and they were smiling and waving at him, signaling for him to come up and join them on the cloud. He kept wanting to go, but he yelled to them to wait a little while because he had to finish his work first. The rainstorm came back again and the thunder was loud, so he slipped back into the envelope of blackness.

The sun was hotter than two stages of hell, and Chris was baking to the bone when the giant Crow warrior sat on his chest and started to bang on his forehead over and over again with the war club. The sun made his eyes want to squint, but he forced them open. The Indian was suddenly gone and Chris gasped. He felt several muscles pull in his back and stomach as he sat up abruptly.

He looked all around. Several buzzards were winging skyward in fright, and Chris noticed the partially devoured corpse of his beloved mount Nighthawk. Tears welled up in his eyes, as he thought about all he and his horse had been through.

On one occasion, Colt had been in a major skirmish with a band of Mescalero Apaches. He was alone, and five Apaches who had been after him had finally cornered him in some rocks near the Mogollon Rim in New Mexico Territory. The two opposing forces had developed a sense of humor about the deadly business. The Apaches would lay down covering fire while one would slither forward to better cover. Chris would stand, despite the covering fire, and shoot at the man moving ahead. His courage was well respected by the tough warriors, and he would sometimes stand and make indecent gestures toward them. He was really very frightened. He could only try to make them so angry that they would slip up and make a mistake. Instead, they admired his raw bravado. Trying to emulate him, the Apache braves started exposing their buttocks and genitals, until one had a private part seriously wounded. The other men teased the aching brave unmercifully, and Chris shouted taunts as well.

Finally, Chris got nailed when he jumped up; this was the scar on his left shoulder, where the bullet had exited at the back of the shoulder blade. His rifle had flown from his hand, and he hadn't had time to reload his pistols. Chris simply flew backward from the impact of the bullets and was slammed against the rock behind him, bruising his back horribly. The Apaches cautiously worked their way forward, and the next thing he knew they were standing on the rocks above him, blocking out the unforgiving sun from his face.

When they jumped down and stood over him, he saw that they were all smiling. The one with the groin injury gingerly sat down next to Chris and lay against the same flat rock. One of the braves took off for several minutes, returning with several herbs and some sap. The warriors treated Chris and his enemy for their wounds side-by-side, handed Chris some jerky to chew on, and disappeared into the afternoon. He had been amazed. It was the first real instance where he had learned how noble the American Indian could be, and how much these men respected courage.

The Apaches knew that he would survive his wounds because of his toughness. But Chris Colt was not so sure. He had fever and became delirious, but he managed to tie himself in the saddle. He literally wrapped his waist with a lariat and tied it to the saddle horn.

Then, leaning forward, he tied his arms around the big horse's neck and weakly whispered, "Take us home, Nighthawk."

The buckskin headed back toward the fort where Colt had been working. The problem was, the fort was ninety-eight miles away. The entire trip was handled solely by the horse. Chris Colt was unconscious most of the time, but Nighthawk kept going. One time, while crossing a river, Nighthawk started to roll, just sensing that his master needed the water and the relief, but then instinctively did not roll, somehow realizing that Colt would have gotten crushed or drowned. Incredibly, Nighthawk made it, and so did Chris.

Now his head pounded with a severe headache, but he kept looking at his beloved mount. Finally tears welled up in his eyes, and he just dropped his head down and cried, quiet but strong, racking sobs, that came from deep inside his beefy chest.

This man bore scars all over his sinewy body, the scars of numerous battles with ferocious enemies. His scars were badges of honor for the many times his bravery had been tested and had passed with flying colors. Unfortunately, a man's attitude and strength is the only testament to the scars he wears in his heart. Chris had just added a new wound to his heart, a deep wound. But, as in the past, he would hurt but he would also heal, and he would survive.

He dried his tears and raised his head, looked at the dead horse again, flies buzzing everywhere, and he fainted.

Chantapeta was nude, and she lay on top of Chris Colt's stretched-out body. Her lips enveloped his, and they kissed long and hard. His eyes opened, as did hers, but she had turned into Sarah Guthrie.

Chris's eyes opened, and he sat bolt upright. It was the middle of the night, and it was chilly. He shivered and looked all around. In the moonlight, he saw the part-skeleton, part-flesh corpse of Nighthawk in the same spot.

Colt thought for a minute and could not figure out where he was or what had happened. He rubbed his eyes and felt a hard, drumming pain in his head. His hands automatically went down to his guns. They were still there.

He got very angry but didn't know why, finally realized the reason: he was very confused. Where was he, and what had happened to him? He remembered dreaming. He remembered crying about his wonderful horse, but Chris could not figure out what was happening. His thoughts were absolutely jumbled and confused.

He tried to stand, and had only made it to one knee when the night sky started to swirl around faster and faster. He felt the ground smack into the back of his head as his eyes closed.

The sun was blazing hot when Colt opened his

eyes again. A coyote lingering near the carcass of the dead horse took off at a dead run, looking back over his shoulder about every twenty yards.

Chris shook his head from side to side and slowly tried to stand, but he got very dizzy and light-headed, so he collapsed back onto the ground. It finally hit him that he and his horse had been shot from the rocks overlooking the trail. He would investigate the rocks, but first he must eat. He was still suffering from amnesia, but he knew instinctively that he had been out for at least several days, probably more. He needed water immediately, then food.

Stifling sobs, Chris dragged himself on his belly to the skeletal remains of Nighthawk. He cut his saddlebags loose from the saddle and dragged his bedroll away as well. He also grabbed his lasso and canteen. The smell was putrid, but that was the farthest thing from Chris Colt's mind. First and foremost in his thoughts was survival.

He drank the entire contents of the canteen, knowing there was a spring-fed natural tank up in the rocks. Next, he dragged out some bacon and flour and coffee. He dragged together some "squaw-wood," as the buffalo hunters called it, tinder that could be bunched together. He also found some pieces of dry creosote and piñon and built a fire. He made bacon, biscuits, and strong coffee.

Chris felt much better after he had eaten, and he rolled himself a smoke, something he did only on very rare occasions. Chris enjoyed a nice cigarette or cigar sometimes, but in his work he was always sneaking close to the enemy and didn't want to have that telltale smell on him.

He carried a small signal mirror in his saddlebag, so he took it out and found a scabbed-over bullet crease running right above his left ear and temple and through the hairline. The whole side of his head and shoulder was covered with dried blood. He used what was left of the little bit of water and cleaned it, poured some whiskey on it from the small flask he carried for just such emergencies, and put a bandage on.

He felt a lot stronger, but he knew he had to take in some meat shortly. He worried about firing his weapons, because he had no idea where the ambushers or any hostile Indian parties might be. The rocks were a good vantage point and had spring water, so that spot would attract a lot of people to the area.

Chris decided to get it over with, so he drank another cup of coffee, then grabbed his rifle and tried to make it to the rocks. He got dizzy again when he stood, so he crawled forward on all fours, resting every twenty or thirty seconds.

It took over an hour to reach the rocks, but he finally made it. Chris drank long from the fresh spring water in the natural rock tank. It was relatively cool and sweet, unlike some of the brackish water he had drunk from rock tanks in Arizona Territory. Colt cleaned his head wound more thoroughly, and rebandaged it. Looking around the rocks, Chris spotted a spent shell from a Sharps buffalo gun, the kind he had seen Buck Sawyer carrying. He was able to walk a little now without getting too weak, so he carefully made a circle of the rocks until he had found what he sought: the tracks of the two friends of the dead rat-faced gunslinger, Buck and Luke Sawyer.

Chris could identify the tracks simply because, for a scout like him, it was like being able to recognize customers' signatures if you owned a small bank. Chris found another spent shell in the rocks, and was thankful how lucky he had been. The two idiots should have checked to make sure he was dead, but they foolishly took it for granted. That would be their undoing, he decided.

Colt checked around the area some more, until he was sure there was something wrong. He couldn't put his finger on it, but there was definitely something amiss. Chris kept looking at everything, trying to pinpoint what was bothering him, but he couldn't.

Suddenly, it hit him. Between the rocks and below the water tank, there were patches of green grass. In the middle of one of these little patches, which were no more than ten feet by ten feet in size, there was a large patch of low-growing cactus. It was the kind Chris hated most, as it would stab you in the lower legs, the barbed needles sticking in your flesh. His horse had hated this kind of cactus, too, and for the same reason.

The only hitch was that cactus would not grow in a green wet patch of soil like that. It had too much water. The cactus would flourish only in sandy soil, with the occasional drenching. Chris walked over and knelt down by the patch. Carefully, he dug around it with his giant knife and flipped pieces of cactus onto some nearby rocks. The work was exhausting and Chris had to rest about every minute or so, but finally he had cleared away all of the pain-causing plant.

Next, the scout dug in the dark wet soil that

had been under the cactus plant. He only had to
go about a foot deep before he hit something with
the blade. Carefully digging it out with the knife
and his hands, Chris uncovered a Cheyenne-
decorated leather parfleche. Another few minutes was all it took for Chris to totally unearth
it. He opened the leather cover and saw a short,
stout Cheyenne bow and a half-dozen steel-
tipped arrows. There was also a bunch of jerky,
which was moldy.

Chris tossed the jerky out and smiled at the
bow and arrows. He handled them, and liked the
feel of the wooden weapons in his hand. They
had been cached there by some clever brave who
probably passed through this area a lot and
wanted to keep an emergency stash.

Colt took the bow and nocked an arrow in it
immediately. He drew it back, but that took all
his strength, he was so weak. He let off on the
string and walked toward a brush pile and some
bushes lying downhill from the spring, where
two cottonwoods and a small patch of green grass
grew.

He made it almost to the brush pile and
stopped, catching his breath. After he had gotten
his breath back, Chris walked up to the pile and
kicked it. He walked around it and kicked again,
and a rabbit exploded out of the pile. Weaving a
zigzag course, the little creature headed toward
the relative safety of the rocks, but Chris had
spent much time with the Indians and knew
their tricks. He held the bow up and drew back
the arrow. Next Chris pursed his lips and whistled, easily imitating the cry of a red-tailed
hawk.

Hearing the sound of the feared predator that

takes so many of its kind, the rabbit instinctively stopped dead and froze in place, shivering in fear, nostrils quivering and little heart pounding. Colt released the arrow, and it sailed over the rabbit's back and stuck into the ground just beyond him. The animal, however, was still paralyzed by fear, and Chris quickly nocked another arrow and drew it back, releasing more smoothly this time. This one took the rabbit through the rib cage and the power rolled him over, the blade sticking into the ground beyond. It let out a squeal and Chris Colt ran to it, quickly dispatching it with a knife strike behind the ear.

An hour later and Chris Colt had another rabbit, after two more near-misses. He took another hour to move back to the dead horse, salvage what he could, and move back to the tanks. He felt renewed, but even more so after he had made another fire by the tank and broiled the two rabbits. Chris ate both greedily, along with some wild onions he'd dug.

He treated himself to another cigarette and went to sleep just as the sun went down.

Chris awakened and just listened. Carefully, he allowed his eyes to open just slightly. He first saw the silhouettes in the moonlight, but after a minute he opened his eyes wide and saw three mule deer drinking from the tank.

He didn't move, knowing that any movement would spook them. He also didn't want to fire his gun, as it still might draw attention. With the patience of the Indians he revered, he waited. After several minutes the three animals started to graze on the grasses near the spring.

Chris knew from his days with the Lakotah

that he could move quietly whenever the deers' heads were down, as they could not see anything but the grass under their faces. The problem was that, with three deer grazing, one almost always had a head up, ears twitching around like radar beacons trying to hone in on any danger sounds.

Using a Lakotah bow-hunter's trick, he watched the tails of the three deer, knowing that a nerve connected to the tail would make each deer's tail twitch upward slightly just before the deer raised its head. Whenever all three had their heads down at the same time, Chris moved closer and closer to the bow and arrows. It took an hour, but finally he was on one knee, holding the bow in his left hand, with an arrow nocked and the bowstring held in the first three fingers of his right hand.

It was early summer, and months away from the rut, so the three deer were all antlerless bucks, having shed them during the late winter. The new racks were just starting to grow. Chris picked out the smallest of the three, as that would be all he needed for now, and all he could handle.

He slowly drew the string back while the three heads were down. One raised his head while Chris held the bow at full draw. The deer's eyes seemed to pierce right through him, but he knew better. It was just checking for danger.

Chris Colt was a strong man, but right now, with the shock and loss of blood, the tension was causing every muscle in his arms and back to shake. Nevertheless, he waited. The deer put his head down. Knowing you should fire weapons higher in the darkness, Chris drew, aimed behind the left shoulder blade of the smallest deer, raised his aim two more inches, took a breath, let it out halfway, and let the string slip from his fingers. The arrow buried itself in the side of the animal, which gave a mighty leap sideways and bounded off after its friends.

Chris couldn't see the arrow hit, but he knew from the release and the sound that he had made a good hit. He also knew that arrows kill by bleeding, not shock like bullets, so he would wait and let the animal calm down, lie down, and bleed to death. If he pursued it, adrenaline would keep the buck going. Chris would be smarter to wait ten minutes or so, so the deer would not feel any pressure to escape. It would lie down and not be able to rise again. If he had hit the lungs or the heart with the arrow, the deer would actually be lying dead already within one hundred yards of him.

Colt saw the gray light of false dawn on the eastern horizon, so he lay down in his bedroll and decided to take a nap for half an hour. He programmed his mind to awaken him in that time. He fell asleep, and opened his eyes to the sight of the morning sun starting to creep up out of its own bed and casting its long slanted rays on the blue-and-purple prairie.

Chris checked for intruders in all directions, then rebuilt the cook-fire and put coffee on to boil. He was able to stand a lot easier this morning, having gained some strength from the food he had already eaten. He went out to look for the deer, and didn't have to go very far. The two-year-old buck had run about fifty yards and dropped over dead, with the arrow through his left lung and the edge of the heart.

Colt rolled him over and dressed him out. As

weak as he was, Colt was still able to drag the animal back to the tank, even carrying it a short distance. He hung it from a limb on one of the cottonwoods, then cut himself a breakfast steak.

Chris had some men to catch, but first he would build his strength back up as much as possible. He also had to report to General Custer with the Seventh Cavalry, so as he fixed breakfast he determined to come up with some kind of plan.

He set his frying pan on the fire and sliced a couple of pieces of bacon for grease. Next, he cut a green stick from the cottonwood tree and poured some flour and water into his coffee cup. He stirred them with his stick, finally swirling the dough he had created around the stick into a small biscuit. He made about five of these biscuits and dropped them into the sizzling bacon grease. He used the spit that had cooked the rabbits the night before and started to roast the steak from the buck's hindquarters. Chris rinsed his cup with a little bit of the boiling liquid and then poured out a cup of hot coffee.

He decided he would have to go on foot across the Great Sioux Indian Reservation in western South Dakota to Fort Abraham Lincoln, where he'd finally meet his new boss. He also decided that the two men would show up there by way of Fort Laramie, which was now due north of Chris and only a day or two away on horseback. Although Chris had had a Minniconjou wife and had spent much time with the Lakotah, he knew that tempers were hot right now. Very hot.

Ever since Custer took an expedition into the Black Hills in 1874 and came back with stories of tons of riches in gold, numerous white men had been killed venturing into the area trying to discover a bonanza. Colt didn't want to run into a war party of young hotheads who didn't know or care about him or his sympathies. He finally decided that it would be best to head back to Cheyenne, the closest friendly place to get a horse. It would still be four hundred miles to Fort Abraham Lincoln, even going in a straight line from Fort Laramie, and he was beyond his reporting date. He didn't want to lose his contract. He was certain the two traders would go first to Laramie, then marry up with a military patrol on its way to Fort Lincoln. If Chris had guessed correctly, the two men were in cahoots with his new boss and the Indian Ring.

Chris Colt had heard all about it, first from some of his friends who were American Indians. A group of Washington bureaucrats, working with crooked traders and Bureau of Indian Affairs agents at reservations, were taking government-supplied cattle, blankets, and other goods. They then sold these and bought cheap imitations that they would then issue to the Indians, pocketing the difference. In some cases the Indian agents simply shortchanged the Indians on the sum they were supposed to be receiving each month, then sold the surplus and filled their accounts with it. The Indian Ring's actions would likely starve out the red man over time. Eventually, the tribes would disappear.

Many people said that Custer was one of the main players in the infamous Indian Ring, and perhaps Chris Colt could now prove it. Anyone who knew what was going on knew that Long Hair desperately wanted the presidency, and he had no feelings other than disdain for the American Indian. He was a known egomaniac as well, and was looking for a major victory in the "Indian Wars" to launch his presidential bid.

If of nothing else, Chris Colt could be sure that the two illegal traders, his bushwhackers, would show up at Fort Abraham Lincoln. He might even luck out and run into them at Fort Laramie or before. They owed Chris for one good horse, plus medical bills. He would make sure they paid their debt—in blood.

His first challenge, however, simply would be to survive and somehow make the trip. The first test of that came right away, as Chris walked over to the tank to fill his canteen with fresh water and spotted some dots in the distance. He ran to the fire and started to kick the fresh dirt pile over it, but decided that would be a waste of time, as the riders would certainly come to this place anyway. Besides, he didn't have time to hide the deer carcass or other things.

He checked his guns and grabbed his Henry, making sure his backup guns were cleaned and loaded. Then he lay down among the rocks and waited, watching the dots grow larger and larger. It was a cavalry troop, but again Chris sensed something wrong. He listened to his intuition, always. In this case it told him to play it easy but careful; to keep his cards close to the vest.

Chris sat up, put more coffee in the pot, and set it on the fire. He had already secured his saddle from the body of Nighthawk and had cleaned it at the spring. He now leaned against it as he seated himself on a log, laid his Henry across his lap, and lit another smoke.

The patrol rode up and ground-reined their horses below the cottonwoods at the base of the rocks. They walked up with a friendly enough demeanor. It was a squad-sized patrol, with one corporal and five privates.

It dawned on Chris suddenly why he was troubled; the patrol was not riding in any type of formation. They had no point, flankers, or rear guard out. He understood that it was just a six-man patrol, and they didn't necessarily have to be in a formation, but it was enough to make him suspicious.

Chris got more concerned when he noticed the men walking toward him without the squad leader issuing any kind of orders to anyone to water horses, watch for bad guys, straighten their gig lines, or anything of the sort. He might just be an inefficient squad leader, but it was one more thing to make Chris wary. All the men walked toward the spring, emptying the remainders of their canteens.

"Howdy," the squad leader said. "Looks like you had yerself a bit a trouble, stranger," indicating the bandage on Chris's head and the dead horse lying out beyond the rocky jumble.

Chris said, "Yeah, I got dry-gulched by a couple of bushwhackers. Both real big, with beards. Got two pack animals with them. Have the look of hide-hunters. Seen 'em?"

One of the privates said, "Nay, laddie, we ain't seen the likes a anybody for all the days we been out an' about."

The corporal gave the man a dirty look and said, "We're with Troop K, Seventh Cavalry. Been out on patrol for a long time."

"I guess," Chris said, fishing, "it's over four hundred miles to Fort Lincoln. I'd think Fort

Laramie or Fort Fetterman would have this territory in their area of operations."

Chris noticed one of the privates off to his left start to reach for his pistol, but another grabbed his wrist and stopped him.

The corporal smiled. "Yeah, well tell that to the old man."

"Who's your CO?" Chris asked.

"Captain Godfrey," the squad leader replied.

"Oh yeah, Ed Godfrey," Chris said. "So you're all with Captain Benteen's battalion. How's the old Son of the Morning Star doing?"

"Custer!" one of the privates exclaimed. "He's a glory-hungry, crazy son of a bitch, and he's gonna get all his men killed!"

Chris smiled and took a swallow of coffee, waiting to see if the man got reprimanded for publicly bitching about his commanding officer. A couple of men chuckled, and that was it.

The corporal said, "How you know so much about the Seventh Cav, mister?"

"Ah, the name's Chris Colt," the scout said. "When I got ambushed, I was on my way to Fort Lincoln. I'm going to be Custer's chief of scouts."

Chris noticed several men acting startled, but the corporal smiled and went on, "So you'll be reporting to either Lieutenant Hare or Varnum. They're the OICs of scouts. There's five other civilian scouts—well, Fred Girard and Isaiah Dorman are considered interpreters, but they scout a little too. There's also the Jacksons, Billy and Bobby, and Charley Reynolds."

"What about George Herendeen?" Chris said.

"He's working as a courier," the corporal said.

Chris heard a gun cocking off to his right and turned to see a red-haired, red-faced trooper pointing a pistol at him. "This is bullshit, Mitch! He's gonna spill his guts when he gits to Lincoln and tells 'em where he seen us! We gotta kill 'im, so quit pussy-footin' around. Now, get shut a that Henry, Colt."

Chris felt anger begin to burn in his ears. His face flushed. "You're making a big mistake, mister," he said. "Sure, it's obvious to me you're all deserters, but by the time I get to Lincoln, you'll be long gone from here."

The man said, "But it's less than fifty miles to Fort Laramie. Sorry, but you gotta die."

Chris started to stand and said, "Now, look."

With that, he swung the Henry up and fired from the hip while diving to his left. He saw flame blossom from the man's gun and heard the crack of the bullet as it passed him by. A big red patch appeared over the man's heart on his dusty blue tunic, as he flew backward, quite dead. Chris cocked the Henry, and as he hit the ground he drew his belly gun with his left hand.

Another private felt lucky and went for his gun, but was clumsily fumbling with the big leather flap over the butt when Chris's left-hand gun spoke loudly. The bullet took the man right through the left cheek, tearing the side of his head off. The man fell to the ground and clawed frantically at the bloody mass where his face had been. He twitched a few times spasmodically and died, after having run away from the cavalry to avoid just such a horrible death in battle.

This scene had a very sobering effect on the other troopers, who all raised their hands. Chris kept them covered with both guns and signaled that they should all drop their gun belts and step away, which each man did quickly and efficiently.

Chris said, "Now, you lily-livered cowards. You bring me that sorrel over there and saddle him with my saddle here. Use the lead lines to tie the other horses together."

"Mr. Colt!" the corporal said pleadingly. "You ain't gonna leave us out here without horses, are you?"

Chris said, "Your friend was going to leave me out here dead, and I didn't see you stopping him. You're playing a rough game, mister, and you shouldn't have picked up the cards if you weren't willing to call or raise."

One of the other privates stepped forward and said, "You talk big with a gun in each hand, and we're unarmed. You ain't leaving me without a horse."

Chris smiled and said, "Partner, if you really had any guts, I guess you'd be back with your buddies you left at Fort Abraham Lincoln, so don't try a brave act now."

"Set those guns down, and we'll see how tough you are," he went on.

Chris laughed, "I'm tough, but I'm not stupid. Speak one more word, and you'll find out how tough I am."

The man, shamed by Chris's talk about being a coward, looked at his cohorts, all of whom were looking to see if he would do anything.

He said, "I told—"

Boom! The Henry roared, and the man went down onto his face with a scream, both hands grabbing at the bloody hole through his right thigh. All the men looked at Chris, as he cocked the rifle with one hand.

Colt grinned broadly and said, "A man is only

as good as his word. If I say something, I mean it. Now, anybody else want to argue?"

The men just stood transfixed, then as one started to shake their heads no.

"Good," he went on. "Get those horses ready. I'll be on my way."

Chris had hated to shoot an unarmed man, but on the other hand he'd had to take bold action against superior numbers. Otherwise they would have had the sense to all go for their guns at once, and he would be dead. Besides that, cowardly men who could leave their friends before an upcoming battle sickened him. He understood that Custer was an ego-driven, self-centered bastard who'd probably get some men killed on his road to glory, but Chris Colt hated cowardice. He himself had felt fear many times. He was afraid every time he confronted danger, but Colt had learned that by conquering that fear and doing what was right you improved and strengthened yourself.

He left the bewildered deserters behind him at the rock tank, their guns lashed to the saddle of the last horse. When he was two hundred yards up the road he unlashed the guns, and they fell to the ground with a clatter. He knew that the ex-soldiers would be watching him intently, as they would most certainly be lost without guns to protect themselves. He checked all the horses and ensured that the lead line of each was tied in a knot to the tail of the horse in front of it.

He was headed north now, toward Fort Laramie, where he would turn in the extra mounts and keep the sorrel for himself. He would send a telegram to Long Hair, then head to Lincoln

with the next troop movement. It wasn't necessary now to return to Cheyenne, and Chris felt
a little bit sad.

He also felt sore. His head pounded like the
receiving end of a miner's doubletree. His back
was sore from slamming into the ground when
he was shot, and the side of his head would probably continue to hurt for several more days anyway. He also would get irritable, because he felt
confused. Chris had seen enough of head wounds
to know that that was a fairly normal occur-
rence. He had seen others lose part of their memory and also have trouble adding and subtracting
things for months afterward. It was natural to
get frustrated over those small details.

He traveled a long way that night before he
went a mile off the road to make camp. He figured he would pull into Fort Laramie early the
next morning. Chris found a grove of cottonwood
around a small spring, which fed a creek. He
built a small fire and had some more venison
steak, which he had packed.

Chris had gone far enough that he wouldn't
have to fear the deserters following him on foot,
although he didn't believe they wanted a part of
him again. Colt was puzzled by men like that.
They felt the same fear he and every other man
felt, but *they* succumbed to it. He wondered how
they would be able to go the rest of their days
knowing that they had sneaked away from their
duties like a thief in the night.

Chris grinned as he remembered a conversation with one of the gunsmiths in his uncle's
firearms factory. The man had been one of the
very first gunfighters ever, winning many battles, until a rifle-toting lawman had missed his

chest and put a bullet through the back of the man's right hand. His youth and his wild gun-fighting days were over, so he decided to settle down and learn a trade. He became a master gunsmith.

The man and young Chris Colt were having a conversation about courage one day when the gunsmith said, "Youngun, the difference betwixt a coward and a hero is about one minute in time."

Chris was perplexed by that statement, and it bothered him for a long time afterward, but he had finally gotten a handle on it. He got into a fight with two brothers whose family owned a farm just outside Cuyahoga Falls. Their family and his had attended the same church, but the two brothers were about the farthest thing you could get from walking the Christian walk of life. They were troublemakers from the get-go.

The two bullies simply beat up everybody, and finally Chris's turn came up. Everyone had backed down from the bullies because they were so tough and brutal—they would chase a person down and beat him senseless. When one of them started to pick on Chris, he tried everything he could think of to avoid getting into a fight. When one of the two, however, made some disparaging remarks about a girl in Chris's church whose father had been arrested for public drunkenness, Chris finally had had it. He was scared—their brutality had become legendary locally—but he was beyond caring at that point.

Chris managed to seem so ferocious in his demeanor alone that the two bullies looked a little unsettled. Colt had heard somewhere that a man using his head has a much better chance in a fight than one who just uses his muscle, so he tried to think his way out of trouble. When the first punch was thrown, it landed square on Chris's temple and sent him reeling to the ground. His right hand closed around a smooth, egg-shaped rock lying on the ground, and he grabbed it without his adversaries noticing.

The two brothers ran up and both kicked him in the rib cage, knocking the wind out of him and severely bruising the ribs. Most boys would have folded over and cried, but this simply made Chris furious. He came off the ground with a fury and tore into both brothers. His fists were swinging so wildly and so quickly, nobody noticed the rock sticking out of the ends of his right fist. The faces of the bullies, however, showed signs of the rock. Within a minute, both brothers were lying on the ground unconscious, each sporting two black eyes and a broken nose. Chris dropped the rock behind his back and nobody ever saw it.

He became the hero of the young girl he had defended, and of the whole community. His repute grew, as did the story of the fight with each telling. In actuality, part of the reason he went off to fight in the Civil War was his worry that the two bullies might try to get retribution. It bothered him to leave like that, but as he grew and gained confidence, he realized how smart he had really been. One thing he never forgot were the butterflies he'd felt in his stomach when he'd had to face the two bullies, and the great fear that had clutched at him. It would have been so easy to start his life out as a coward back then; instead, Chris Colt chose to act like a man. That decision made him a hero.

It was well short of noon when Chris Colt caught sight of Fort Laramie. It was also well short of noon when Luke and Buck Sawyer, ever uneasy and vigilant, caught sight of Chris Colt approaching Fort Laramie. At precisely the same moment, they made the decision to light out cross-country for Fort Abraham Lincoln, instead of waiting three more days for the supply train, which was carrying fresh goods from Denver.

The garrison surgeon fixed Chris up pretty well—he said the head wound had been healing nicely. Colt sent a telegram to Custer, explaining about the ambush and saying he would travel to Abraham Lincoln with the next available troop movement, which was to be in three days. A short, terse reply came back from the Boy General to leave immediately by the shortest and quickest route possible.

Chris was able to hang on to the sorrel after turning in the other horses, saddles, and making the report about the deserters. He got resupplied and decided to take off the next day, giving himself one more chance to rest and recuperate. He decided to keep quiet about who had ambushed him, because of the duo's obvious tie-in to Custer.

What he didn't know was that the pair of swindlers had another ambush planned for him. They couldn't afford to let Colt get to Fort Lincoln. Number one, they were making tons of money hauling trade goods for General Custer and buying and selling where they were directed. Number two, and more importantly, was the fact that George Custer would have them both snuffed—and damned fast—if they allowed anyone or anything to let the cat out of the bag.

The two men didn't know how long Colt would stay at Fort Laramie, but they would go slightly north and wait.

There was a new trail called the Texas Trail that had just been run by some cattlemen from Lone Star country. But the most common route would be heading north toward the Black Hills on the Cheyenne-Deadwood stage road, which cut back to the east at the Hat Creek stage station about forty-five miles due north of Fort Laramie along the border. Either way, they figured they would spot him from the highlands over the headwaters of Rawhide Creek, which ran south down into the North Platte River. From there they could plan an ambush.

Wherever, they could not let the scout get to Custer. He *had* to know they had ambushed them. If they could kill him north of Laramie, they'd make it look like Indians had done it. Hell, Luke thought, Lieutenant Grattan and thirty-nine soldiers from the fort had been killed right there at Laramie twenty-two years earlier, and plenty of white men had been killed since. Nobody would even investigate. Sure, this time they would do the job right.

In fact, Chris Colt planned to head due north of Fort Laramie to and through the Black Hills, then head a little more northeast to Fort Abraham Lincoln. He had no plans to be ambushed by those snakes again, and he also had to be constantly on the lookout for the numerous Lakotah (Sioux), Chyela (Cheyenne), and even Crow patrols in the area. Many warriors were riding around with their ponies' tails tied in knots, and allies or not, Colt didn't want to end up with his scalp hanging on the end of someone's coup staff.

Colt left Fort Laramie the next morning at first light. The Texas Trail actually ran into the Cheyenne-Deadwood Trail a little bit north of Laramie, but thousands of cattle had been pushed up the trail from Texas to Montana, so it was easy going. He had decided he would alternate between a trot and a fast walk, then break for lunch and a siesta to rest his head some more. Then he'd push on.

By mid-morning he was paralleling the high ridges just east of Rawhide Creek, and it was there that the two brothers first spotted him and decided to set up their ambush just a little further north. They took off at a dead run for a mile, then picked out a spot that rose up a little over the trail but was a bit lower than the ridge line. They figured he would show up in about half an hour, and they were right. But they were just learning about Christopher Columbus Colt.

The tall rider got closer and closer, and both men lay down under the bushes they were using for hiding spots atop the bluff. Both men hid beneath bison hides, so their gun barrels wouldn't accidentally emit any sunshine glints. The scout trotted the horse closer and bobbed up and down in their sights. He was almost in range of the Sharps, but suddenly he veered off to the east and went out of range. He kept riding northward, but veering sharply to the east at the same time. Both men were completely puzzled. They had taken every precaution, yet somehow he had still seen them.

Chris saw a bluff up ahead that would make a perfect spot for an ambush with a big Sharps or even a Spencer like the other one was carrying. He had no idea if those two polecats were anywhere about, and he figured it was more than likely they had gone, long before, to Fort Abraham Lincoln. In any event, he was not about to get shot from ambush again. At least, not by them. His eyes were peeled for any sunlight glints off of rifle barrels, but he saw none. Still, the bluff would be an excellent spot to lay low and fire at him from ambush, so Chris swung the sorrel out toward the east and made a big arc around the rise, keeping himself well out of rifle range.

"That sorry sumbitch!" Buck exclaimed. "How in the hell did he know we was here?"

"Mebbe he didn't," Luke answered. "Mebbe he's jest bein' careful. We plugged him oncet. Mebbe he don't cotton to havin' too damn many bullet holes through his skull."

Buck chuckled. "Mebbe so. Leastways, now we kin foller 'im and figger out jest where and when we wanna make a perfect ambush."

The two men returned to their horses and took off after Colt, keeping well back behind him. They didn't want him to turn around and spot them. And that's how the journey continued, with Chris Colt traveling ahead and the two bushwhackers following at a distance.

On the third day out, Colt decided it was time to investigate the people who were following him at a distance and leaving the little dust puffs he could just make out when he shinnied occasional trees to check his backtrail. One night he set up camp in a grove of piñons not too far from Devil's Tower, and built his fire. He then left it burning while he crept back on his own backtrail and located the fire of the Sawyer brothers. He didn't want to tip his hand, so he didn't go all the way to their fire, just close enough to see the glow on the trees. It was a considerable glow, at that.

Chris remembered a talk he had had with his ex-father-in-law one time, when the old man had said, "Wise Lakotah build small fire, keep close and warm all over. Enemy no see. Stupid *wasicun* [white man] build big fire, burn one side, freeze other, signal his enemies."

Chris knew that it had to be the Sawyers following, and he decided that they deserved a lesson. He didn't want to kill them, as he wanted to let them marry up with Long Hair so he could see what developed. The next day, he had plans for them. He thought about what he'd do, and started to laugh to himself.

"C'mon, Red," Chris said, turning the horse back toward his own campfire, "let's go get some shut-eye. Tomorrow's going to be a fun day."

The next day started with a brilliant red sky in the eastern sky at daybreak.

Chris took a swallow of coffee and said, "Damn, going to storm today, Red. Guess it's going to be tougher on the Sawyers than I even planned it would be."

He was saddled, fed, and ready to go about fifteen minutes or so after daybreak. The only difference was that, on this day, he would change his morning routine. Chris didn't pour water or loose dirt on his fire, as he always did. Smoke started to pour out of the heretofore smokeless fire.

Colt swung up on the army sorrel and trotted off toward the open prairie. He meandered in a general northeasterly direction though, staying low with the curvature of the land.

The two men, in their own camp, didn't notice Chris anywhere, as he stuck to trees and arroyos. They did notice the smoke from his campfire, so they stayed by their fire and drank coffee. Luke, in fact, made jokes about the stupidity of a cavalry scout who would have so much smoke coming from his cooking fire.

After an hour the pair finally started to get suspicious, and after another hour they took off toward Chris's campfire.

Smoke still swirled out of the fire as they rode up to it, but the mesquite was burned up and no ashes from it were visible. The two brothers assumed that Colt must have just decided to leave his fire burning, or had forgotten to put it out. Now, they worried about how long ago he had left.

Buck said, "Sumbitch! Dammit, we better get the hell down the road and catch up to 'im. Ain't no tellin' how long ago he lit out."

The two brothers took off, leaving the smoking campfire behind them. As soon as they had dipped out of sight, Chris Colt, wearing a big grin, rode out of the trees and dismounted. He got out his pot and made a pot of coffee. After pouring out a cup he extinguished the fire, then poured the balance of the pot on the hot embers.

Several other pairs of eyes had watched all of this from a distance. One pair, dark eyes encircled by copper-colored skin, had a wise look. The eyes smiled as they watched Chris Colt completely extinguish the fire, then kick the embers around to make sure it was out. The same eyes had been watching since the first smoke went up. The wise set of eyes smiled again as Chris Colt leisurely set out on the trail of Buck and Luke Sawyer.

The men with the dark eyes mounted their horses and followed Colt at a distance. They were curious and felt this would indeed be an adventurous day. The tail of each of their horses hung in a knot. The one with the wise eyes reached down and adjusted the sheepskin anklet on his right shin. It covered the bullet scar from a long-ago battle. He always wore it. He had a secret. Everybody thought that he could not be touched by bullets. They all thought he was blessed by spirits that protected him. They knew that his medicine was strong. Everyone looked up to this Lakotah war hero, the strongheart with the name of Crazy Horse.

Luke's eyes scanned the ground in front of him, as they followed the telltale tracks of the red horse. He would have expected the scout to have an Appaloosa, the kind of horse scouts used because they could turn on a dime and give you nine cents change. They were exceptionally good in the mountains, which is where it really counted in his line of work. The Army usually crossbred Morgans with standardbreds, and preferred those for remounts. They also used Arabians and thoroughbreds, but they liked the Morgan cross the best, especially when they bred to get mules.

Luke and Buck kept watching the ground for the telltale tracks of the cavalry-shod sorrel. The ground was all plains after a short distance, and they simply had to look down occasionally to see the tracks in the tall grass.

"Hell!" Buck yelled suddenly, looking up.

Luke looked ahead and saw a giant torn-up trail on the plains ahead. The trail was all dust and trampled-down grasses, one foot deep and about a mile wide. Thousands of buffalo had been along here and had just about destroyed any chance the two brothers had of following Chris Colt.

After ten minutes of sorting his tracks out among all the split-hoof tracks of the bison, however, they suffered another setback when they found a spot where the scout had gotten off his horse and done something with the mount's feet. They could tell Colt had covered the hooves with something, as the tracks showed no sign of shoes, nor any clarity on the edges.

Luke said, "Wal, don't matter. This here trail's headin' north, and he's headin' northeast to Fort Abryham Lincoln. We know that, so let's jest head there our own damn selves."

Buck said, "Ya think he seen us, when he left his fire goin'?"

"Naw, jest bein' careful. He ain't no dummy. Jest in case anyone was follerin' him his fire'd make 'em think he was still in camp."

That evening, the two brothers made camp at the base of Crow Buttes, near the northwestern corner of South Dakota Territory. They didn't see the tall figure on the distant horizon behind them, as the sky grew dark. If they had, they might have just kept on going or tried to set up an ambush. Anxious to catch up with the clever scout, who they were sure was ahead of them, and trying to make their goal of Crow Buttes, they rode well into the evening.

* * *

The men of C Company of the Seventh Cavalry sat in formation and listened while the big blond-haired sergeant held a metal contraption up in his right hand.

He yelled, "The British curb bit is very heavy for a bit, and is also just as powerful as the American 'Shoemaker bit' that many of you have been using up to now. The construction of such a bit is all metal, and the weight of the bit, along with the bridoon, is two and three-quarter pounds. Those of you who have not switched to the British curb bit and still have the Shoemakers will switch bits prior to getting in the chow line. It's more severe than the German curb bit we tried, and the old man likes it the best."

Two of the privates sat on the ground in the midst of the formation, and one whispered to the other, "I can't believe we haven't eaten yet, and the son of a bitch is talking to us about what to stick in our horses' mouths."

The sergeant continued. "Now, you lucky bastards you, I know we have all been out on patrol today, but every man who does not have a British curb bit properly affixed to his mount's headstall will do so before jumping into the chow line this evening. Squad leaders, you are to inspect all bits before allowing any trooper to chow down. Do I make my damned self clear?"

"Dammit," the private hissed between his teeth, "who's runnin' this tribe a red niggers, anyhow?"

Inside the garrison headquarters building, Custer watched out the window along with his adjutant, Lieutenant Bill Cooke. He watched the troopers from his brother Tom's company as they got instructions about a new bit to be used, and wondered if they would bring him victory when they eventually cornered the Sioux and Cheyenne to teach them a lesson. He held Colt's latest telegram in his left hand, and he wondered if the new chief of scouts would help contribute to the victory. If I can only pull it off, he thought, I'll become President of the United States of America. The *power*, what power I'll have if I achieve the presidency! Long Hair stared out at the prairie and wondered where Colt was now, and what he was doing.

Chris kept his horse trotting toward Crow Butte's outline on the night sky, just knowing that the two brothers would predictably make camp on the land mass, or by it. When Chris arrived, he couldn't locate the campsite right away, so he simply rode carefully around in circles until he smelled wood smoke. He rode upwind toward it. The two men had found a buffalo wallow at the base of one of the hills and built a small greasewood fire in the bottom.

Knowing now what he wanted, Chris rode off and around the base of the butte, plunging his horse up the other side.

Knowing that the two foolish *wasicun* would make camp at Crow Butte, Crazy Horse held his charges well back from the buttes, not wanting to get careless and be spotted by the wise one— the one who was married before to his wife's cousin, Chantapeta. The man had put leather boots on his horse to hide the tracks from his iron shoes, but the other two were very easy to follow, and Crazy Horse knew that this Colt had his paint on. He saw that Colt wore a white ban-

dage around his head, so these two men probably
had wounded Colt somehow. Crazy Horse
grinned as he decided they must have done it
from ambush, because he could not see either
man counting coup on this wise one, Wamble
Uncha, or fighting him head-on. Crazy Horse
could see the outline of the buttes against the
night sky, but he couldn't make out the lone
rider climbing the butte on the sorrel horse.

When he and his men got closer, Crazy Horse
would stop the war party out on the prairie and
leave one man with the horses. He would lead
the rest of the men in closer to locate the *wasicun*
and stay back and have fun watching what Wamble Uncha would do to the other white-eyes.

Chris held back and peered over the edge of
the wallow, as the two brothers ate jerky, hardtack, and drank coffee by their fire. He grinned
as he listened to the two men brag to each other
about all the things they were going to do to him
when they caught up to him.

Luke finally lay down in his bedroll and was
snoring within minutes. Colt grinned again as he
noticed that Buck was up to something. Buck
crept over and checked Luke carefully to ensure
that he was asleep. Then he went over to his
pack, which had been diamond-hitched on the
mule he was leading. Reaching inside one of the
boxes, he produced half a bottle of whiskey and
sat back down by the fire. He pulled at the
amber liquid and belched loudly. Buck froze as
Luke stirred in his sleep, then relaxed as the
snoring resumed. Chris shook his head nega-
tively as the ex-skinner took another swig at the
neck of the bottle. Chris thought to himself how

low the man had to be to hold out on his own brother.

In time, Buck hid the bottle in the box again, almost all of its contents now working its way through his system. He finally curled up in his blanket, head on his saddle. When he had lain there unmoving for ten minutes, Chris started to crawl down on his belly.

Halfway up the butte, behind several bushes and rocks, Crazy Horse and several of his men watched with amusement, while the brave *wasicun* called Colt crept down the side of the wallow toward the two men.

Suddenly Buck sat up like a shot and Chris Colt froze in place, less than ten feet away and slightly off to Buck's right, clearly in the man's line of sight. Colt didn't move an inch, but watched the trader through squinted eyes.

Chris didn't want the firelight to reflect off his eyeballs, the shine alerting the man just feet away. In the manner of the Native Americans who had taught him so much, Colt didn't look directly at Buck Sawyer or Luke. Instead, he looked at the spot on the ground right next to them. If he did look at them, it was only for brief glances. The Lakotah, Apache, and several other nations believed that one could feel, or actually sense, a person's eyes if one stared at another. Chris reasoned it out and remembered times in his life when he had gotten a shiver as if someone were watching him behind his back, and it turned out to be true.

Buck didn't notice Chris, for the moment. The big trader pulled out some makings from his left shirt pocket and rolled some tobacco. He lit his cigarette and laid his head back on the saddle, staring up at the stars. He dragged smoke deep into his lungs and then let it drift out his nostrils. Chris still didn't move an eyelid as he watched the big man start to drift off, cigarette in his mouth.

The wind came from behind Chris and a little to his left, slipping down the side of the wallow and into the scout's nostrils. Chris smelled bear, and he suddenly came alert. Chris knew what he was really smelling.

Just when the cigarette was almost ready to burn Buck's lips, his eyes popped open and he tossed the butt into the burning fire. Then his eyes closed, and he was snoring within a minute's time. Chris waited a few more minutes and slowly crept forward. He made his way to the fire, moving at a snail's pace. At the fire, he stood and grabbed a burned-out coal and walked over to the sleeping figure of Luke. He bent over and lightly drew a mark across Luke's throat with the ember. The snoring man reached up and brushed at his throat, then went back to sleep.

Chris always carried moccasins in his saddlebags for just such an occasion, so it was in his moccasins and in utter silence that he crawled back up the edge of the buffalo wallow and grabbed something hidden in the sod. Chris returned to the sleeping form of Luke Sawyer with a cross made of piñon and lashed at the crux with leather thongs. He had carved the letters RIP on the horizontal crossbar. Instead of dulling his own knife, Chris withdrew Luke's from his sheath. Then he dug a hole just beyond his head and buried the end of the cross in it, tamping it down as quietly as he could.

Chris stood at the base of Luke's feet and admired his handiwork, smiling to himself. He decided not to do the same with Buck, as he would save another surprise for him. He did, however, remember the bear smell he had been smelling every time the wind blew from the butte toward him. With that in mind, Chris carefully bent down and reached into Buck's pocket, retrieving the pouch of smoking tobacco.

He crept over to Luke and, finding another pouch of tobacco in his pocket, gingerly pulled it out. He held up both tobacco pouches and displayed them to unseen parties in the direction of the butte. Chris tossed both pouches of tobacco toward the butte, and both pouches disappeared into the darkness over the lip of the wallow. Seconds later, a Lakotah arrow whooshed through the darkness and stuck into the ground between Chris Colt's feet. Chris smiled, displayed the arrow over his head, and tossed it into the darkness in the direction of the tobacco pouches.

Out on the side of the butte, Crazy Horse grinned in the darkness and signaled two warriors ahead to fetch the tobacco pouches. He marveled at Chantapeta's widower, wondering how the *wasicun* could know of their presence.

Chris left the wallow and used a circuitous route to head back toward his horses. He knew the Lakotah, like the Apache, admired courage, but that didn't necessarily mean they wanted to sit down by a fire and eat buffalo hump together and swap war stories. He returned to the campfire he had made atop the butte and fixed himself a quick meal of coffee, biscuits, and a pheasant he had shot with his bow from his horse earlier in the day.

At first he was going to move off elsewhere to

sleep a little that night, but he decided that the two men would never even consider looking for him on the butte. The Lakotah knew where he was and would continue to watch him no matter where he went, but obviously, at least for now, they were enjoying the show. He had thought he'd smelled the heavy scent of bear, but he realized quickly that it was the more familiar smell of bear grease used by the Lakotah to keep their hair shiny, attractive, and manageable. They bathed often and kept themselves clean, much cleaner than any of the soldiers Chris worked for. Still, bluebellies ironically referred to the Indians as "filthy savages."

Colt rolled up in his bedroll for a few hours of sleep, making a mental note to awaken himself at first light. It was actually a habit of his anyway to awaken a little before dawn, so he was sure he would, although he would only have had about four hours sleep.

Dawn came quickly, and Chris snapped himself to consciousness. He looked down from his perch and saw that the two men were still asleep.

He relieved himself and saddled up, checked his guns, then drank water from his canteen and ate cold jerked venison. Chris ground-reined the sorrel, then crawled to the edge of the butte to watch the two men below. An hour later, Chris still knelt motionless under some mesquite, and the two brothers finally awakened. Seeing the cross and the stripe across the throat of his brother, Buck started cussing like crazy and kicking logs from the firewood pile.

Luke still wasn't quite awake, as yet. A minute or so later, though, he was totally shaken when it dawned on him what had happened. It took another minute for him to realize there was something wrong with him, and he dug the little piece of broken mirror out of his saddlebags and started screaming when he saw the black mark across his throat. At first he thought it was dried blood and was totally hysterical, clutching at his windpipe and making gurgling sounds. This kept on until Buck came over and gave him a swift kick. Buck then reached out and scraped some of the black off of Luke's neck and held it up in front of his face.

"I don't care!" Luke screamed. "Don't you know he coulda kilt us both, jest like that?"

"I don't give a damn!" Buck screamed back. "He's jest tryin' to scare us, and it's workin' with you, idjit!"

"It don't matter," Luke replied angrily. "He's lettin' us know he *coulda* kilt us. It's bad enough the country's crawlin' with red niggers. Now we gotta put up with this Colt character. He ain't human, I tell ya. He's a devil. It gives me the creeps!"

"Hell," Buck went on, "let's pack up and git outta here. We gotta really watch fer redskins from here on, and watch close fer this Colt feller, too. When we find 'im, believe me, we'll make 'im pay. In spades!"

Chris watched as the two men loaded up their pack mules and horses and took off. He waited until they were well off in the distance before he left the butte, but first he turned toward the adjoining butte and waved. On the other butte, separated from Colt by a small saddle of land, Crazy Horse, hiding under some mesquite himself, grinned broadly. He knew Colt couldn't see him or his men, but the *wasicun* knew they were there watching him. Colt disappeared over the edge of the butte, and Crazy Horse signaled for his dispersed warriors to assemble around him.

In 1876, numerous battles had already been fought at Slim Buttes, but Chris figured the two brothers would be in too much of a hurry to avoid the hills. He decided he would chance it and circle out past them, to give them another surprise at Slim Buttes. Colt stayed out further to the west and kept his cavalry mount at a fast trot, alternating with a canter. It was about thirty-two miles cross-country to Slim Buttes, and there was some woodland when they got closer. Chris would have enough cover to slip ahead.

That afternoon, Colt found a spot that would be just right for his plans for Slim Buttes. What he didn't know, however, was that Crazy Horse also thought Slim Buttes would be the best place to plan an ambush for these crazy *wasicun*.

Colt found a small hill before the buttes, from which he planned to shoot numerous holes through the supplies being carried on Luke's and Buck's pack mules. If he got a chance, he'd also punch some holes through their canteens.

Crazy Horse had taken a different route, swinging wide to the east to set up his ambush just before the hill where Chris Colt lay hidden. He figured that the two brothers would keep their eyes on the buttes. It was a place where enemies might hide; he would surprise them in the open space before the buttes.

The two brothers arrived within the hour, and rode into a draw that naturally funneled them past Chris Colt. Crazy Horse didn't have anyone follow Colt, as he was sure the white man would follow the other two. Colt guessed that the Indians who had seen him back at Crow Buttes were after the supplies and scalps, and would follow the white men with the pack animals. He had no idea it was Crazy Horse, the already famous Oglala Lakotah war hero.

The two brothers rode side-by-side up the draw, and Chris Colt's Henry boomed from the nearby hill off to their left front. One of the boxes on the second pack mule exploded with a bullet's impact, and pieces of it and its contents flew sideways as the mule reared and lurched sideways. A second shot hit the pack on the lead mule just as the Lakotah ambush opened up. Warriors dashed out from both sides of the draw, most attempting to rush in and touch the *wasicun* before killing them to count coups. Counting coups in a battle was much more important than killing an enemy.

The two men hardly knew what was hitting them, as rounds poured at them from all directions. Chris Colt wanted the two men dead, but in a pinch they'd be on his side, no matter how bad they were. With that thought in mind, he started pouring shot after shot into the positions of the Lakotah ambushers. No choice. He jumped on his horse and rode into the ambush, to help the low-lifes fight off the Lakotah warriors.

Chris plunged down the hill and into the draw, putting his heels to the horse's ribs and drawing his Colt .44. He poured fire at the figures coming from both steep sides of the draw.

He saw Luke go down, with three bullets in his massive frame. Buck flew backward, with two bullets slamming into his chest as Luke fell. Both men lay dying on the ground as Chris reached them. His horse took a rifle bullet through the side of the head and did a somersault at full gallop, with Chris Colt kicking out of the stirrups. His feet hit the ground at a run, but his speed was too fast, and like his mount he too did a somersault, firing into the chest of an attacking warrior, upside down, while he somersaulted.

More warriors poured through the draw. Colt put his last bullet through the shoulder of one. He yanked his big Bowie knife out and faced the charging warriors, while reaching down into his boot with his left hand. He yanked out a Colt Third Model .41-caliber pearl-handled derringer, cocked it, and fired point-blank into the face of a charging dog soldier. The warrior dropped like he had been hit on the head with a two-hundred-pound sledge hammer, his eyes crossing in death as if he were trying to view the bullet that had just split his eyes and skull.

Chris dropped the gun and swung his big knife, turning from side to side, facing ten warriors who now surrounded him with various weapons. He jumped and threw his body sideways into the chests of the two closest braves, knocking them both down, their wind leaving them in a simultaneous rush. He rolled to his feet and slit open the abdomen of another brave who had ventured in too close. The warrior rose up on his toes to grab at his stomach, then crumpled in a heap.

There seemed to be a momentary standoff, as the remaining warriors circled him slowly, taunting him. Chris knew that ultimately he was going to die, but he would do it as a warrior. He heard a horse approach behind him, and he turned to glimpse the war-painted face of Crazy

Horse, just before his pony slammed into Chris and knocked him in one direction, his knife in the other. Warriors jumped on him from all directions and pinned him to the ground.

Crazy Horse spun the horse around and walked him back to Chris Colt, smiling at the captured *wasicun*. Chris was dragged to his feet and his hands were quickly bound behind his back with rawhide, the end of the thong then looped and tied around his neck.

Crazy Horse wore his familiar anklet, a single hawk feather in his hair, a breechcloth, and a stone behind his left ear, as was his custom. He had a zigzag line of war paint, like red lightning, that started at the top of the middle of his forehead and went down to a point below his chin. Other than that, he wore only his weapons. He also had covered himself and his horse with fine dust, another of his customs before battle.

He was magnificent and proud as he rode his painted horse and faced Chris Colt.

Crazy Horse spoke in Sioux. "You are the one they call 'Wamble Uncha,' who is blood brother to the Minniconjou. Do you know who I am?"

Chris said, "You are Crazy Horse of the Oglala, son of the mighty warrior Worm, who gave away his name to you because of your many brave deeds in battle. It has been almost as many winters as toes on your feet and fingers on your hand since you were called Curly. I have heard much about your courage and the blessing in battle you have from the Great Mystery, but I must have heard lies. You must only fight enemies who are tied up and held for you by your fellow warriors."

Crazy Horse grinned.

"They call you 'Colt'?"

Chris nodded.

"Colt does not like to be tied, and tries to start fires in my heart with his words, so I will untie his bonds," Crazy Horse said.

Chris grinned at the wise warrior.

Crazy Horse said, "Your bonds will be cut, for now, if you give your word not to flee or to fight."

Colt said, "You are my enemy. If you cut my bonds, I will fight you and your warriors."

Crazy Horse grinned again, "You speak like Lakotah."

Chris responded, "I am Lakotah and Apache, but I am also *wasicun*."

Crazy Horse said, "Why did you fight us when we attacked these white-eyes? They were your enemies."

Chris looked at the two men, who were either dead or very close to it.

Chris said, "They are white and so am I. There is a war between our people. You are my enemy."

Crazy Horse said, "Where do you go? Do you go to join Long Hair?"

Chris said, "Yes, I will be his chief of scouts."

Crazy Horse seemed disturbed, but not shocked.

He spoke again, "You were married to one of my people, and you ride with our enemies, the Crow and the Arikara?"

Chris said, "I have my reasons."

Crazy Horse thought for a minute and said, "Then they are honorable reasons. Your wife and daughter were killed by the Crow dogs. You and I are enemies, but we are also brothers."

He nodded, and the bonds on Chris's wrist and neck were cut.

Chris rubbed the circulation back into his wrists and said, "It is not polite to speak of the dead."

Crazy Horse continued, "This is true. I hope we do not meet in battle. I do not want to kill you."

Chris laughed and said, "You won't."

Crazy Horse responded, "Meet you in battle?"

Chris said, "No, *kill* me in battle."

Crazy Horse laughed as he slid his left leg over his horse's neck and slid off the right side, the side the American Indians mounted on, opposite of the white man. He walked over to Chris Colt and handed him the reins to his war pony.

Chris took the reins and stared at Crazy Horse, a questioning look on his face.

Crazy Horse said, "A gift. If I have to meet you in battle, I will take it back."

"If you meet me in battle," Chris said, "you will only need it to ride the spirit trail."

Crazy Horse smiled.

Chris reached down and picked up his Colt .41 derringer. He dusted it off and cocked it, breaking the barrel open sideways. He reached in his gun belt and pulled out a handful of .41 bullets. Chris started to hand them to Crazy Horse, but stopped just short.

He said, "A gift for my enemy. Your word you will not use this against *wasicun*?"

Crazy Horse nodded.

Chris showed him how to load the little gun and how to cock it. Several braves helped him lift the lifeless body of the sorrel and remove his saddle. He also removed his bridle.

Crazy Horse sat on the ground and pulled out one of the tobacco pouches Chris had tossed to him the night before. Colt recognized it and grinned again. Crazy horse lit a pipe, then offered smoke to the four points of the compass. Chris sat down across from him and accepted

the pipe. They both smoked in silence, then
Chris got up, saddled up, and left without looking back.

When he had gotten out of sight of the Lakotah, he pushed the pony into a canter. He wished
he didn't have to go far, as the war horse had
been pushed hard this day already. However,
Colt didn't want any of Crazy Horse's braves to
decide to come after him this day. Crazy Horse
would not have control over them if they really
wanted to kill. White men couldn't understand
the concept of Lakotah self-government. The
title "chief" was simply that—a title. Many
called Crazy Horse "a war chief," but in actuality he was a war *hero*. The older, more experienced men in the tribe governed after a fashion,
but everyone listened to the shamans, the so-
called medicine men, such as Sitting Bull. The
spiritual leaders were the important ones in the
Lakotah nation, and the chiefs were men with
wisdom. There could be many chiefs in one village, but that didn't mean they were all the boss.
All the elders ruled the tribe with common sense
and experience, under the watchful eye and advice of the shamans. White men could never get
the hang of it, or the understanding, as they
could never govern themselves that way. For
them someone always had to be in charge, so
they just couldn't grasp the Lakotah concept.

In any event, Chris wanted to get as far away
as possible, riding until long after dark before
making camp, then rising before daybreak each
day until he had arrived at Fort Abraham Lincoln.

Chapter 3

>>>>>>>>>>>>>>>>>>

Son of the Morning Star

Several days later, Lieutenant Cooke entered Custer's office and said, "General, we just got word from our scouts that Christopher Colt's on his way in."

"What's his ETA, Bill?" Custer said.

"Ten minutes, sir," the adjutant said.

"Okay, have him come in here when he arrives," Custer said. "I'm going to run over to my quarters and change my tunic. I was going to anyway. I spilled some coffee on this one."

Custer went out the door behind Lieutenant Cooke and headed toward his quarters. He had no intention of greeting his new chief of scouts in a normal, or almost normal, blue tunic. He had not spilled coffee on his clothes at all. He just wanted to make a big splash when Colt saw him. Colt was not that important, but he had begun to establish a reputation as a warrior among warriors, and Custer was secretly anxious for his approval. He put on a tailored fringed buckskin jacket with his rank of brevet general on the shoulders, then topped that off with a red sash around the midsection. He checked out his beard and blond hair and, his vanity satisfied, returned to his office.

Libbie, his wife, was given a quick hug and kiss on the way out. As an afterthought, Custer stopped and summoned his two dogs, with whom he used to hunt antelope. He would let them lie on the floor in front of his desk, another symbol of the power he held. Often, while out on campaigns, the two dogs, which were crosses between greyhounds and Irish wolfhounds, would chase antelope. Custer would leave his command and follow the hounds in their chase.

Libbie's voice stopped him. "Hey, Cinnamon, why did you change? A girl coming to your office?"

His face flushed, as he turned.

Custer said, "Nobody's coming in, darling, except my new chief of scouts, Christopher Columbus Colt. I just wanted to look fresh—and please don't call me Cinnamon."

His wife, Libby, was making reference to the nickname given him by some of his friends, because of the cinnamon oil he often used in his blond hair. He had also been nicknamed "Curly" by other friends because of his naturally curly hair, which curled all the more when he let his hair grow long.

Custer returned to his office and waited for Colt to arrive.

In a few minutes, Cooke entered Custer's office and said, "Excuse me, sir, but you'd better come out here and see this."

Custer got up from behind his big engraved mahogany desk and walked out the door, pulling fringed buckskin gloves on over his hands and placing a plumed campaign hat on his head.

He stepped out onto the parade ground and, for the first time, set eyes on Chris Colt, riding up on a horse. Custer was astounded, for the tall, dark-haired scout rode in on a Sioux war pony, a black-and-white paint with three bright red coup stripes around each of the two forelegs and red handprints on each rump. The horse also had several bald eagle tail and wing feathers braided into its mane. A single wing feather adorned the war pony's braided tail, which was tied in an overhand knot.

To Custer's eyes, Colt presented an imposing figure. He wore his buckskin shirt with fancy beadwork and porcupine quillwork, as well as fringe. He also wore his flop-brim leather hat with its beaded hatband, boots, jeans, guns, and bowie knife in its beaded and fringed sheath. His Cheyenne hunting bow and arrows lay tied on the back part of the saddle skirt, across his bedroll and over the saddlebags.

Custer said, "What are you, a white man or a red nigger?"

Colt smiled and stared into Custer's blue eyes. "I'm your new chief of scouts, General. Christopher Columbus Colt. I had a little run-in with Crazy Horse, and he gave me this war pony of his to ride here, because they shot my mount out from under me."

Custer looked like he was about to deliver a baby, straining with stomach cramps and the veins sticking out in his forehead and neck. In fact they didn't just stick out, they bulged. Somehow he regained his composure before he spoke.

"What the hell do you mean, Crazy Horse gave you his mount? What are you, a damned traitor?"

Chris Colt swung off his horse and slipped the thong off his six-shooter, ignoring the cocking of numerous cavalry rifles and speaking between clenched teeth. "General, you may be my boss, and I'm sure you didn't mean to word it the way you said it, but anybody who suggests I'm a traitor better back up their words with firepower."

Custer was taken aback for a minute, as he looked at Chris Colt standing there in front of him in a gunfighter's crouch.

Used to taking charge of uneasy situations quickly, Custer cleared his throat and said, "You insubordinate bastard, I'll have you court-martialed!"

Colt grinned. "Can't, General. I'm a civilian scout, not a soldier, and I haven't even signed a contract with you yet. You can refuse to hire me, but you can't court-martial me."

Chris thought quickly. He knew Custer didn't dare back down or apologize. He would lose face in front of all his soldiers. And Colt wanted to be there in the campaign against the Lakotah and Cheyenne. He had to think fast, very fast, if he was to restore a balance of power but not lose out entirely.

Colt said, "General, I thought you'd want to hear my report about the deaths of two traders I tried to save on the way here. Name of Luke and Buck Sawyer."

Colt detected a quick faint reaction in Custer's eyes, but Custer masked it quickly.

"Sawyers, huh?" Custer was nonchalant. "Yeah, that's too bad. They've carried trade goods in and out of here a number of times. I will need a full report in private, Colt. Let's go to my office."

They walked over to Custer's office and an orderly followed them within seconds. He carried two china cups, hot coffee in a silver pot, and cream and sugar in silver bowls. This all arrived on a silver tray. Chris and Custer both took cups of coffee black.

The General dismissed the orderly from the room. "Maybe I was a little harsh, Colt, but you have to admit that is quite a shock, having your new chief of scouts ride in here on a painted Indian horse and tell you it was a gift from your biggest enemy. You've heard about Crazy Horse's most recent victory?"

"Yes I have, General, but he wasn't in charge of it. He was just the bravest warrior in the battle."

Again Custer eyed him suspiciously. "How do you know?"

"My job, General," Colt replied.

"Well, tell me about the Sawyers." Custer had forced a smile by now. "How were they killed? Did they talk to you? Where are their supplies? And tell me how you came to ride in here on a horse owned by no less than that red devil Crazy Horse."

Chris and Long Hair went through two pots of coffee as the scout told him about the events with the Sawyers, Sarah, "Rat-face," the Crows, and the Lakotah. The two men plainly did not like each other, but there were things about Custer that Colt did admire. For instance, he could tell that Custer was not a coward, a trait that Colt absolutely despised in a cavalry commander. Custer was egomaniacal and manipulative, though, and Colt dreaded the mere thought of working for him, much less his becoming President.

Chris was very careful not to tip his hand about the Indian Ring, or Custer's involvement. He also kept from Custer his knowledge of Luke and Buck's letter of introduction from Custer, and of their crooked trading.

The Boy General was less sure why he didn't like Colt. What he didn't realize was that he actually feared Chris Colt. He feared, admired, and respected the quiet strength that Colt displayed—that self-assuredness that he never really felt himself. Colt didn't need the security of the military. He was a loner who could challenge a general to a gunfight if he wanted to, or even earn the respect of a hell-bent-for-leather warrior like Crazy Horse himself. Colt was rough stock. He was a real hero.

From the time he was a child, George Armstrong Custer had wanted people to look up to him, to consider him a hero. He still wanted that more than anything. No matter how many victories he had in battle, he always wanted more. He still didn't feel like he measured up to a man like Chris Colt. What Custer didn't realize was that, in his quest for so much recognition, he actually *had* become a hero in the eyes of most. He was vainglorious. He was a rapist and a racist. He was an egomaniac. But in battle, he had proven himself a hero time and again. Custer was a hero in everyone's eyes except his own.

Now he was in the presence of a man who had conquered fear and acquitted himself well in battle, but who was also moral and principled, self-disciplined and secure in himself—areas in which Long Hair was conspicuously lacking.

Custer spoke. "You may have a problem here, Colt. Luke and Buck have another brother named Will, and he was definitely the leader in the family. He's in Bismarck right now, and he'll come gunning for you when he hears about Luke and Buck. He's a giant of a man, but he has lightning speed with a six-gun. He's also killed a man in a bar fight with his hands and feet."

Chris said, "Why would he come after me, General, if all he hears is that I tried to rescue his brothers from an Indian attack? It doesn't make sense."

Custer's face reddened, and he quickly responded, "I just mean that Will is the type of man who will blame you for not saving his brothers. And I'm sure he's heard about your troubles with them in Cheyenne. They communicated all the time."

"How do you know that, General?" Chris asked innocently.

Again Custer reddened. "Why, I had people keep track of them. You know, they traded a lot with the Indians and all. I just wanted to make sure they were on the up and up."

Chris said, "Were they?"

"As far as we could determine," Custer responded matter-of-factly. "Never saw any large numbers of repeaters in the hands of hostiles, or any telltale signs like that. But you just never know."

Chris said, "No, General, you sure don't. You never know when one or two people might put their own interests above the welfare and lives of an entire race of people. That's probably about the lowest level any skunk could sink to."

A glare came into Custer's eyes and his stare quickly met Colt's taunting grin, but again the General checked himself. "Absolutely right, Colt. Well, anyway, welcome to the Seventh. Unfortunately we started out on the wrong foot, but that's the past now. It's a good thing indeed you gained the confidence of that red scoundrel Crazy Horse. Maybe we can trick him right into a trap."

Colt stood and walked to the door. "I'm a scout, General Custer, not a turncoat who tricks his friends."

"Friends!" Custer fumed. "What do you mean by that? Do you claim that heathen killer as a *friend*? How can you scout in a campaign against him with such divided loyalties?"

"I don't have divided loyalties," Chris replied. "If Crazy Horse and I meet in battle, we'll each try our damnedest to kill each other. We both understand that, so I don't have any divided loyalties at all, General. Not at all."

"Well," Custer said sarcastically, "just to clarify this, Colt, whose side *are* you on, anyway? Who *is* your loyalty to?"

Chris smiled and said, "America, General. The United States of America."

Colt left Custer staring.

He reclaimed his war pony and asked where the livery was. The trooper pointed to a long stable area, and Colt easily swung onto the horse's back. He rode over to the post stables and met the NCOIC, the NCO in charge of the stables.

"You'll be the new chief of scouts, Colt, what

braced the old man?" the sergeant said. "Name's Muldoon, and this is my stable. Want anythin', you just ask me."

Chris stuck out his hand and shook with the big, crusty NCO.

Colt said, "Nice to meet you, Sarge. Chris Colt. I could use a bait of grub for this old war horse here. He carried me a good piece and was a mover the whole time."

Muldoon looked at the animal. "I was gonna ast ya iffin he really was the property of old Crazy Horse, but I can tell he was."

Chris said, "Oh?"

Muldoon said, "Hell, yeah, look at those straight cannon bones, and lined up even as hell with the edge of his hindquarters. He's put together, too, and stands sixteen hands tall. He shore dint start out as no Sioux pony. Look at his hooves—straight ahead, not pigeon-toed or cow-hocked in the least—and more important than all that, look at that head. Looks Arab, don' it?"

Without waiting for Chris to answer, he went on, "Look at them alert eyes and them ears. No bulges over the eyes, either. I'll git shut right quick of them nags with big lobes over the eyes. Too smart. They always turn out to be killers, every damn one of the sons of bitches. Always tryin' to figger out ways to git your ass off their back an' onto the groun'. Hate them smart bastards."

Chris finally cut in, "So how do you know this was Crazy Horse's, by all that?"

The man looked at Chris like he had asked the dumbest question in the world.

Muldoon said, " 'Cause it's one damn fine piece of horseflesh. Crazy Horse dint become the legend he is 'cause he's stupid, ya know. Yer stall'll be the third one down this aisle. When yer in garrison here, this horse'll be treated like a French whore. He'll be bathed and brushed, grained and hayed. Give 'im a good alfalfa/grass hay mix, and I always mix corn with oats and a few other goodies when we grain 'em. Want 'im shod?"

"Yeah," Chris replied, "I'd love it. I can see he'll be in good hands with you, Sergeant Muldoon."

The beefy NCO puffed his chest out a little and threw his shoulders back.

"Well, that's my job," he said, "I'm in charge of the mounts for the Seventh Cavalry. You name this horse, yet?"

Chris said, "No, no, I haven't."

Muldoon looked at the horse a little bit. He closed one eye and walked around the animal, like an artist studying a painting.

"War Bonnet," Muldoon said, "That's what ya oughta name 'im, War Bonnet."

"Okay," Chris said, smiling and looking at the horse appreciatively. "Good name, Sergeant. He's War Bonnet from now on."

Muldoon said, "He'll be shod the next time ya see 'im. Now, he's a stud, and they don't make good mounts. Ya want me to de-nut 'im? Geldings make the best mounts. Mares're too bitchy, and studs'll jump off a cliff or go through a barn wall to give it to a mare that wants it."

Chris said, "No, don't have time for him to heal. Custer'll be wanting me out scouting, probably before sundown. I'll wait, but thanks. Which way's the dispensary? Got to get my dressing changed."

"Out the door, do a column left, and go fifty feet," Muldoon said, "Yer there. There's three saw-bones: Dr. Lord, Doc Porter, and Dr. De-Wolf. All good. Don't let 'em cut off anything what's s'posed to stay."

Muldoon laughed uproariously at his own joke as Chris Colt left the stable with a smile and a wave of his hand.

He walked down to the post dispensary and was pronounced fit enough not to wear a bandage anymore. He'd probably survive, so long as the rations didn't poison him.

He asked where the scouts were garrisoned, and found it was a building next to the stables. He went there and found one scout snoring loudly on a bunk. Chris picked out an empty bunk and tossed his bedroll, war bag, and saddle-bags onto it.

He heard voices, and five scouts walked in the door. One was a half-breed, and the other four were Crows. One of these four was quite young and Chris recognized him immediately. It was Runs-Too-Hard, the young Crow whom Chris had caused to lose face in front of his fellow warriors after the attack on the Guthrie family and the rape of Sarah.

Runs-Too-Hard raised the Spencer in his right hand, cocked it, and pointed it at Chris's midsection. Chris didn't move. He just grinned.

The half-breed's green eyes twinkled under a heavy lock of black hair. Seeing Chris's clothing, he addressed him in Lakotah. "Watch him. Hothead."

Chris gave a nod and looked over to the young Crow.

Runs-Too-Hard spoke in very broken English. "You die now. I kill."

He stood directly to the left of the half-breed and was in the very middle of the rest of the group. Chris didn't have time to think. He had to react. He dropped flat on his back, his gun already drawn when his back slammed into the floor. A split-second before he hit the floor, a blink of an eye after the rifle had boomed over his head, his gun bucked in his hand, and a giant blossom of blood appeared in the middle of the Crow brave's chest. The warrior's body went through the door of the barracks, and Runs-Too-Hard died flat on his back in the dust.

The half-breed and other scouts all dived for cover, their hearts pounding like drums. Chris was scared inside, but he sure wasn't going to show it. This was an excellent opportunity to establish himself as the boss among all the scouts. He slowly walked to the door and looked at the dead scout, as he ejected his spent bullet and dropped another cartridge into the revolver. He holstered his gun. The other scouts got up and followed him outside, as soldiers, guns in hand, poured from buildings all over the post; not the least of whom was Long Hair himself, wanting to be at the front of the fight.

Colt looked down at the dead man lying in a pool of blood and said calmly, "Next time you want to shoot a man, shoot him. Don't talk about it."

With that, he turned and started to walk back inside, but was halted by Custer's voice. "Colt!"

Chris turned around and said, "Yes, General?"

"What the hell happened?"

Colt grinned and winked at the commander. "I fired him, sir."

Custer shook his head, a small smile appearing at the corners of his mouth. Chris turned and walked into the building. Medics and a doctor ran to the dead scout, while the other Crows and the half-breed entered the building. The half-breed walked up to Chris and offered his hand. Chris smiled warmly and shook it. He worried that the others might see that his knees were shaking, but he had been through similar things before and knew better.

The half-breed said, "Michel Bouyer, but everyone calls me Mitch."

Colt said, "Nice to meet you, Mitch. You're the interpreter. I've heard many good things about you over the years. I'm the new chief of scouts. Name's Colt, Chris Colt."

Speaking with a very thick French accent, Mitch said, *"Mais oui,* Colt, I have heard much about you, too. All good, but, *pardon-nez moi,* how could you have heard anything about *moi*? I am not so much."

Chris smiled again and said, "We hear about each other. Your brother John was hanged about six years ago for killing another scout, but I heard the other scout needed killing. Your ma was a member of the Santee tribe of the Lakotah Nation—what you people call the Sioux. Your dad was Baptiste Bouyer, a fur trapper and trader for the American Fur Company. You're married and have children, been in the mountains since around 1849, speak fluent Crow and Lakotah, spent most of your time around the Yellowstone, Fort C.F. Smith, and have spent a lot of time with the Oglala Lakotah, Snakes, Bannock, and Crow, mainly trading furs. I also know that, just this year, you came off a campaign with General John Gibbon in Montana and he said that next to Jim Bridger, you were the best guide in the whole country."

"*Sacre bleu!*" Mitch said, laughing heartily. "You know almost as much about me as I know about you, Monsieur Colt. Here are four of your scouts: White-Man-Runs-Him, Half Yellow Face, Hairy Moccasin, and Goes Ahead. There ees also White Swan and Curley, who are also Crows, but zey are out on patrol weeth Captain Custer. There are beaucoup Arikara scouts, too, but zey are not worth a sheet. Zat one asleep zare is Scabby Face. He ees Arikara. Zat Crow you keeled, Runs-Too-Hard, was hired yesterday, but I knew he would not last one month. He deedn't like you much, *n'est-çe pas?*"

"Didn't look that way," Chris said without elaborating. "*Captain* Custer? You said captain."

Mitch smiled, "Good man, Captain Tom Custer, zee general's younger brother. Commands Troop C."

Chris smiled. "Yeah, I have heard good of him, too. Won the Congressional Medal of Honor in the Civil War."

"*Oui,*" Bouyer said. "Zee general ees very proud of heem, too. He weeshes he could win that same medal, and even says that Tom should be zee one who ees zee general, but Tom Custer he worships zee general. He ees too moody, anyway."

Chris said, "Do you know Will Sawyer?"

Mitch made a face and said, "He ees a very bad customer. Do you know Touch-Zee-Clouds, zee Minniconjou Sioux war chief who ees good friends weeth Crazy Horse?"

Chris said, "I saw him at my sundance ceremony. He's seven feet tall if he's a foot."

"You are right, *mon ami*," Mitch said. "I have seen Touch-Zee-Clouds many times, and he *ees* seven feet tall. He was measured by two missionaries. Zees Will Sawyer could look Touch-Zee-Clouds in zee eyes. He ees very fast weeth a gun, and very tough in a fight with hees fists. He has two smaller brothers, Luke and Buck, who are also very bad, but not as tough."

"Not anymore they aren't," Colt said. "Crazy Horse and his men saw to that."

Mitch said, *"Très bien,* zees country will be much better without those two. Maybe Wakan Tanka weel smile on us and get rid of Will, also. Zey are especially bad for our friends, my mother's people."

Chris smiled, "What do you mean 'they'? Are you talking about the stealing of supplies for their reservations, and switching them with inferior goods?"

Mitch looked around and whispered, "Be careful, Monsieur Colt. Do you know who ees zare partner?"

Chris smiled and said, "The Son of the Morning Star himself."

Mitch carefully looked around again and said, "We must not talk of zees, my friend."

Chris said, "I won't. I'll just keep checking. The information we pick up may be used at some point to protect the Indians, if Custer doesn't treat them right in the future. You just never know what the future might hold."

Mitch smiled cannily. "Chris Colt, you are a

scout for zee same reasons I am, my friend: to protect my mother's people."

Chris grinned and said, "And the people of my late wife and daughter. I better go brief the old man on Runs-Too-Hard, then check on my horse. Talk to you later, Mitch. Glad we'll be working together."

"Me too, Monsieur Colt," Mitch said.

Chris said, "Please call me Chris, or just Colt."

Mitch smiled and said, "*Oui*, or just Wamble Uncha?"

Colt grinned broadly and winked, walking out the door. He went to Custer's office and reported to him about the shooting incident. Custer seemed satisfied. He didn't seem to care about an Indian anyway.

Colt returned to the stable and saw Sergeant Muldoon. Muldoon was as happy as the first time Colt had seen him.

"C'mere Colt," he said. "Lemme show ya somethin' what's right purty."

Chris followed the big sergeant down one of the rows of stalls to two side-by-side stalls, where he saw two large, very well-groomed chestnuts with white blazes and white stockings. Both horses were very spirited and seemed to be full of energy. The size and look of them clearly showed them to be thoroughbreds.

"Vic and Dandy?" Chris asked.

"Aye," Muldoon answered. "Ya heerd a the old man's mounts, huh? Pretty, ain't they? He'll ride one one time and the other another."

"Beautiful horses, that's for sure. How's War Bonnet doing?"

Muldoon beamed and lit a pipe he had been

carrying in his hand. He walked quickly toward War Bonnet's stall, with Chris following. Colt smiled when he saw his gift horse. The horse was clean and shiny and had a fresh bed of straw and a crib full of green hay. A wooden trough in the corner showed he had been fed grain, and he had fresh clean water in a trough running through the stall. It was obvious that his mane and tail had been curried and he had been cleaned and brushed, but the curious thing was that he was still wearing his coup stripes, hand-prints, and eagle feathers.

Colt said, "He looks wonderful, Sarge, but how did you clean him so thoroughly without removing his paint and feathers?"

"We did," Muldoon said enigmatically, with a hearty laugh. "I figgered that old War Bonnet here was the pride a Crazy Horse, and he decorated him up thet way. Iffin you ain't a half-breed, you shore seem to act and look like one, so I figgered we'd keep him Indian fancied-up like this fore ya all the time."

Chris smiled and patted his horse. "Yeah, I like that. Thanks. Thanks a lot."

Despite the fact that Colt felt cautious after the loss of two horses in such a short period of time, he was really starting to admire the horse given him by the Oglala war chief. He even liked the name War Bonnet.

Colt met some more of the scouts at dinner time, after which he hit his bunk and decided to catch up on the sleep he had been missing for a long time. The next morning he got out of bed before daybreak and saddled up War Bonnet, deciding to look around nearby Bismarck. The town was about the same as other frontier towns, with false-front buildings, a few brick ones, and a helter-skelter system of streets that had evolved as the town grew in size.

He saw a restaurant called the Frontier Café that boasted a big sign in the front window advertising homecooking. That sounded like something Chris could appreciate as much as the sleep he had just gotten.

He really was feeling healthy already. His head no longer hurt, and he felt rested. That was until the auburn-haired beauty walked into the room to wait on him. He thought he was going to suffer a seizure, as his breathing came out in pants and his heart pounded heavily in his chest.

The top of her full head of red hair would touch him right about the chin, and the simple gingham dress she wore could do nothing to hide the curves of the body underneath it. Her lips were full and her cheekbones high, and despite the proud uplift of her chin, she had a warm smile that would make anyone feel welcome. The thing that caught Chris Colt's breath, however, were her bright green eyes. They penetrated through his stare and went right inside his head, traveling all the way deep into his soul. He felt he could have closed his eyes tightly and those green eyes still would have shot right through him.

"Coffee, sir?" she asked, with a voice like crushed velvet.

"Thank you, ma'am," Chris said, nodding.

He wished he had taken a bath. He wished he had brushed his teeth longer and combed his hair better. He wished he didn't feel like he was about to tangle with a war party of angry Apaches.

She poured him a cup and they stared at each other, smiling uneasily. She accidentally poured too much into the cup, the overflowing liquid making Colt jump up and bump the table into her, which overturned the entire pot of coffee. She screamed and grabbed a napkin, trying to clean up the spill. Colt grabbed another, also trying to wipe up the coffee.

"How clumsy of me," she said. "I'm so sorry, sir."

Chris said, "You? It was totally my fault. I'm sorry, ma'am."

They stopped wiping and looked up at each other, first grinning, then both breaking into an embarrassed laugh. They ended up sitting down at the next table and just laughing. It was infectious, and the more they giggled, the harder it made them laugh.

Finally stopping, Chris said, "This your place, ma'am?"

"Yes it is," she replied, sticking out her hand for him to shake. "My name's Shirley Ebert. Are you new in town? Are you staying?"

"Yes and no," he replied. "I'm the new chief of scouts for General Custer at Fort Lincoln. My name is Colt, ma'am, Christopher Columbus Colt, but folks call me Chris."

"Any relation to the famous Colonel Colt?" she asked.

"My uncle."

"Well, Mr. Colt."

"Chris, please," he requested.

"Fine. Call me Shirley, too," she responded. "Can I get you some breakfast, Chris?"

"Yes, ma'am," he said. "I sure am ready for some home cooking."

"What would you like?" she asked.

He looked into her eyes and didn't answer for a second. Both of them blushed.

Chris broke the silence by saying, "It's up to you, Shirley. You decide."

"Okay, I'll surprise you. And it's on the house, since I almost scalded you with hot coffee."

Chris laughed and blushed again. "Shirley, it would have been worth getting scalded just to meet you."

He shocked himself with the statement, and felt that he shouldn't have said a word. This time he *really* blushed, as did Shirley, but she gave him a smile and a look that promised volumes of love poetry in just a glance. When she left the room quickly, Chris wondered if he had offended her.

Chris heard footsteps on the board sidewalk outside, and the door opened suddenly. Three cowboys walked in, but each wore his gun low and looked more like a gunslinger punching cows than a cowboy who could handle a gun. They were followed by Goliath himself. The giant behemoth who walked in the door had to be Will Sawyer. He was every bit of seven feet in height, toes to hair, and looked as broad in the shoulders as he was tall in length. He wore a Colt .45 Peacemaker in a low-slung holster and was filthy, with a long, unkempt beard.

He looked over at Chris and said, "You the one that owns that red nigger horse outside?"

Chris said, "That's my horse at the hitching rail, Sawyer."

Will angrily said, "How do you know my name?"

"Lucky guess," Chris said with a smile.

Colt could tell by his attitude that this man had come in the door wanting to prod him. He'd probably heard all about the various troubles Colt had had with his brothers.

"Who are you?" Will asked.

Chris took a sip of coffee and said, "I believe you already know my name."

Sawyer responded, "Yeah, I know who you are: Colt, the cowardly son of a bitch who ran out on my brothers and let them get massacred by the redskins."

Colt looked over at Will and said between clenched teeth, "Sawyer, I know you must be distraught over the sudden death of your brothers, so I'll let that slip, but nobody questions my courage or honesty. Nobody."

Sawyer stood up and said, "You sawed-off son of a bitch. Nobody, but nobody, ever talks to me like that. I'll call you and anyone else anything I want. You wanna do somethin' about it?"

Chris said, "Not really. I just came here to enjoy a quiet breakfast."

Sawyer walked forward a little and said, "Wal, in fact, we don't cotton to no red nigger-lovers around here, and yer a liar and a coward. Now git out of this restaurant."

"No, you leave, Will Sawyer, right now!" Shirley demanded, as all eyes turned toward her in the doorway to the kitchen.

Will just stared at her, hands on hips.

She continued, "This is my business, and you may bully people all over this county, but you aren't going to do it here. Understand?"

He walked at her, but she just stuck her chin out defiantly, folding her arms in front of her.

As he walked across the room he said, "Nobody talks to me that way, man or woman."

He was stopped in his tracks by Chris Colt's deep, quiet voice, "If you even look at her cross-eyed, Sawyer, it'll be the last thing you ever see."

Will Sawyer spun around in a gunfighter's crouch, ready to draw, but found himself staring down the barrel of Chris Colt's weapon. Viewed from the business end, the muzzle looked like a cannon. Will moved his hand away from his holster, as if it had a diamondback rattler in it.

Will said, "That ain't fair, you coward. You got the drop on me."

Chris laughed and said, "Fair? Tell me, Sawyer, how many seven-footers have you ever picked on?"

Sawyer just stared flames of hatred at the rugged scout.

Colt said, "Now you and your pals there unbuckle your gun belts and let them drop to the floor. Shirley, step back into the kitchen where it's safer."

"No," she said, and stood her ground.

He smiled at her, then looked back at Will Sawyer, who said, "Yer real damned big with that six-shooter, Colt. I wish I could git my hands on ya. I'd show ya."

Chris said, "Well, it's obvious to me that you've been planning on trying that, so we are going to go outside and I'm going to let you try it."

Sawyer looked at Colt and gave out a big laugh. "What? Are you kidding me? Are you really crazy enough to fight me? Do you know I'm seven-foot-one inch tall, and weigh three hunnert and sixty-five pounds?"

"No, I didn't know that," Chris replied. "I'll have to pay more attention to how big they make the piles behind the livery stable from now on."

Nobody laughed, least of all Shirley, who looked like she was ready to cry.

Finally she spoke. "Chris, please? You can't fight him. He's a monster. He killed a man in a fight with his bare hands."

Sawyer and his friends chuckled.

Will said, "Now ain't that sweet, boys. She's all worried about Chris's health."

Chris said, "I'm worried about her being treated with respect, so when we're done, you will apologize to Miss Ebert for the disrespect you've shown her."

Inside, behind the stone-cold face, Chris was scared to death. This man was a monster and he loved to fight and kill. Colt had taunted the giant purposely. He wanted to make him angry. A mad man fights like a fool. He also wanted to make him unsure. More than anything, though, Chris Colt was at that point he sometimes reached where he just didn't care about the odds. Sawyer had insulted this beautiful woman, and Chris just wanted to rip his head off.

Will Sawyer spit on his ham-sized hands, then rubbed the palms together.

He rolled up his sleeves and said, "Ya jest tryin' to show off fer Shirley here, or are ya really gonna go outside and fight me? C'mon, Colt, I'd love it."

Chris signaled the others out the door of the café with his gun, and then followed them. Shirley ran up behind him and pulled on his right arm, spinning him around. Colt looked into those entrancing green eyes and almost melted.

"Please don't?" she pleaded.

Sawyer and his cohorts were outside. Chris just smiled at Shirley, swept her into his arms, and kissed her passionately. When he stepped back, she had tears running down her cheeks, but she was smiling bravely. He removed his gun belt and handed it to her with his Colt.

Chris said, "If any of them goes for a gun, shoot him."

"If I can't talk you out of it, and you're bound and determined to do it, I want you to go out there and kick Will Sawyer's ass."

Chris winked and turned, stepping out the door. A fist like a Thanksgiving turkey smashed into his lips and drove him back through the door.

With that, the numerous people walking up and down the street rushed over to see if the massive Sawyer was going to kill yet another person, or just disable one as he had done so many times before.

Sawyer stood on the dirt street in front of the sidewalk and laughed, along with the cowpunchers. Just then, as all the women watching screamed, Chris Colt's body came flying head-first out the door. He slammed up into the surprised Will Sawyer with his head and shoulders, the momentum knocking Sawyer back about six feet. He wiped a smear of blood from his nose and looked at it on his finger. This seemed to anger him, but he still hadn't been knocked off his feet.

Chris stood up and shook his head from side

to side, clearing the cobwebs both from Sawyer's punch and from head-butting the monster.

He backpedaled as Will Sawyer charged in, growling like a bear and swinging both arms. Chris's deft moves seemed to anger Sawyer even more, and he suddenly stopped, panting heavily.

Chris, still wanting to make Will blind with anger, taunted him. "Keep swinging, Will. Maybe the breeze will give me a cold."

Will roared and rushed forward, kicking at Chris's right knee as hard as he could. This was what Colt had wanted, as he jumped forward and up in the air, smashing his elbow into Will's nose with his body weight totally behind it. He felt the cartilage give way under his elbow. Seeing as Sawyer's right foot had been swinging up into the air, this blow knocked the big man flat on his back, knocking the wind out of him. Chris rolled over beyond the prone bully and came up on his feet.

Will Sawyer had never before been knocked off his feet, and it made him even crazier with fury. Colt danced from side to side as Sawyer now tried to snap punches at his head. Sawyer kicked again at Chris's knee and missed, but his boot grazed Chris's right thigh and that alone was enough to severely bruise it and almost knock Colt off-balance. Sensing his weakness, Will rushed forward, and Chris spit right into his face. This totally caught the giant off-guard, and he halted in mid-stride to wipe off his face. Chris punched straight up, not an uppercut but a straight right landing underneath the chin of the big man. It sent the giant up on his tiptoes, as his upper and lower teeth cracked together, knocking several loose. He grabbed his bloody mouth, blood streaming over his hands from his broken nose.

In a total blind rage, Will Sawyer ducked his head, with his arms outstretched, and charged at Chris with a mighty roar. Colt grabbed his hair and pulled his head into a front headlock and simply backpedaled, kicked his feet up in the air, and landed on the ground, driving the behemoth's head into the ground. He let go and tried to roll away, but Sawyer reached out and grabbed him by the hair, smashed a wicked blow into Chris's rib cage. Chris knew the blow had broken at least one rib. He kicked free and rolled for his life, holding his left elbow over his broken rib and facing the giant. Blood was still streaming from Will's nose as he rose to his feet, and his eyes were swelling shut.

Chris knew he couldn't do much. He was simply in too much pain, and he knew he couldn't afford to take another punch from the monster, or he would be dead. He stood in front of the post that held up the corner of the veranda over the café and weaved slightly. Will Sawyer, face pulped, sides heaving, faced him with his head bowed forward, his fists doubled up at his sides.

Quietly, Sawyer seethed, "I'm gonna kill you, you son of a bitch."

Chris said, "No, you're going to apologize to Miss Ebert."

Roaring again like a mad bull, Sawyer ducked his head and charged again as hard as he could. Chris waited until the last second, dropped to the ground, tripped Will with his left foreleg, and watched as Sawyer went headfirst into the corner post, driving the six-by-six off its foundation several inches and making everyone on the sidewalk run to get out from under the veranda. It held, but Will Sawyer lay facedown on the street in front of the wooden sidewalk, out cold.

Chris roughly grabbed the hat off one of Sawyer's cohorts and walked over to the water trough. He dipped the hat into the water and filled it. Then he walked over to Sawyer and dumped it all over the back of his head.

Sawyer got up on his knees gasping and shaking his head from side to side, trying to figure out where he was, who he was, and what had happened. Chris grabbed him by the hair and tilted his head up. The man was almost out on his feet and had no fight left in him, at least not in his body, although maybe in his mind.

Colt said, "Now, as I told you, you owe Miss Ebert an apology."

Will shook his head again and looked up at Chris, then at Shirley, a very blank and faraway look in his eyes. "Huh? Oh, I'm sorry, Shirley."

His eyes rolled back in his head and he fell backward, unconscious. Chris left him there and walked into the café. He bent over and retrieved all the gun belts of Sawyer and his cohorts. Carrying them outside, he got his own gun and belt from Shirley and tossed the others to the gunslingers.

Chris said, "Take your friend and yourselves and get out of town."

One of the gunslingers had a scar running down his left cheek from the corner of his eye to the corner of his mouth. It puckered the whole face when he spoke, smiled, or moved any facial muscle at all.

He quickly strapped on his gun belt and said, "You made a big mistake, mister. You may be able to fight with your hands, but I fight the way it counts, and nobody tells me what to do."

Chris smiled and said, "This is a mistake partner. You can walk away from this right now. I don't mean being yellow, I mean just you and me forgetting it, because it's nothing important."

The gunfighter's hands hovered over his pistols, and he said, "Not a chance."

The entire crowd ran away from the two men as quickly as possible.

Chris said, "Mister, I'm better with a gun than I am with my fists. This is your chance. Leave."

"Uh-uh," he responded, "time for you to die, Colt."

"You've had your chance," Chris said. "You climbed in the saddle. You're going to have to ride this horse."

The gunfighter drew, and there were two explosions when his gun was halfway out of his holster. He stared at Chris Colt, the smoke coming from the barrel of Chris's gun. He looked back down at his stomach and saw the two bloody spots above his belt buckle. He grinned, then saw the sky fly in front of his eyes and felt the back of his head ram into the ground. He looked at one of the puffy clouds overhead, shaped just like his father with a club raised in his hand, just ready to strike him when he was a young, tow-headed boy.

Chris came up and looked down into the man's face, and he heard a voice from behind say, "Look at that! You could cover both bullet holes with a silver dollar, and he shot both shots quicker'n anybody else could shoot one."

The gunslinger squinted his eyes and looked at Chris weakly. "Don't hit me again, Pa."

He closed his eyes and heard a voice say, "He's dead."

He felt a twinge of panic, then felt and heard nothing at all.

Chris was sad. He hated to kill anybody, but the man had asked for it and Chris had had no choice. It didn't matter, though, as he still hated to kill anyone, no matter what the reason.

A man stepped up out of the crowd, a six-pointed star under a crescent symbol on his black-and-gray tweed jacket. The badge said MARSHALL on the crescent and BISMARCK, N.D.T. on the star portion.

He said, "Mr. Colt, did I hear? I saw the whole thing. It was a righteous shooting."

"Thanks," Chris said and shook hands with the marshal.

The marshal looked at Shirley, who had walked up to Colt's side, and said, "Morning, Miss Ebert," tipping his Stetson. "You want Will Sawyer arrested for anything? I understand you had some kind of problem with him, too."

Shirley said, "No thanks, Marshal."

She took Chris by the arm and escorted him into her café. They went into the kitchen, and she had him sit down on a stool. Shirley started to prepare eggs and a large steak. She pulled a baked potato out of a pot covered with a towel and put it in the oven to heat it up.

She went to a cabinet in the corner and pulled out some towels, tape, and other items, and went over to Chris.

"Take off your shirt," she commanded.

Moaning, Chris complied, as she helped him with the tight leather war shirt.

She felt his ribs, and secretly admired Chris's

build. She also was amazed at the scars all over his torso. He winced when she pushed on his injured rib.

She felt all over it carefully and said, "It's broken. Do you want me to get the doctor, or do you want me to mend it?"

Colt said, "You don't have to worry about it. I'll have the regimental surgeon patch me up at the fort."

"Nonsense," she said. "I can bind it if you want, or I'll be happy to get Doc Fedders. Now, what do you want?"

Chris raised his arms and folded his hands on top of his head. Smiling, Shirley pulled out a rolled-up long cloth bandage and started wrapping it tightly, very tightly around Chris's chest and back. He smiled at her.

She smiled back, saw the question on his face, and said, "My father was a regimental surgeon in the Civil War, and was town doctor before and after that."

Chris asked, "Where?"

Shirley said, "Youngstown, Ohio."

Chris winced and said, "You're kidding. I grew up in Cuyahoga Falls, and fought for the Ohio National Guard in the Civil War."

"Where's Cuyahoga Falls?"

"Right next to Akron, on the Cuyahoga River."

"Aren't you too young to have fought in the war?"

Chris smiled and said, "I lied about my age. I *was* young, too young."

She finished wrapping his rib cage and went right back to her cooking.

Chris wondered how she was able to complete everything and not burn a thing, even while wrapping his ribs. She put the steak, eggs, and potato on a plate and headed toward the door to the dining room.

She turned her head and said, "Follow me."

Chris started to follow her and she turned at the door to the dining room, putting her back against the swinging batwing doors and saying, "You might put your shirt back on, Chris."

Chris got embarrassed and meekly said, "Oh," pulling on his war shirt and following her out.

He sat at a table and she was gone like a flash, only to return with a steaming pot of coffee and two cups. She set them down on the table and Chris poured out two cups, while she walked to the door and put the closed sign up, just as four people almost reached the door. She smiled politely and turned her back. Shirley turned back around and locked the door, then sat down with Colt.

"Aren't you going to eat?" he asked.

She smiled softly and said, "No thanks, I ate already. I'll just enjoy my coffee and watch you."

"Why did you close? You don't want to lose business."

She said, "I do right now. Maybe you could go through all that and not be affected, but I'd like to relax my brain."

Chris grinned and said, "You're a *wonderful* cook."

"Thank you," she said. "Besides, I want to spend some time alone with you right now."

Chris blushed again.

She went on, "You must think I'm very forward. I've just met you and we've already kissed. I've closed my restaurant, and I'm sitting here alone with you. This has never, ever happened to me in my whole life."

"Me either," he said between bites. "And I don't think you're anything like forward."

"What *do* you think?" she asked.

He said, "About you?"

Shirley nodded.

Chris said, "I think you're absolutely wonderful, Shirley."

This time *she* blushed, but Chris was familiar and confident with her now.

He went on, "In fact, you are the most beautiful woman I've ever met in my entire life." Chris couldn't believe he'd told her that, but he was too honest, and he really believed it.

Shirley just stared into his eyes for a few seconds. His food was almost devoured already, which was a very good thing, because Shirley moved around the table and swept his plate and cup and silverware to the side and sat down in his lap, kissing him with all that was in her. He responded in kind.

When she had returned to her seat, Chris dropped his head and looked down at the floor.

"What's wrong?" she asked.

"Have you ever been married?" Chris asked.

"No," she replied. "Why?"

He said, "I lost my wife and daughter to the Crows a while back. It'll probably take me a long time to get over."

She responded, "I know about it. Did you love her?"

"Yes, I loved her very much," Chris replied. "How did you know about them?"

Shirley laughed and said, "Chris Colt, don't you realize what a hero you are here? All over?

You're becoming a legend. Everyone knows about the tragedy, and you probably will never get over it, but you don't strike me as the type of man who will let tragedy make you stop living."

"I'm not," Chris said. "But I don't want any feelings I develop to be disguised by the pain."

Shirley said, "Then don't let them. You're a man, a real man."

Chris smiled and walked around the table, sweeping her up in his arms. He pulled her close and held her in a long hug. He then tilted her head up, swept her hair back slowly, and kissed her softly and tenderly.

They stepped back from each other and just stared deep into each other's eyes. Chris kissed her lightly, then walked toward the door.

"I better get back to the fort," he said. "I've been waiting for Custer to send me out ever since I arrived yesterday. What do I owe you for the breakfast? It was great."

She said, "You'll never pay for one of my meals."

Chris smiled. "I have a feeling I will, one way or the other."

She chuckled. "Nice to meet you, Mr. Colt."

"It was a pleasure meeting *you*, Miss Ebert."

A short while later, Chris reported in to Custer, and the General seemed quite angry.

Colt said, "Something bothering you, General?"

"I don't like hearing about my troops, civilian employees, or civilian contractors going into a town next to my post and getting into fistfights and gun fights, Colt," Custer said.

Chris whistled and said, "You sure hear about things fast, General Custer. It just happened a

little while ago, and I did all I could to avoid a
fight. They started the dance, so I played the
fiddle."

"So I've heard," Custer said. "But I don't like
it. Anyway, you've certainly made an enemy of
Will Sawyer now, and he won't rest until you're
dead."

"Well, that was his decision to become my
enemy," Colt replied. "If he wants me, I
shouldn't be hard to find."

"To matters at hand," Custer said, walking
over to a map.

He pointed at the map and said to Colt, "You
seem to be close with the Indians. Tell me.
We've been getting reports of Sitting Bull assem-
bling all kinds of tribes together somewhere in
the area of the Yellowstone, maybe in the Big
Horn Mountains. We've heard estimates that
maybe even as many as one thousand, five hundred Sioux and Cheyenne have banded together
to fight us, and they're all under Sitting Bull,
that red son of a bitch. What have you heard
about it?"

Colt laughed and said, "General, I don't know
where you've gotten your information, but it
could get you killed."

Custer's face flushed with anger, and he said,
"Killed? By primitive indigenous warriors?
Ha!"

Chris went on, "General Custer, many tribes
have formed a giant encampment under Sitting
Bull, but not to attack. It's for mutual protection,
and the actual numbers are far different from
what you have had reported to you. There are
six major tribal circles, with five being Lakotah—what you call the Sioux—and one being

Chyela—which you call the Cheyenne. General, there are over fifteen thousand people in the encampment with Sitting Bull. Many tribes have joined: both Northern and Southern Chyela, Arapahoes, Brules, Sans Arc, Yanktonais, Blackfoot, Oglalas, Santees, Minniconjous, and Hunkpapas. They were on the Powder River, then the Tongue, now they have struck camp and are moving to the Rosebud. They're planning a giant inter-tribal sundance ceremony, and Sitting Bull is going through it himself."

"How do you know all this?"

Chris laughed. "It's my job to know."

Custer went on, "Well, I just can't believe there are anywhere near that many Indians assembled. Even if there are, I'm going to kick the shit out of them. I've heard of this sundance ceremony, but what the hell is it?"

Chris removed his war shirt, and a concerned look came over Custer's face when he saw the tight bandage around Chris's rib cage.

Chris smiled and said, "The fight this morning. Sawyer did manage to break one of my ribs."

Chris showed Custer his sundance scars and explained the significance of the ceremony.

The presidential hopeful winced. "Put on your shirt and follow me."

They walked out the door and into the next building. It was obviously the garrison briefing room, with a number of large maps covering the wall. The room was filled with chairs and uniformed Army officers.

The officer seated closest to the door hollered, "Ten-hut!"

Custer just as quickly said, "Carry on!"

The men had jumped to their feet at attention,

but relaxed when he told them to carry on. All watched, however, as Lieutenant Colonel Custer sat down in a large leather-backed chair facing the two largest maps.

Once seated, he said, "Gentlemen, this is our new chief of scouts, Christopher Colt. Those of you who have not met him can do so when the briefing is concluded. He rides a paint horse, which was a gift from that red devil Crazy Horse. He just told me an incredible thing that he believes: There are fifteen thousand red niggers in the great Sioux encampment. Now, I find that very hard to believe, but on the other hand Colt has impeccable credentials as a scout, so I do give some credence to his estimates. In any event, I don't care how many braves that coward Sitting Bull wants to surround himself with, we'll still carry his head on the Seventh Cavalry guidon."

The men in the room applauded, and a couple of the younger ones, some lieutenants, cheered.

Custer went on. "Mr. Colt thinks the hostiles are much tougher than we estimate. Does he believe we can carry Sitting Bull's head on our guidon?"

"Yes I do, General," said Colt. "But I can guarantee you Sitting Bull is no coward, and I think it is critically important that you do not underestimate the fighting ability, resolve, and intelligence of these men."

Custer got angry at that. "They are not *men,* Colt, they are *animals,* and they deserve to be exterminated. In any event, half our officer corps isn't sure what's going on half the time, so we will have a briefing on the entire Sioux problem and what military actions have been and will be taking place. I can promise you all this, however: Sitting Bull's head will be displayed on our company guidon before it's all over. Lieutenant Cooke, start the briefing."

Bill Cooke walked up to the front of the room and addressed the group of officers. "General, gentlemen, what is discussed in this room is classified information, and is not to leave this room. As most all of you know, we are leaving tomorrow morning and heading west for the Tongue River area to engage hostile forces of Sioux and Cheyenne, under the command of Sitting Bull. They will be beaten into submission and moved onto reservations."

Several heads turned toward Chris Colt as he chuckled at this remark.

Cooke continued, "The operations officer will brief you on the concept of the operations and our specific mission, as well as the general's plan for our participation. The quartermaster, as well, will brief us on how we will keep our forces fed, supplied, and resupplied during the course of the operation. He will explain the entire logistical part of the operation.

"First, however, I will give you an overview of the campaign, and the history behind it. The commander in chief, because of certain political considerations with the upcoming election, has seen fit to make General Custer sit here while the rest of the overall command has proceeded into hostile territory and has engaged hostile forces in several skirmishes. However, every one of you knows how persistent the General is when he decides to accomplish a mission, and the President has finally given the go-ahead for the Seventh Cavalry to take off for parts west and do our part to resolve this dangerous situation. Being the Seventh Cavalry, we will do the major part of the resolving. In other words, we will kick some red asses."

All the officers cheered, while Colt sat there thinking to himself about the stupidity of underestimating your enemy's potential.

The briefing continued, as Lieutenant Cooke explained the background to the present problems with the Lakotah, Arapaho, and Cheyenne, at least from the Army's point of view.

Cooke explained that Sitting Bull enjoyed the rare distinction of exerting leadership as a religious leader, as well as being a war and a political chief. His influence extended beyond his own tribe, the Hunkpapa Sioux, to the other Sioux tribes. The Hunkpapas ranged from the lower Yellowstone to Fort Peck. Moreover, when these tribes came together with their kinsmen to the south, in the Powder and Bighorn country, Sitting Bull commanded still wider attention and more respect. Even the Northern Cheyennes and Northern Arapahoes, who often traveled with the Sioux, responded to his leadership.

Hatred of white Christians, as Cooke explained it, had caused Sitting Bull not to yield or to compromise, or even to negotiate, with the U.S. Cavalry. Whites had heard of him as early as 1865, when he prevented the Hunkpapas from talking peace with General Sully and led a battle against U.S. forces stationed at Fort Rice on the upper Missouri.

After Red Cloud left the warpath in 1868, and made his "X" on the Fort Laramie Treaty, Sitting Bull's name began to appear with growing frequency in the white man's newspapers as

leader of the hostile Sioux. Other chiefs were
also mentioned from time to time, such as
Black Moon, No Neck, Black Twin, Four
Horns. The name that was heard the most,
however, was that of Crazy Horse of the Oglalas. He was a cunning, fearless, and ferocious
warrior in pitched battles with the cavalry, yet
he was not a prominent decision-maker in the
Sioux's war planning. Also making names for
themselves were the war chiefs of the Hunkpapas, Gall and Rain-In-The-Face.

Rain-In-The-Face, Chris knew, had been tricked
not long ago and arrested under a flag of truce
by Medal of Honor winner Captain Tom Custer,
now seated just three rows behind Colt. Rain-
In-The-Face managed an escape, and vowed he
would cut Tom Custer's heart out someday and
eat it. Almost all of the Lakotah and Cheyenne
knew of this promise.

Starting in the early 1870s, Sitting Bull headed
everyone's list, however, as the embodiment of
Sioux hostility. Chris knew the medicine man
was regarded in the same way by the members
of his own nation.

Colt noted that Cooke's references to the Sioux
or Cheyenne didn't refer to them as their own
nations, although that was how the Lakotah and
Cheyenne saw themselves. The Sioux, as the
French and the Americans called them, were a
nation comprised of various *tribes* of Lakotah,
such as the Teton, Minniconjou, Yanktonais,
Oglalas, Hunkpapas, San Sarcs, Blackfeet, and
Brules.

Red Cloud still remained the most powerful
Oglala chief. In peace, he became famous with
the military as a major pain in the ... major

point of contact between a trooper and his McLellan saddle.

The governmental policy toward the Sioux was simple: Lure them onto a reservation and subserve them to the apparatus of Indian administration. The groundwork had been laid by the Treaty of 1868, which defined the Great Sioux Reservation—roughly present-day South Dakota west of the Missouri River—and promised free rations and other presents to those who would affiliate with an agency. Success of the reservation program, however, depended in large measure on firmly attaching Red Cloud's Oglalas and Spotted Tail's Brules to an agency. As the government's best Indian negotiators discovered, these two chiefs were as formidable in diplomacy as in war. The second part of the plan was to "punish" the rest of the "renegade hostiles" and force them onto reservations as well.

Chris Colt listened to this briefing with bitter humor, for he saw how much the white government officials of America underestimated the intelligence and resolve of the Indian. Incident after incident still hadn't awakened them, either.

A treaty stipulation of major import was that the Sioux agencies be built on the Missouri River, so that supplies could be forwarded quickly and cheaply by river steamer and so that military surveillance could be easily carried on. General Sherman chose retired Gen. William S. Harney for the mission of supervising and administering to the Great Sioux Reservation, and during the summer of 1868 Harney established the Missouri River agencies—the Grand River Agency (moved, and renamed Standing Rock Agency, in 1875) for Hunkpapas, Blackfeet, and

Yanktonais; the Cheyenne River Agency for Minniconjous, Sans Arcs, Blackfeet, and Two Kettles; and the Whetstone Agency for Brules and Oglalas. The Crow Creek and Lower Brule agencies served Lower Brules, Yanktonais, and Two Kettles as well.

Red Cloud and Spotted Tail, on the other hand, had absolutely no desire to go to the Missouri River to pick up supplies or to live. For years, their tribes had hunted the Powder and upper Republican country and traded at Fort Laramie. Despite the treaty, whose contents had been badly explained to say the least, they insisted on picking up their rations and presents at an agency located somewhere near Fort Laramie.

For almost five years Red Cloud and Spotted Tail lobbied the government, even traveling to Washington to meet with President Grant. After that, having a personal interest, Grant sent numerous emissaries from the White House to meet with the two chiefs, and eventually the government gave in to many of the demands and requests of the Sioux. Late in 1873, and after several interim locations, agencies for the two tribes were built on the upper reaches of White River. The sites were in Nebraska instead of on the Great Sioux Reservation. These were so distant from both the Missouri and the Platte that they made supply expensive and military oversight difficult.

According to possibly inflated official figures, some nine thousand Ogalas, two thousand Northern Cheyennes, and fifteen hundred Northern Arapahoes drew rations at the Red Cloud Agency, and about eight thousand Brules drew rations at the nearby Spotted Tail

Agency. On the Missouri River, about seven thousand Indians attached themselves to Grand River Agency and another seven thousand attached themselves to the Cheyenne River Agency. Three thousand were at Crow Creek and Lower Brule.

Agency Indians actually accounted for only a small number of these thousands of Sioux, Arapahoes, and Cheyennes. For many of them, the lure of the old ways proved as strong as the lure of the white man's supplies, tobacco, and coffee. And nothing really prevented them from sampling both. They shuttled between the agencies and the camps of hostile tribes.

Colt, whittling a toothpick from a chair splinter, wondered what some of the great warriors he knew would think of being referred to as "agency Indians" in the manner and context they were being referred to. The government must figure that once a treaty was in place and a reservation established, those Indians participating would be "tame." The scout thought that that thinking would be akin to thinking that you could pet a grizzly once he had been bound by chains.

Chris drew stares again, as he chuckled once more. Tame agency Indians, he thought.

Cooke rattled on, undaunted.

These people, observed Col. David S. Stanley, pass half their time at these agencies and half in the hostile camps. They abuse the agents, threaten their lives, kill their cattle at night, and do anything they can to oppose the civilizing movement, short of eating all the provisions they can get.

In the spring of 1870 General Hancock, De-

partment of Dakota commanding officer, had stationed two infantry companies each at Grand
River and Cheyenne River and one each at Crow
Creek, Lower Brule, and Whetstone. General
Hancock found this to be an inefficient operation, because there were not enough troops. His
recommendation that the agencies be moved to
the forts fell on deaf ears.

In the fall of 1873, thousands of Sioux and
Cheyenne from the north descended on the Red
Cloud and Spotted Tail agencies and rioted at
the locations. There were several killings, including those of the chief clerk at Red Cloud
and an infantry lieutenant, Levi Robinson. Both
agencies, the lives of their men constantly at
risk, called urgently for help.

Despite problems in the BIA, early in March
1874, under General Sherman's orders, Colonel
John E. Smith led a major expedition of nearly
one thousand cavalry and infantry from Fort
Laramie, in a punishing winter march to White
River. The hostiles, according to Lieutenant
Cooke, "fled in a cowardly fashion" back to Powder River, and the problem was over. General
Smith created a new post named in honor of the
slain Lieutenant Robinson. It became a key military base in the war shaping up with the Sioux.

Numerous events continued to shape the war
that many were now calling "Sitting Bull's
War." The reservation Indians were still primarily mobile warriors who took advantage of beef,
food, blankets, and clothing from the U.S. government, yet returned to their tribes off the reservation whenever they felt like it to fight
against white settlers and the U.S. Army.

Chris Colt tried to keep from laughing outright as he heard all this explained.

In any event the briefing continued, explaining events from Custer's staff's perspective up until the current year of 1876.

General Sheridan felt that military victory against the Sioux and their allies would be inevitable. Success depended on a quick move against the enemy while they lay vulnerable in their winter camps and before they had received the usual spring reinforcements from the agencies.

"Unless they are caught before early spring," Sheridan warned, "they will not be caught at all."

It took until February 8, however, for General Sheridan to be able to signal the advance to his subordinate generals, General Terry in St. Paul and General Crook in Omaha. At first, intelligence reports came in stating that Sitting Bull had made winter camp on the Little Missouri River, and General Terry felt that Custer could make a quick strike against him with the Seventh Cavalry. But newer intel came in, saying that Sitting Bull was actually two hundred miles further west. This meant that the Custer attack would have to be given up, and that an expedition involving considerably more preparation would need to be organized.

Heavy snows had slowed the flow of supplies to the Seventh Cavalry at Fort Lincoln. General Terry finally resigned himself to a spring or even a summer campaign.

Meanwhile, General Crook managed to have an expedition assembled at Fort Fetterman, Wyoming, by the end of February, 1876. It numbered almost nine hundred officers, enlisted men, and civilians. Crook had brought his pack trains from Arizona, while five trains of eighty mules each, supplemented by about eighty wagons, hauled forage and other provisions. Crook assigned command of the expedition to Colonel Joseph J. Reynolds, CO of the Third Cavalry. Crook himself also accompanied the operation, which moved out of Fort Fetterman on March 1 and up the old Bozeman Trail.

The worst adversary turned out to be the weather. For four days, from March 7 to 9, a "norther" pummeled the command, piling up snow and sending the temperature below zero. The wagons had been left under infantry guard on Crazy Woman's Fork, and the troops had to bivouac without tents. They went down the Tongue River, then Crook turned east, toward the Powder.

On March 16, the scouts spied a pair of Sioux headed east. Three hundred men moved out with Reynolds in the early evening to follow them. The remaining two squadrons and the pack trains stayed with Crook.

During the night Reynolds' scouts discovered a Indian village, numbering about one hundred lodges, in a cottonwood grove beside the Powder River. At first they thought the village belonged to Crazy Horse, but it turned out to be Old Bear's Cheyennes and some visiting Oglala Sioux under He Dog; in all, about two hundred warriors and their families. Colonel Reynolds planned to strike and destroy the village, which he attempted. Another troop seized the village's pony herd of six to eight hundred head, but the Sioux and Cheyenne counterattacked. The troops withdrew with two friendly losses. The "savages" recaptured most of their pony herd.

Lieutenant Cooke paused to mention that General Custer would have handled that attack differently from Colonel Reynolds, who had ended up with a total of four killed and six wounded, plus the loss of the pony herd and the colonel's humiliation.

Reynolds rejoined General Crook with the rest of the command and together they returned to Fort Fetterman, where General Crook brought charges against Reynolds for mismanaging the Battle of Powder River. He stated that Reynolds' failure had led to the failure of the campaign and the return to Fort Fetterman. Sheridan, the leading exponent of winter campaigns, blamed it on "the severity of the weather."

Cooke paused again. General Custer was in agreement with Crook. The hostiles needed to be taught a lesson, no matter *what* the time of year.

The strategy of the summer campaign evolved easily from the plans and movements already made in the winter campaign. Crook would once again push northward. Colonel John Gibbon would move eastward from Fort Ellis, Montana. The Seventh, General Custer having been asked to sit it out, would finally be allowed to move out from Fort Abraham Lincoln, join forces with the other units in Montana, take the hostiles of Sitting Bull under fire, and defeat them.

Since the Indians were mobile and their location indefinite, the plan would be for the columns to act independently, each searching for and, if possible, engaging the enemy. The idea was for Custer to sweep the hostiles westward toward the Bighorn River, so that Crook could drive them back on Custer. Gibbon, patrolling the north bank of the Yellowstone, would intercept any that tried to flee northward toward the Missouri.

The Sioux campaign of 1876 was modeled after the successful Red River campaign of 1874–75, with major units working in blocking and pincer movements to harass and tire the Indians. Also paralleling the Red River strategy, Sheridan proposed to place all the agency Indians under military control and to build two forts in the hostile country, one at the mouth of the Tongue and the other at the mouth of the Bighorn River.

Chris drew some eyes as he bent over, but he had just dropped his toothpick and was looking for it. He also wanted to hide the moistness that had appeared in his eyes, because he knew that the strategy being planned would work eventually, simply because of the sheer numbers of the U.S. military. He thought about the pride and nobility of the red man, and the white man's inhumanity toward him. He spotted the toothpick and sat up, hiding his emotions as he heard the end of Cooke's remarks.

Gibbon was first in the field. The "Montana Column" pushed off from Fort Ellis on March 30 and plowed through deep snow in the Bozeman Pass to the Yellowstone. The column consisted of six companies of the Seventh Infantry and four troops of the Second Cavalry—about four hundred and fifty men in all.

It wasn't until May 17 that the expedition from Fort Abraham Lincoln was ready to march. Terry, not Custer, commanded. Lieutenant Cooke cautioned every officer in the room that what he was about to say was "for your ears only." The delay was due to the fact that the General had allowed himself to be drawn into partisan political strife, stirred up by the Belknap scandal in Washington. He had testified before a congressional committee hostile to the administration and had angered President Grant. For a long time Custer had had to endure the humiliation of being left behind, but finally Grant gave in and allowed him to go. The problem, however, was that he would go only as commander of his regiment.

The "Dakota Column" consisted of all twelve troops of the Seventh Cavalry under Custer, two companies of the Seventeenth Infantry, one of the Sixth Infantry to guard the supply train, a detachment of the Twentieth Infantry serving three Gatling guns, and about forty Arikara Indian scouts. Altogether the command numbered about nine hundred and twenty-five officers and enlisted men, of whom the Seventh Cavalry accounted for some seven hundred.

Lieutenant Cooke, to Chris Colt's delight, finally shut his mouth and introduced the quartermaster, who discussed logistics at great length. Provisions would be hauled in one hundred and fifty wagons and also would be forwarded by steamer up the Missouri and the Yellowstone to the mouth of Glendive Creek, where three companies of the Sixth Infantry from Fort Buford would create a supply base. Also, even though pack transportation had never been attempted in the Department of Dakota, the wagons would carry two hundred and fifty pack saddles that could be used on the wagon mules should the occasion arise.

The briefing finally ended and the men broke for mess. They moved to the officers' mess as a group, and Chris ate with Second Lieutenants Varnum and Hale, who it turned out were supposed to command the Indian scouts but made it clear to Chris Colt that he would have free rein to run the scouts in any way that he saw fit.

This was one bright spot in the day for Chris and he concluded that maybe these two officers would survive if Custer tried to tangle with Sitting Bull, like he knew he would. Chris had served at a number of military posts now and had seen numerous commanders and officers, especially out in the field. The better ones never acted like they knew it all; but instead would rely heavily on the advice of their NCOs and scouts. Those who didn't many times ended up quite dead.

After chow, Chris located Mitch Bouyer and told him to pass the word that Chris wanted to meet with all the scouts on the parade ground in one hour's time.

Chris said, "I want you to translate my words for me."

An hour later, the scouts, the two second lieutenants, and Chris met on the parade ground. Instead of having them stand in military formation like the cavalry had done, Chris decided to make them more comfortable by forming a circle. Everything Indians did, especially the Plains tribes, was centered around the circle, which represented the Earth and Nature itself. Circles were religious symbols and villages were always formed in a circular pattern. Chris had the scouts sit down cross-legged in circles of fifteen men each. The circles made up another circle, surrounding him and Lieutenants Varnum and Hale on the parade ground.

Colt also had Mitch Bouyer standing next to him. When Colt spoke, he would stop every few sentences, while Mitch Bouyer translated for him. Colt spun slowly around so each little circle felt he was directing his attention to them. The men already appreciated the way Colt was treating them, and went a long way toward introducing Colt to them as their new boss.

While Mitch Bouyer translated, Chris said, "My name is Wamble Uncha, One Eagle, the name given me by the Minniconjou circle from the Lakotah Nation. My *wasicun* name is Chris Colt. It will be easier for the Crow and Arikara, with your tongues, to say my name 'Colt,' so call me that. You know that I have been made your new chief. If Son of the Morning Star himself comes up to you and gives you a command, you will ask me first before you do it. If you are not given food or bullets or anything, you will come to me and tell me. If anyone tries to give you orders, tell them you work for me, and they can argue with me if they don't like it.

"Tomorrow, we will go out toward the lodges of our enemies."

One scout in particular, Dirty Bear, had listened to all Chris had to say with particular interest. He stood at this last remark and spoke as Colt recognized him.

"I am Dirty Bear. Colt, you say you are called Wamble Uncha by the Lakotah, but now you say they are our enemies. I do not understand this."

Chris smiled as Dirty Bear sat down. "I have been hired to lead you to scout the Lakotah, Chyela, and Northern Arapaho, so they are my enemies in war, but they are also my brothers. Crazy Horse must do as he must do, and One Eagle must do as he must do, but if we meet in battle we will try to kill each other, although we call ourselves brothers. Can you understand and respect this?"

All the Crows looked at each other and nodded in agreement, giving grunts of approval. Following the lead of the Crows, the Arikaras responded the same way.

Dirty Bear again stood up and again Chris let him speak. "You say we will go towards the lodges of our enemies tomorrow. *Where* do we go?"

Chris said, "I will tell you each day where we must scout, and where we are going."

Dirty Bear sat down and Chris continued, "We are not soldiers, and we do not march like soldiers. Our job is to scout for the soldiers. We must find sign and read what Mother Earth is telling us. We must find all her words, even those that are whispered and hidden under rocks and leaves. We must decide what Mother Earth is saying to us with her words and tell this message to the blue-coats with Son of the Morning Star. When you find sign, you will report it to me before anyone. How many here are the sons of the same father?"

Two Arikaras raised their hands, and two Crows did as well.

Chris looked at these men and said, "When you are sent out to scout for columns, you men who are brothers will not travel together, but one will always stay with the main column of troops while the other scouts. That way two brothers will not be killed at the same time."

He continued to address the rest of the troops. "Tomorrow morning, Son of the Morning Star will wear his finest skins and will be mounted on Vic or Dandy. His soldiers will be wearing clean uniforms, and their horses will have fresh iron on their feet. They will all have many bullets, sharp knives, and clean weapons. They will march away from the fort while the band plays their song 'Gerry Owen,' but we will not be with them."

A murmur went up around each circle, as the scouts looked at each other trying to figure out what their crazy new chief was talking about.

Chris continued, "Our job is to move ahead of Son of the Morning Star and find the signs of our enemies. Our job is to keep the long-knives from becoming ambushed by our enemies. Our job is to move ahead of them and look for sign, so we will start tomorrow morning. We will leave one hour ahead of the column."

Charley Reynolds, one of the handful of scouts who was not Indian, said, "That's bullshit, Colt. What are we going to scout for, tracks of cows from farmers living on the outskirts of Fort Laramie?"

Colt said, "Maybe you should be chief of scouts, since you know more than me."

"Maybe so," he said.

Chris said, "You Charley Reynolds?"

"Yeah," Charley said. "What about it?"

Chris said, "I've heard you're a good scout. You'll head the lead patrol of scouts in the morning."

Charley Reynolds grinned, as Colt went on.

"By the way, if you were a war chief of the Lakotah or Chyela, where would you pick a spot to ambush the cavalry if you knew they were coming to attack you?"

Charley smiled and said, "I get the point, boss."

Chris grinned.

He said, "All of you will be here ready to leave when Father Sun peeks up from under his buffalo robe and looks at the prairie."

Charley laughed and said, "For us non-Indian folk, does that mean about an hour before sunup, Colt?"

Chris winked and said, "See you in the morning."

The scouts all dispersed, except for one Crow who walked up to Chris and said, "I am Crow. My name Curley. Son of the Morning Star is fool and get us all killed, maybe. What you think, Colt?"

"I think you're right, Curley," Chris replied. "But I told him I will scout for him and so did you, so if we go into battle and must die, we will die."

"This is true," Curley replied. "Maybe, I think Chris Colt will keep his scouts alive."

"If I can," Chris said. "See you in the morning. Don't sing your death song just yet, Curley."

All the scouts went off to their horses, equipment, and families, to make preparations for the long journey they would begin in the morning.

All of them except for one.

There was a cottonwood grove with a running spring about four miles out from Fort Lincoln to the northeast. That was where Dirty Bear headed his cavalry mount after the assembly. While he rode, he thought back to his childhood. Red Cloud himself had led the attack on his village, and Dirty Bear remembered how his brother and he had fled to the hiding place they used by the stream. It was a cutaway into the bank of the stream and the weeds grew long and thick, bending down and covering their hiding place. From there they were able to look out and watch the attacking Lakotah. From their hiding place across the creek, in the bank, they watched as their mother and two sisters were stabbed to death. They watched as they saw their father die, scalped by a Lakotah warrior. The two frightened boys watched as they saw their entire village being wiped out.

The older brother had lived but eight summers then, and Dirty Bear, whose name then was Thistle, had only lived six summers. The two boys went off to raise themselves, and Thistle's older brother was in charge. Because of their tough upbringing they not only survived, they both became mighty warriors. The one problem, though, was that both boys, then men, always felt displaced. They felt like they didn't belong. The two wandered from Crow band to Crow band. Thistle grew into manhood and was eventually renamed Dirty Bear by one band he and his brother stayed with for a while. His older brother had been renamed as well, but Dirty Bear only found this out not long before the killing of his sibling. He had been called Bull Calf, but he too took a different name when he achieved manhood. He had been called Two Bears, but Dirty Bear could no longer say his name. It was wrong to say the name of one who has gone beyond. He could no longer say the name of, or see, or talk to his brother, who had been killed in a knife fight, a fight with Christopher Columbus Colt.

His hatred for Colt ran deep, and his hatred for the Lakotah was just as deep. A friend of his would help him to get rid of both Colt and the Lakotah nation. He would be waiting in the cottonwood grove to get the latest news from Dirty Bear. His friend would make a plan, now that the Seventh Cavalry was going to move out. His friend was smart, and he was big, the biggest man Dirty Bear had ever seen. He was the white-eyes who the *wasicun* called Will Sawyer.

Colt rode War Bonnet into Bismarck and tied him up at the hitching rack located in front of the Frontier Café. He walked inside and sat down at one of the checkercloth-covered round tables. A minister and his wife sat in one corner of the café, and two men who looked like they were probably wagon drovers ate in the other corner. Between mouthfuls they were having a friendly argument about something, but Chris couldn't tell what it was from their whisperings. In the middle of the café a man and woman sat eating; Chris figured they could well be the town banker and his wife.

Shirley came out the door carrying two plates, and she spotted Chris immediately. She winked at him, and beamed as she served the banker type and his wife. She hustled back to the kitchen and returned with two cups to pour out coffee for the couple, then freshened the coffee of others in the room.

Shirley walked over to Chris and smiled down at him, saying, "May I help you, sir?"

"Yes you may," Chris replied. "May I have one large kiss, well done?"

She giggled, drawing everyone's attention. She blushed and shrugged her shoulders, then set her pad down, lifted Chris by his arms, and threw her arms around his neck. They kissed long and hard, while everyone in the little restaurant stared in amazement. One of the drovers whistled when they had finished.

The other drover broke the awkward silence by blurting out, "Ma'am, does that go with every order?"

Everybody in the café laughed for a long time.

Chris sat down and Shirley, still embarrassed by her own actions, said, "Don't order. I'll surprise you."

Colt thought to himself that this was one incredible woman. A heap of fun. He thought whoever married her would be happy for the rest of his life. Then he got a panicky feeling as he realized he was thinking about a woman and marriage. He felt like getting up and running out the door. Colt caught himself and settled down. He sat there and looked out the window and tried to think about the upcoming campaign.

Shirley walked out the door of the kitchen carrying a large steak, baked sweet potatoes, and sliced tomatoes. She set the platter down and hurried back to the kitchen, returning with a basket of biscuits, a plate of butter, and the pot of coffee. She set these down and poured Chris a steaming cup of hot coffee. Then she went around and once again freshened the cups of all the other customers.

After Colt and Shirley's antics, all eyes in the room were on them as she sat down across from him. He savored the meal, thinking that it was one of the best he'd eaten in a long time.

"Ma'am," Chris said, "you are one fine cook. This food is delicious."

She said, "Thank you, Mr. Colt, but make sure you save some room for dessert."

"Dessert?" Chris said. "What dessert?"

She stood and said, "You're about ready. I'll bring it to you."

Shirley started into the kitchen, but was stopped by a tug on the arm by the banker's wife. She grinned up at Shirley and gave her the "naughty, naughty" sign while giggling. Her husband tried to act as if nothing were happening.

Shirley said something unintelligible to the woman and the woman nodded her head. The café owner walked back into the kitchen and came out a few minutes later carrying three slices of hot apple pie, with slices of cheese melting on top of them. She gave one to the woman, then set one down in front of Chris and had the other herself.

The banker's wife said, "Shirley, can I have some more coffee, please?"

Shirley said, "Sure," and started to jump up.

The other woman held her hand up and smiled broadly, saying, "No, Shirl, you stay right there and relax. I'll get it."

Chris reached across the table and took Shirley's hand in his. They both smiled at each other.

He said, "Shirley, I have to leave in the morning."

She got a concerned look on her face and said, "Where? For how long?"

"I'm going out with Custer on a major campaign in Montana," Chris said sadly.

She said, "How long will you be gone?"

Chris said, "I don't know. Months."

The banker's wife came up and poured coffee into Chris's cup and Shirley's. Shirley had tears showing in her eyes, but she gave a brave smile and said, "Thanks."

Chris thanked the woman, too, and she went around the restaurant and freshened everybody's coffee.

Shirley said, "How long will you be gone? How long do you *honestly* think?"

She had tears streaming down her cheeks now.

Chris said, "You want it soft or real?"

Shirley said, "I hate dishonesty. You be totally honest, even if it's going to hurt."

Chris lingered over his coffee and said, " 'Shirl,' did she call you?"

Shirley said, "Yeah, some people call me that for short."

"Shirl, I have a strong feeling about this one," he replied. "I believe that a lot of us won't be coming back from this campaign."

He heard her breath catch, and more tears filled her eyes and rolled onto her face, but she sniffled and straightened her back.

Shirley said, "If you believe that so strongly then it's going to happen that way, but I know one thing for sure."

Chris said, "What's that?"

She smiled and said, "*You* definitely *will* be coming back."

Chris said, "Yes, I do believe I will. Those of

us that survive probably will be gone for several months, though."

Shirley smiled now and whispered, "I don't care. I can handle several months, a year, whatever. Just as long as I know you'll be coming back."

"Only death could keep me away from here," Chris replied. "From you."

She grabbed his other hand in hers and stared into his eyes.

Shirley said, "You and I just met yesterday and I feel, I feel . . ."

"You and I fell in love yesterday," Chris said softly. "And I'm scared."

She said, "Why?"

Chris replied, "Because I'm deeply in love with you, Shirl, after knowing you just two days. I'm scared because I lost my wife and daughter not that long ago, and I'm afraid of mistaking the wrong feelings for love."

"You haven't," she said. "I love you, too, Chris, and I'll be here when you get back. If you need time to sort out your feelings, I'll still be here."

"I'm going to go," Chris said. "But I'll see you when I get back."

Chris felt awkward. He usually was so much more in control of himself, of the situation. Now he almost felt paralyzed. He stood up, and Shirl did too. Chris looked around the room at the other diners, and now he felt self-conscious.

Shirl put her arms around his neck, and they hugged.

She whispered, "Don't leave me tonight. Stay with me."

He looked into her eyes and smiled, then gave her a small kiss on the end of her nose.

Chris sat back down and said, "How about another piece of that delicious apple pie?"

Shirley smiled from ear to ear and went to the kitchen, returning with the rest of the pie, a knife, and extra plates. The other diners helped to make it disappear quickly.

Chris had to slip away in the middle of the night without waking her. He didn't want to go through another awkward moment with another good-bye. However, he found a little garden around the back porch of her little house, which was attached to the back of the café. He took out his knife and cut one of the roses in the garden. He sneaked back into the house and set the rose down on his pillow, then sneaked back out.

Crossing the prairie due west of Fort Lincoln was uneventful. The column made relatively good time. It was May, and Custer had orders to rendezvous with General Terry on the Yellowstone River in Montana in early June. The timing was fortunate, in that it allowed Chris Colt to ride out and check on each of his scouts and evaluate their ability. So many were assigned to Custer's main battalion, so many to Major Reno's, and the rest to Captain Benteen's.

During any operation against the Sioux and Cheyenne the three battalions would be separated, and it was important to Chris that he find out who were the good scouts, who were the loafers, and so on, so that he could evenly distribute them to each unit. He himself would remain with Custer and his battalion.

One thing that bothered Colt was the sign he kept finding of lots of Indian movements toward the Yellowstone River country. That was where they were headed, and it was where Sitting Bull had his massive encampment that kept getting larger and larger.

Since Custer had run his mouth in Washington, the Seventh Cavalry was coming into the roundup at the last twenty miles, so to speak. Other things were already going on in the Yellowstone country.

For the second time, on May 29, 1876, Crook had marched from Fort Fetterman, driving up the old Bozeman Trail. His command was comprised of ten troops of the Third Cavalry, five troops of the Second Cavalry, two companies of the Fourth Infantry, and three companies of the Ninth Infantry. He had over one thousand men in his command. One hundred and twenty wagons and one thousand pack mules carried supplies. Crook established a base camp on Goose Creek, a tributary of the Tongue River, on June 14, and he was joined there by one hundred and seventy-six Crow and eighty-six Shoshoni Indian scouts and volunteer fighters.

By June, the enemy area of operations held a lot more Sioux, Cheyennes, and Arapahoes than it did in the winter. The Black Hills issue, which had worsened conditions at the agencies, and the government's attempt to take away their freedom, had started an unusually large spring migration of agency Indians to the camps of the "hostiles."

Later, the army, professing ignorance of the increase in enemy strength, blamed the failure of the campaign on the Bureau of Indian Affairs' negligence in reporting the warriors' exodus from the agencies. Pointing out that each of the converging columns was itself strong enough to cope with the five to eight hundred warriors the Indian Bureau estimated were absent from the reservation, General Sherman implied that knowledge of their real numbers would have changed military plans and averted disaster. All past experience, however, showed that agency Indians swelled the hunting bands every spring. On May 30, Sheridan telegraphed Sherman that "information from Crook indicates that all the agency Indians capable of taking the field are now or soon will be on the warpath." Actually, the generals worried much less about the enemies's strength than about their reluctance to stand and fight conventionally. Campaigns usually failed because the Indians could not be caught and engaged in battle. Besides, chances of encountering any significant portion of the warriors at one time were remote. The generals hoped that grass and game could not long support very large gatherings of the hostile Indians.

After the successful Reynolds battle, the Cheyennes fled down Powder River and joined forces with Crazy Horse. Together they moved northeast and joined forces with Sitting Bull, Black Moon, Gall, and Lame Deer. Cautious because of the soldiers' attack on the Cheyenne, the chiefs resolved to stay together for common defense. They moved down the Powder, the Tongue, and the Rosebud. Two other Sioux tribal circles, Sans Arc and Blackfoot, formed. The Cheyenne contingent grew with the accession of parties under Lame White Man, Dirty Moccasins, and Charcoal Bear. Scatterings of Brules, Yanktonais, Northern Arapahoes, and Santees attached themselves to the other circles. Throughout April and May, warriors and families, singly and in groups, had straggled in from the agencies to swell the village further. Every few days, seeking fresh grass for the vast pony herd, the Sioux and Cheyenne moved camp. They also sent out hunting parties in every direction to fill the camps' occupants with meat.

In mid-June, as Chris Colt had predicted, the Hunkpapas held a sundance ceremony on the Rosebud. Sitting Bull went through the ceremony, after giving up fifty pieces of flesh. Before actually doing the sundance, warriors many times would cut little pieces of flesh off their arms and legs, or both. The Hunkpapa spiritual leader experienced a vision, and in it he saw the image of many soldiers "falling right into our camp." He described them as "dead soldiers who will be gifts of God."

Immediately after the sundance, the Indians moved across the Wolf Mountains and formed the giant encampment on No Name Creek, which flows into the Little Bighorn. On June 16, men from the many hunting parties finally discovered the *wasicun* soldiers and brought word of the many soldiers on the upper reaches of the Rosebud. Thinking about the soldiers falling into the camp in Sitting Bull's vision, warriors from all the camp circles assembled that night and rode back to the Rosebud.

On that same day, General Crook left his wagon train column and crossed from the Tongue to the Rosebud. The next morning, while his Wyoming column took a smoke and a coffee break, the Lakotah attacked. The Crow and Shoshoni volunteer warriors held the Sioux off for almost half an hour until the cavalry troops got organized. After the initial attack, the soldiers did a little better. The cavalry eventually took the high ground in the valley, and some other units of infantry occupied the bluffs south of the valley. The fighting raged on, as attack after attack rippled up and down a battle line some three miles in length. The broken terrain, filled with hills, ridges, and ravines, caused the fighting to occur in little pockets and effectively prevented good central command.

Crook sent one troop from the Third Cavalry to seize the village, then began to mobilize the rest of the command to follow and be ready to support the Third Cav. All the units in the battle line came under heavy pressure. Trying a retreat from one part of the line, Lieutenant Colonel Royall and three troops of the Third Cavalry he commanded were badly mauled and almost cut off, before Crook sent two companies from the Ninth Infantry to reinforce them.

Another troop's commander was shot off his horse and gravely wounded, so his troopers all but gave up. Sioux swarmed toward the wounded captain. But some of the volunteer Crows and Shoshonis raced to the rescue of the wounded officer and got into hand-to-hand combat.

Royall's experience persuaded Crook that he couldn't support his other units, so he dispatched an aide to cancel any offensive movements. Trying to make a strategic withdrawal, one of the troop commanders moved his men west, then got off the main trail and charged up and downhill cross-country. Ironically, this placed his troop behind the Sioux and Cheyennes. Effectively surrounded by that accidental action on the part of the cavalry, the Lakotah and Chyela broke off the fight and abandoned the battlefield.

The Crows and Shoshonis had performed much better in the battle than the soldiers, a battle that lasted six hours. More than once the Indian allies saved the troops from being overrun, besides preventing the Army captain from being captured or killed. Because the Sioux and Cheyenne withdrew, as was their custom, and Crook ended up occupying the battlefield, the colonel tried to claim the Battle of Rosebud as a victory. In actuality, he had effectively and totally been defeated by the Indians. Though only twenty-eight soldiers were killed and fifty-six wounded, thirty-six Lakotah and Cheyenne killed and sixty-three wounded, Crook still retreated from the battlefield and formed a defensive position at his supply base on Goose Creek, refusing to patrol anywhere until reinforcements had arrived. The Rosebud battle was a tremendous moral, emotional, and strategic victory for Sitting Bull, because one of the major military units against him had been effectively immobilized, defeated, and demoralized.

Not knowing anything about Crook's operation or defeat, General Terry and the Dakota column made their battle plans. He and Gibbon, who met on June 9 aboard the supply steamer *Far West* on the Yellowstone River, agreed that the finds of Gibbon's Crow scouts made it unlikely that any Sioux would be found east of the Rosebud. Even so, Terry wanted to confirm this conclusion, and on June 10 he sent Major Marcus A. Reno and six troops of the Seventh Cavalry to scout the Powder and Tongue valleys. During Reno's absence, Gibbon concentrated his command on the Yellowstone River near the mouth of the Rosebud. The infantry and all the wagons stayed at the newly-formed supply base at the mouth of the Tongue River, while Custer, relying solely on pack transportation, advanced the rest of the troops of the Seventh to the mouth of the Tongue to await Reno's return.

Going beyond his orders, Reno led his troops westward from the Tongue to the Rosebud, where he discovered the trail to Sitting Bull's village. While Crook clashed with Crazy Horse near the head of the Rosebud, Major Reno's men were examining abandoned campsites forty miles downstream. Reno turned around there and went down the Rosebud to the Yellowstone. General Terry was furious when he found out that Reno had gone further than he'd been instructed to go—the major could have alerted the Lakotah and Chyela. General Terry decided to reassemble his cavalry units at the mouth of the Rosebud, but first started Gibbons and his infantry back up the north side of the Yellowstone River.

On June 21, General Terry held a final strategy meeting aboard the *Far West* to work out final details of the battle plan. The main thrust of Terry's plan was to work out a strategy that would contain the Indians. These cavalry generals were so accustomed to the hit-and-run tactics of the northern plains tribes, they could only picture all the times that these warriors had struck quickly and run off, eluding U.S. military pursuit. The fundamental order of attack was based on the fact that the Crow and Arikara

(Ree) scouts had seen many columns of smoke near the Little Bighorn River.

Custer and the Seventh Cavalry would march up the Rosebud and then drive down the Little Bighorn River from the south. Gibbon's troops would cross the Yellowstone River, then ascend the Bighorn River and enter the Little Bighorn Valley River from the north. Custer was expected to strike the blow after Gibbon had a chance to move into a position to block the flight of the fleeing "cowardly redskins" to the north. Gibbon felt he could reach the mouth of the Little Bighorn no sooner than June 26. Custer was to travel the entire length of the Rosebud before crossing over to the Little Bighorn River, and was to continue past the major trail leading toward the giant encampment. General Terry made these orders very specific, because he wanted to make absolutely sure that he had blocking forces in place before the warriors could flee once again, eluding the American military forces.

Because of this fact his orders were specific, but the written orders were also ambiguous to some extent. General Terry was trying to be polite, so to speak. Nevertheless, he made sure that Custer and Gibbon were given copies of the written orders to ensure that they would be totally clear on the fact that he wanted them to block both ends of the valley and bottle the giant force of hostiles between them.

Chapter 4

>>>>>>>>>>>>>>>>>>>>>>>

Beyond Purgatory

By the beginning of June, Shirley Ebert had really started to miss Chris Colt. In the weeks after that, she talked to every person she knew at Fort Lincoln and in her café who had any news at all. There had been several battles with the Sioux and numerous skirmishes, but no word about Chris. She did know that General Custer constantly sent letters by courier to his wife, Libbie—Elizabeth Bacon Custer.

She passed a number of tear-filled nights worrying about Chris, but she also knew he was the type of man who would always come out on top. Though she couldn't help but worry, she believed deep in her heart that he would not be killed. Shirley had learned, years before, to pull herself out of worry and negativity by believing that things would always turn out for the best.

The scout really missed Shirley himself, but his life and the lives of others were dependent on his being clear-headed and single-minded in purpose. His job and the work of his men was most important before any battle began.

Chris Colt tried to see Custer several times,

but the general was always too busy to talk with him. Chris wanted to let Custer know that he was dealing with a force that could bring death to him and his men.

As the operation moved closer to Sitting Bull, Chris and his scouts stepped up their security efforts. Colt was seeing sign everywhere. He was also upset because several Sioux had been added as additional scouts, and Colt was positive they were spies for Sitting Bull. He couldn't fathom any other reason they'd have wanted to work as scouts, side by side with all their enemies: the *wasicun,* Crows, Shoshonis, and Arikara.

While Chris was getting increasingly alarmed that Custer was taking things too lightly, he had no idea that horrible events had taken place back in North Dakota and were actually bringing his love much closer to him. Unfortunately, she was getting closer to him in a way no one would have wanted for her at all. No one but Will Sawyer, the ruthless giant.

Shirley awoke at three o'clock in the morning to be told that Chris Colt had been brought in by ambulance wagon to Fort Lincoln. The cavalry corporal that came to summon her said that Colt had taken two arrows in the midsection while fighting against the Sioux on the Yellowstone River. He was lingering near death, at the post dispensary. The regimental surgeon said that if he could make it through that night, he might have a fighting chance.

Shirley dressed as quickly as she could, after showing the corporal where the coffeepot and cups were. Once dressed, she rushed out and joined the corporal behind the restaurant and climbed into his buggy. A three-quarter moon and the Big Dipper hung low over the early-summer sky. But they and the Milky Way were nothing but a blur, because Shirley was crying so hard. She tried to be brave and hold it in, but the man she had just fallen head-over-heels in love with was lying at death's door in an Army dispensary just a few miles away. She couldn't help it. It just wasn't fair.

Shirley's father worked hard, very hard, as a blacksmith in Youngstown, Ohio. Her mother was a housewife and she, too, worked very hard. Shirley had lost two brothers in the Civil War, both fighting for the Union, and that had just about destroyed her parents. It was also probably the reason, Shirley knew, that she had isolated herself from men. There were some who might have piqued her interest as marriage prospects, but because of her brothers' deaths she set very high standards for men she would court. She didn't want to get "too" close to somebody and love them, then get hurt again.

Yet the feelings she had for Chris Colt were so overpowering that she could not help but let her guard down. When she first saw him, something in her heart snapped. She was finally in love, and now she could not bear the thought of losing Chris, too.

Before reaching the fort, the corporal suddenly pulled off the road onto a double-rutted wagon road through some trees. He pulled up quickly on the reins and stepped on the brake lever of the buggy. Shirley looked around and was caught totally off-guard. Two men ran out of the trees, and when she saw that the closest was Will Sawyer her heart sank, and she immediately panicked. She tried to react, but powerful hands grabbed her and jerked her from the buggy. Sawyer threw her onto the ground while she kicked in vain. He started to blindfold, gag, and tie her, while another pair of hands groped her breasts.

Many people from back east didn't really understand the code of the West, but there was a very strict unwritten law. No matter how tough an hombre you were, you just didn't molest women. Because women were such a rare commodity out west, this was, in effect, a societal self-defense mechanism. There had been numerous cases of outlaws actually lynching other outlaws for having sexually assaulted a woman. For this man to fondle Shirley's breasts while she was being tied and gagged, well, that really put fear in her heart. What kind of desperate monster could this be?

She was lifted up and tied on a horse, then led, at a fast trot, while the three men abandoned the buggy. She had no idea where she was being taken, she just worried about being knocked off the horse by a low-hanging branch across the trail, an image that kept appearing in her mind's eye.

The men led the horse for hours, and Shirley tried to listen for sounds of waterfalls, streams, echoes from rock formations, anything she could think of, but it just turned out to be hour after hour of hard riding. Finally they stopped, and then Shirley got really frightened. She was pulled off the horse and untied. Her blindfold and gag were removed. She rubbed her chafed wrists briskly and tried to restore the circulation.

Will Sawyer walked over and stared at her

with a look that chilled her all the way to her bones.

He said, "Missy, I'm a gonna leave ya untied, but iffin ya try to run on me, I'll tie yer purty little arms under the horse's belly an' ye'll ride to Yellowstone Territory thet way. Ye'll live, iffin ya do what yer tole. If not, I'll jest beat the ever-lovin' hell outa ya, and ye'll still do it my way. Iffin ya scream, wal, we're in Injun country right now, so go head an' scream an' see where it gits ya. Unnerstan'?"

She nodded her head meekly, tears filling her eyes. Ironically, some of her tears fell because, even if she had been duped, she now knew that Chris was not dying. That alone gave her floods of relief.

Will walked up to her with that evil look in his eye and said, "Get naked."

She set her jaw, fighting back tears, and shook her head no.

The giant grabbed her and started to remove her clothes, with all the other men watching, mouths open. He raped her right there in front of them, while they built a fire and set up camp.

When he had finished, he addressed his cohorts. "I'm the only one to touch her. I don't want spoilt goods. Unnerstan'?" There was eager nodding all around.

He looked at her and said, "Fixin's are in that saddlebag yonder. Fix our supper."

She glared at him and said, "Chris Colt will kill you, Will Sawyer. He'll cut your black heart out."

He looked at her a second and chuckled, then said, "Fix our food, woman."

She got out the flour, coffee, bacon, and hardtack, and started the meal. Shirley tried to figure out a way she could come up with some kind of poison, but she couldn't.

She wanted to curl up on the ground in the fetal position and cry her eyes out, but she would not let herself do that. Somehow, some way, she would endure whatever she had to endure and survive. She knew that Chris Colt would live, and she would live, and somehow they would be reunited, so until then she would do whatever she had to do to survive. In the meantime, she would not stop trying to find a way to escape.

It continued like that for a number of days. Sawyer would take her whenever he felt like it. She would prepare meals for the desperadoes, and they kept moving further west. Now they were much closer to Christopher Columbus Colt. Because of that, Shirley felt renewed. He was such a special man, such a hero, she just knew that he would save her. All she had to do was survive, but that in itself might turn out to be a tall order.

A good tracker can look at sign and tell you all kinds of things about a person or animal, but an *excellent* tracker like Chris Colt can read tracks and sign and tell you an entire story. He can put several tracks together with some bent grass and pieces of fabric and clearly envision the person or animals that made those signs. He knows where they came from, where they were going, and why.

Thus Chris Colt saw signs in the current tactical area of operations that to him were like the open page of a newspaper. He knew from the signs that nobody was in a hurry to run anywhere. They were congregating together for strength. Colt found signs of large parties of hunters. He found gut piles on one hunting party trail from fifteen antelope and twenty-five deer. This had been no expedition to feed just a couple of tribal circles. It had to have been only one of many hunting parties. *Thousands* were being fed.

Colt found where the antelope had been killed, and from the sign was able to visualize the hunt itself. He found a watering hole with a lot of pronghorn tracks around it. Not too far away there was a series of small mounds of dirt, maybe ten feet in diameter and four or five feet high. He found the tracks where the warriors had crouched behind the clumps and used mesquite to make a kind of natural fence-line, turning the immediate terrain into a funnel's mouth. On a bush behind the farthest clump still hung one of the several feathers that the hunters had displayed.

Antelope have eyesight like binoculars, so the hunters stayed well hidden. The main brave hid behind the clump with the feathers, knowing that the antelope, the fastest land animal on the North American continent, has one weakness: curiosity. Curiosity has killed more than the cat; it has also killed many pronghorns. The antelope being a herd animal, many had come to the watering hole and spotted the feathers blowing with the prairie breeze. Closer examination of the bush showed Colt a tiny thread of red, so he knew that the brave had also placed a streamer of red cloth to attract the curious animals. He could picture the antelopes moving closer and closer to the feathers and ribbon, trying to figure out what it was. When they had ventured far enough into the ambush, all the hunters, on a prearranged signal like the whistle of a marmot or a prairie dog, would have fired their bows and arrows and taken a number of the herd.

He also found places along the banks of several of the streams and rivers they scouted where bull-hide boats had been dragged ashore, mule deer gutted nearby. Again Chris visualized how the deer had been taken so easily. The Lakotah hunters had in their bull-hide boats a small platform on which they placed a fairly large, very flat rock. They would place a small fire on the rock and back the fire with another flat rock. They would then paddle up to deer either watering or feeding on the lush grasses in the river bottoms at night. Deer are hypnotized by bright light, so the bull-hide boat hunters would quietly paddle right up to them, then fire their arrows at point-blank range from behind the fires that hypnotized them with their light.

The signs told Chris Colt something else. A group of Lakotah and Cheyenne who were traveling fast and light and eluding the cavalry would not be using a bunch of big, round, cumbersome buffalo-hide boats. They wouldn't even *have* a supply of bull-hide boats. Not unless they had a large, fairly permanent encampment nearby.

That large encampment was indeed there, nearby, and Chris could sense it. He didn't know that the woman he loved was nearby as well. He only knew that he had a tremendous sense of foreboding. Christopher Columbus Colt was a man of the wilderness, and a warrior. He knew to trust his instincts. He would ride with his rifle across his saddle horn until the uneasy feeling went away, or until he was dead.

The phony corporal, Will called him "Otis," had changed clothes and now wore cowboy duds, but Shirley noticed that he rode what looked like a cavalry horse. She'd seen plenty of just such horses, and the trooper-issue McLellan saddles. Based on that, and a certain surly demeanor she'd seen before at Fort Lincoln, Shirley assumed that the man was a deserter. Otis was very large and had one front tooth missing.

The other man, Rip, was one of the cowboys who had accompanied Will Sawyer to her café when he'd gotten into the fight with Chris Colt. He had blond hair and a little boy face. In fact, many women would have looked at this man and thought him to be quite innocent. His twin cross-draw pearl-handled Colts, in silver-studded black holsters, looked plenty evil enough. Shirley was mildly surprised when she realized that while he was dressed for punching cows, his hands were slender and uncallused. He also stuttered when he spoke.

They arrived at the confluence of a large river and a fast-flowing stream. She didn't know it at the time, but the river was the Yellowstone. She also didn't know that they were less than a half a day's ride from her hero. They made camp on a small knoll overlooking the apex of the two watercourses, and they stayed there for two days. The men took turns watching all the time, so Shirley assumed that either there were a lot of unfriendly Indians close by, or they were waiting for someone.

Late in the afternoon of the second day, an Indian man came to their small camp to meet with Will Sawyer. She could tell that they were speaking about her, and she felt a lump in her throat. Would she be sold or traded to this Indian?

They struck camp, and Shirley felt the instinctive tensing she'd learned to associate with Will Sawyer touching her. He, for the first time in days, tied her hands to the saddle horn, and Rip led her horse. They rode until well after dark when Shirley started to smell wood-smoke. At first the scent was very faint, but it kept getting stronger. They started up a small hill, and she could hear the faint sounds of many horses. As they got near the top the sounds got louder and louder, and in the moonlight she looked from atop the rise, down onto thousands of horses in a giant herd. Beyond that, she saw flickering little lights dotting the breadth of a large valley.

She could tell that these were the lights from thousands of Sioux and Cheyenne lodges. The outline of many of the bison-hide lodges were individually lost in the distance. The sheer quantity of lodges, and the countless horses in the pony herd, were truly awe-inspiring. She could hardly take in the sweep of it all, even as her mind attempted to see it as a daylight panoramic view.

The men got off their horses and immediately began to gather sticks for a fire. It was then that Shirley noticed that each of the men was carrying a white flag on a long stick. They started a fire and sat around it in a circle, holding their truce flags. Within minutes Lakotah warriors, paint on their faces, appeared in a circle around the small group. They pointed guns and arrows at the Crow and Americans, and the men stood. Shirley was still tied to the saddle horn, and the lead line was now held by Will Sawyer.

She sat up straight, chin stuck out defiantly, deciding not to show fear or scream out, no matter what. She felt that Chris Colt would let these people torture him and would never cry out, no matter what. Nor would she. She was Chris Colt's woman.

The Lakotah spoke, with much gesturing, with Shirley's captors, but at the drumming of hoofbeats all the Lakotah went silent. They stared in the direction of the hoofbeats as a large steeldust horse and rider rode up to the fire circle.

The brave was large and very well muscled, and had a red zigzag lightning bolt starting at the top of his forehead and running straight down to the chin. Shirley scanned his items: he had a single hawk feather, breechcloth, knife, war club, and an anklet on one leg. The man was covered in fine gray dust and was obviously highly revered by the Sioux.

He spoke in broken English to the first Indian, who was called Dirty Bear. "You are Crow? Why you come?"

"We bring gift to the Lakotah," Dirty Bear said. "We bring *wasicun* woman, and I bring you gift of knowledge. I am scout for Long Hair. He is close, and comes with many Long Knives. We—"

The large man interrupted. "Boss you? What name boss you?"

Dirty Bear said, "He is son of the snake. Is named Colt."

The lightning-faced one swung his leg over the neck of his horse and hopped down. His bone-

handled knife was in his hand before anyone
could even see him draw it.

He stood face-to-face with Dirty Bear and
snarled, "I am Crazy Horse, of the Oglala Nation! You call my brother son of snake! You die
now, Crow dog!'

Will Sawyer grinned and said, "Crazy Horse,
huh? I heerd ya got big medicine, but ya shore
don't wanna kill ole Dirty Bear, on account a
he's got all kinds a stuff to tell ya about Custer."

Crazy Horse grinned at Sawyer and stabbed
straight into Dirty Bear's lower abdomen. The
Crow's face twisted as he tried to speak. Crazy
Horse grinned into his face and stared deep into
his eyes.

The famous Oglala warrior said, "Crow dog,
you betray men give word to."

Crazy Horse spit into the man's face and Dirty
Bear died, slowly sliding off the end of the Lakotah's blade.

Will Sawyer's eyes never left Crazy Horse.
Shirley stared at the Sioux legend, knowing that
this famous man was Chris Colt's friend. He had
just proved it beyond any shadow of a doubt.

Sawyer said, "But he could a told ya all
about—"

Crazy Horse interrupted, "He lie to friends! I
not believe anyhow."

Shirley understood. At this moment she could
appreciate the simple but profound logic struggling out of the lips of such a sinewy tower of
frontier violence. He walked to her and brought
his bloody blade up quickly, cutting through the
rawhide bonds. He roughly grabbed her and
dragged her off the horse, walking over to his
while she kicked and struggled feebly, in tow.

He took a leather braided rope from the back of his horse and made a loop in one end, slipping it over her neck. Grabbing another piece of rawhide rope from his parfleche, he tied her hands, then turned toward Sawyer.

He turned his head and said to her, "Stand."

Addressing Sawyer, he said, "What name?"

Will said, "Sawyer, Crazy Horse."

Crazy Horse said, "What want?"

Will said, "Wal, I heerd ya say yore brothers with Chris Colt, but him an' me ain't exactly friends. Now I see ya got real strong feelin's bout yer friend, so we won't discuss my problims with him, but me and jest these two friends here been wantin' ta do some minin' on Sioux lands, so we brought ya this white woman as a gift. She's kinda crazy, so ya can't believe nothin' she says, but she'd be good under yer buffaler robe. Know what I mean, chief? What we want is ta mine in the Black Hills and not be attacked by no Sioux or Cheyenne."

"I am Chris Colt's woman, Crazy Horse!" Shirley cried out.

Crazy Horse glanced at her, then looked at Sawyer, saying, "She talk true?"

Sawyer laughed and said, "Naw. I tole ya, she's a little bit teched in the head."

Crazy Horse said, "Not believe you. You go."

Rip said, "Now wait, we brung you reports on old Custer, an we—"

Crazy Horse's arm whipped up from his side and the blade twirled in the air before it buried itself to the handle in the man's throat. Rip clutched at it and fell backward, kicking around on the ground. Shirley's stomach turned over, but she refused to allow her face to betray the fact.

Otis's eyes opened wide, and his head swiveled from side to side in fear. An arrow swished through the darkness and buried itself to the feathers through his right lung. Another arrow knifed through the chill of the night and stuck in his breastbone. A third went through his heart, and he dropped dead in his tracks. Three of the Lakotah warriors around the circle renocked arrows.

Will Sawyer looked all around him and started to draw his pistols, but froze at the sound of several rifles being cocked. Crazy Horse walked up to him and looked up into his face.

The Oglala said, "You brought gift, so I give you one: your life. Go."

Will Sawyer did not have to be given another invitation.

He mounted up as quickly as possible and rode off into the darkness, but not before hearing the frenzied words of Shirley Ebert haunting him from behind. "Chris Colt will hunt you down and kill you, Will Sawyer! Think about that!"

A hint of a smile crossed Crazy Horse's handsome face. He grabbed the lead rope on Shirley and jerked her behind his horse. Then he vaulted onto the back of the steel-dust gelding and led her toward the giant encampment.

She had to run to keep up with the slow trot of the big captured American horse. The rope had little slack. In the darkness, Shirley kept falling, but she would immediately roll and get back onto her feet. I will survive, she decided, no matter what.

Chapter 5

>>>>>>>>>>>>>>>>>>

At the End

"**B**ut, General, you will take you and your men into certain death," Chris Colt insisted. "I am telling you. There's more Lakotah, Sioux, and Cheyenne out there than you can imagine. One of our Crow scouts, Dirty Bear, has been missing, and we have reason to believe he could have gone to Sitting Bull and told him whatever he knew about your plans or movements."

"First of all, what proof do you have that Dirty Bear has gone over?" Custer asked in an angry manner.

Colt said, "Some of the better scouts didn't like or trust him to begin with; then, after he turned up missing, I found out that he's the brother of the Crow warrior I killed in a knife fight when I saved Sarah Guthrie."

Custer paced back and forth, looking at the floor of his tent, then stopped and said, "Doesn't matter, Colt. He wouldn't know anything anyhow. We'll proceed and set those red niggers into flight, no matter how many there are."

"General Custer!" Colt fumed. "They are *not* running! Listen to me. You are going to get all your men killed!"

A man came to Custer's tent door, preventing the screaming tirade the Boy General was about to launch into.

"Come in, Mr. Kelly," Custer snapped, and took some messages and letters that had come in by courier.

He leafed through them and pulled out three letters from his wife, Libbie. He also pulled out a large envelope that read *Hand-Carry; Delivery* URGENT. Setting down the letters from his wife, he handed two letters of his own for Libbie to the courier, then opened the message and read it, his eyebrows arching every few seconds. He set it down and blew a long breath through pursed lips.

"Mr. Colt," Custer said, "I'm afraid I have some bad news. Didn't you have some interest in a Miss Ebert from the Frontier Café in Bismarck?"

A deeply concerned look on his face, Chris replied, "Yes, I did. I do. What's happened?"

Custer went on, "Well, it seems that Miss Ebert has been missing for some time now. The sheriff's posse found tracks of Miss Ebert and one man getting into a buggy and leaving. Two days later they found an abandoned buggy a few miles out of town, and tracks indicate there were three men and they all departed on horseback. The tracks of one of the three indicated that it was an extremely big and heavy man."

Chris said, "Will Sawyer."

Custer continued, "That's what the sheriff believes."

Chris said, "I have to go find her, General."

He started for the door.

Custer yelled, "Sentry!"

A guard ran through the doorway with his rifle at the ready.

Custer continued, "Mr. Colt, I'm sorry. I know how you feel, but I cannot spare you right now."

Colt turned, and Custer nodded at the sentry, who removed Colt's gun from his holster from behind.

Through clenched teeth, Colt addressed the "General" by his true rank. "Colonel Custer, I have to go."

Custer said, "And I have said you cannot. I give the orders around here. I'm sorry, but I cannot risk the lives of my command for the sake of one person."

"One *kidnapped woman!*" Colt shot back. "Besides, I quit. You can't give me orders now."

Custer said, "Seize him, guard! Colt, if you go wandering around in this area now and get captured, you could compromise my entire operation."

The guard, joined by two others who had also entered the tent, grabbed Chris by his arms and put irons on him.

"You can't do this, Custer!" Colt raged. "I'm a civilian!"

Custer smiled and said, "No, right now you're a liability."

Chris demanded, "To your operation? Or to your crooked deal with the Sawyers and the Indian Ring, you self-loving son of a bitch!"

This last remark hit Custer where he lived. It showed on his face, and the three sentries stared at the General with a funny look on their faces. He stormed over to Colt and punched him in the face. Colt flew backward along with the guards and landed against the wall of Custer's tent. The side of the tent caved in on them, and soldiers came running to their commander's aid. Colt was finally picked up and brought outside, where Custer walked up to him as he was being held by several troopers.

Custer whispered in Colt's ear, "Too bad you said that, Mr. Colt. You may just have an accident while you're a prisoner. Maybe one of these red niggers, like that one you mentioned, will sneak in here and slit your throat."

Custer stepped back and Colt said, "You shouldn't have hit me, Custer. It's going to cost you."

"Are you threatening me, Mr. Colt?" Long Hair asked.

Colt grinned and said, "Yes."

Custer, looking around at his men and apparently showing off for them, said, "Be kind of hard for you to do anything to me, Mr. Colt, chained to a wagon." He laughed, and his men followed suit, trying to butter him up.

Colt stared at Custer through angry eyes and replied, "I don't have to do anything to you, Long Hair. Your own ego will get you killed, and these good men here too."

Colt looked at the gathered troopers and saw some of the color drain from their faces. Custer laughed nervously.

He said, "Sergeant of the guard, take him away, chain him in a wagon, and put him under double guard."

Colt was dragged away, chained, and locked in one of the emptier supply wagons. He was furious, and his mind was made up. Chris Colt was truly in love with Shirley Ebert, and he was going to rescue her, wherever she was.

There were several problems, though. Number one, he didn't know if she was still alive or dead. Number two, he had to somehow get out of the irons. Number three, he had to escape from the Seventh Cavalry without getting shot. Number four, he had to keep from being discovered and killed by thousands of angry Lakotah and Chyela and Arapaho who were all over this country. Number five, he had to locate Shirley before he could rescue her.

Chris looked out the back of the wagon and tried to analyze his situation. He was in a covered wagon with some containers in the front near the box, and piles of Army blankets between him and these. His hands were in iron shackles, and a chain ran out a hole in the side of the wagon floor, around the axle, then back into the wagon. It was padlocked.

His eyes scoured the floor of the wagon bed. Colt's mind dashed from one thought to another. He decided to close his eyes and sleep, letting his mind work on the problem in his subconscious. Within a minute he was asleep, his back against the side of the wagon.

His eyes popped open, and he strained them to see in the darkness. Someone had placed a blanket across his legs, and as his thoughts drifted back he remembered someone doing that during the night. Chris couldn't see the sky, but by the shadows and the chill he assumed it was probably the middle of the night. His ears strained for a sound he could distinguish from the usual ones, for he knew that was what had awakened him.

A hand appeared from under the wagon and placed a bone-handled Lakotah knife on the edge of the wagon bed. Chris looked outside and saw a sentry looking out into the darkness with his back to the wagon. Colt looked at the knife and recognized it. It belonged to Mitch Bouyer.

Chris whispered, *"Merci."*

A tap came on the floor of the wagon. Mitch had probably heard about Shirley's kidnapping, and then figured out the rest. Like Colt, Bouyer was one of those who can read a story from just a few signs.

Having retrieved the knife with his foot, Chris Colt sat still and listened. He could hear telltale sounds under the wagon, and figured that Mitch was working on unlocking the big padlock that held the two ends of the chain together. Pretty soon he heard a noise, and he looked down. Both sides of the chain were slowly being fed through the hole up into the wagon, a link at a time. Chris helped by grabbing the chains and carefully pulling while Bouyer pushed from below.

Once both ends were up, Chris saw Mitch's index finger pop up through the hole. It disappeared, then popped up again, and this happened four more times. Chris knew he was asking for five minutes to get out of the area. Mitch Bouyer was taking a terrible risk, just out of loyalty to a new friend. Mitch could never discuss this with anyone, or even let on that he condoned it. Custer would have him shot.

Colt waited ten minutes, thanking God that his hands were shackled in front of him rather than behind his back. Carefully slipping the chains through his shackles, he quietly leaned over to the pile of blankets and grabbed several. He formed several of them into a figure of himself, seated and leaning against the side of the wagon in sleep. He took one blanket with him and silently slid on his belly to the end of the wagon. He looked out and saw another sentry ten yards out to the right side of the wagon, leaning against a sapling and holding his Henry repeater by the end of its barrel. Chris realized that he was asleep.

He looked out the other side and spotted another sentry, sitting on a log, with his head bobbing forward every few seconds. The one behind the wagon was carefully scouring the darkness in front of him.

Chris went out the back of the wagon head-first, then curled back underneath it. So far his cuffed hands weren't hampering his movement too much. He slithered on his belly and crawled forward under the bed, to emerge underneath the box. He saw some men sleeping, without a tent, around the embers of a fire. He crawled right through their midst, figuring that would be the last place anyone would look. He finally got far enough away that he could come up into a crouch. He spotted the line of tents and picked out Custer's, assuming that that was where they had put his weapons.

It took half an hour, but Colt finally stalked to within one tent of Custer's. There was one lone sentry in the front of the tent, and he too was nodding off on his feet. Chris made it to the rear of the tent and removed his boots. Using Mitch's knife, he slowly, carefully slit the side of the tent and crawled inside. Custer was snoring, and he never even stirred as Chris checked around the tent. Chris did find his weapons, to his great relief.

Colt strapped on his gun belt, then found the extra ammo that he had carried in his pocket.

He crawled out the back of the tent and pulled his boots back on. From there, Colt made his way, crawling and crouching, to the remuda of horses. There were numerous sentries guarding the picketed mounts, and Colt had to cover himself with the blanket he had kept from the wagon. He crawled into the horse herd, looking for his horse. Colt crawled under and between the legs of numerous mounts, but after half an hour managed to locate War Bonnet. The paint stood out like a sore thumb amongst the brown, black, and gray horses.

He had located his horse, but Chris still had to find the bridles. He crawled through the remuda until he had found the saddles and tack. He was fortunate indeed, as he found not only his bridle but his saddle as well. His bedroll was still attached, as were his saddlebags. Chris covered the saddle with the blanket and made the long crawl back to his horse.

He slipped on the bridle and saddle and then, hiding behind War Bonnet's neck, carefully led the paint to the edge of the herd. Chris tied the horse to the picket rope and took off on his belly toward the closest sentry. Every time the man walked back and forth his back was exposed to Chris for a count of sixteen to eighteen. When even his back was turned Colt kept crawling forward, at other moments freezing on the dark ground, the green blanket thrown over his body and head.

Finally Colt got close enough, and the guard again turned his back. Chris came off the ground like a cougar and threw the blanket over the man's head and upper body. His right fist pounded into the sentry's temple, and he dropped as if he had been poleaxed. Colt took the trooper's cartridge belt for his Henry and left the unconscious man lying there, covered with the blanket. He had wanted to escape without hurting anyone, but he knew this young man would simply wake up with a headache in a few minutes or so.

He crouched down and ran to War Bonnet at the picket line. Chris untied the reins and lifted the line up with his rifle barrel, leading the horse underneath. Colt led him away and into the shadows. Now he had to figure out how to sneak away from the command. Chris chuckled to himself as he mounted up on the magnificent paint and rode back toward the line of command tents.

Once there, he rode right down the row of tents, his Henry carbine in his right hand, the butt resting on his right thigh. When Colt had reached the spot where all the scouts were camped, he looked at the clumps of sleeping bodies around the campfire. He finally spotted what he was looking for: a high-back, high-cantle Mexican-influenced saddle. It was Mitch Bouyer's. Chris stopped his horse and pulled Mitch's knife from his boot. He took careful aim and threw it. It turned over several times and stuck into the ground about two feet from the interpreter's head. Mitch reached out and grabbed the knife and pulled it under his blanket, now a seemingly lifeless form. Chris grinned and waved, and saw one hand peek up from the bedroll and wave back.

Colt rode toward the main sentry gate and

spotted two troopers coming out to greet him as he approached. They halted him.

Chris said in a low voice, "Hi, boys, the old man has sent me out on a volunteer scouting mission. We got word that Sitting Bull's camp isn't but two miles from here."

"Two miles!" one said. "Dammit to hell in a Conestoga wagon, but I thought you were put under arrest."

Chris laughed and said, "Why in the hell do you think I got volunteered for a suicide mission like this?"

The two men looked at each other, then Chris, then started laughing.

They stepped aside and the first speaker said, "Good luck, Colt. I'm sure glad I'm not you."

Chris nodded and tipped his hat at both of them, then walked away into the darkness—and the hottest Indian country he'd ever even been near.

Once away from the Seventh Cavalry, Chris quit worrying about the possibility of getting caught. As Custer had said, not even one person could be spared for anything, let alone a whole patrol to look for a civilian who had escaped. He could care less what Custer would do to him if he was caught or turned himself in. All that mattered was that the woman he loved had been kidnapped, and was either lying murdered or being held prisoner somewhere. Chris had to find her. Afterwards, he had to find Will Sawyer and kill the giant.

Chris rode south and tried to decide where he should start looking. It was close to daybreak, and he had to decide *something*. Colt thought about the Indian Ring and the Sawyer brothers.

What if Will Sawyer had kidnapped Shirley and tried to trade her off to the Lakotah or Chyela, just to get revenge against Chris Colt? He had to locate the giant Indian encampment. That, Chris thought, will be the easy part.

He pushed his horse for the Little Big Horn Valley. He knew they had to be there. Colt thought about what an insane mission he was on, but it didn't matter. He was beyond scared this time, so in love was he with Shirley Ebert. That was all that mattered to Chris. He forced himself to remember what day it was. It was early morning on June 25, 1876.

He rode, alternating between a canter and a fast trot. Just after daybreak, Colt found the scalped and mutilated bodies of Dirty Bear, Otis, and Rip. He also found the tracks and sign of Shirley, Will Sawyer, and the Lakotah warriors. If Chris had seen the new steel-dust Crazy Horse was riding, he would have memorized the horse's hoofprint, but he hadn't. He followed Will's tracks just far enough to satisfy himself that he was heading back east at a fast pace. Chris also saw that Shirley had been led off behind a horse with a line tied to her. He saw where she had fallen, and he could even tell that a rope had been placed around her neck.

Colt could not believe the incredible beauty and majesty of the sight of the giant encampment. He saw tribal circle after tribal circle for miles, with early-morning cooking fires sending hundreds upon hundreds of little columns of smoke skyward throughout the whole valley.

Chris Colt climbed down from the saddle and tightened the cinch. He stood in front of the big paint and pulled on each foreleg, to stretch the hide and not have any of it pinched under the tightened girth strap. Next, he checked his bedroll.

The Cheyenne warrior came out of the ground, and Colt hardly had time to react. The last thing he wanted to do now was create even more hard feelings, but he had to defend himself. Colt drew his pistol and smashed it across the face of the charging warrior, buckling the man's knees under him and sending him up in the air and onto the ground flat on his back.

The next one came from behind a small mesquite clump and attacked, bow raised, ready to shoot. Instead of firing, Chris did a somersault toward him, the arrow passing inches over his tumbling body. His foot came up, as he rolled over and kicked the brave in the kneecap. The man bent over in extreme pain and Chris's other foot came straight up and caught him flush under the chin.

Two more attacked at the same time, and Colt grabbed his rifle from the boot and swung the barrel into the midsection of the brave on his left, then butt-stroked the second one in the face. The first was still bent over, with the wind knocked out of him, when Chris bashed him in the shinbone with the barrel. He then took the brave's weapons and tossed them down the hill.

Holding guns on the wounded warriors, Chris quickly disarmed all of them. He used rawhide thongs to tie each man, running a stick between each man's elbows and behind his back. The wrists were tied to the sticks in front and then were tied across the front of the body. Chris used his razor-sharp knife and cut lengths out of his lasso. He tied each length around the neck of one warrior. He then tied the rest of the lasso to all of them and mounted his horse.

It almost looked like he was being led down the hill by a team of warriors, as he headed the braves toward the encampment with ropes around their necks, all tied to his one single rope. He held his rifle across the saddle with his other hand, knowing that the Indian-trained horse would follow these men as he directed them to walk.

Soon warriors, children, old men and women were staring in wide-eyed wonder at this insane *wasicun*, bringing four Chyela prisoners right into the camp.

Chris told the Chyela, in their tongue, to take him to the lodge of Crazy Horse. By the time they reached the Oglala tribal circles they had already ridden through the Hunkpapa, the Blackfoot, the Minniconjou, and the Sans Arc circles. The Oglala circle was the next one to the north, followed only by the Brule and the Cheyenne. After having traveled through so many circles, Chris Colt was amazed that nobody had pulled or shot him off his horse. On the other hand, the horse he rode was easily recognized as Crazy Horse's prize possession, and the word had probably already gone around about the gift Crazy Horse had given to a *wasicun*. More than one rifle was pointed at Colt, though, and numerous little boys ran up and tapped his leg, trying to count coups on this big white-eyes. Chris waited for one of those eager young lads to put an arrow through him, hoping to collect his first scalp.

Christopher Columbus Colt was about the

very last thing on the mind of George Armstrong Custer. He had been getting word from all the scouts about how many hostiles were in the area, and yet was not cautious or even concerned. He was excited. This might be the day he would achieve fame. He had been given very specific orders to wait to enter the valley of the Little Big Horn until Gibbon had the opportunity to reach the other end and bottle up the Sioux. Custer had no intention whatever of carrying out such an order. He believed that Gibbon would beat him to the punch, kill or capture Sitting Bull, and get all the credit. Long Hair, although his hair now didn't fit that description, had to have this major military victory against the Sioux to clinch his bid for the presidency of the United States. He just *had* to have it.

Terry's expectation was that Custer would not follow the Indian trail west from the Rosebud, but continue in the direction he had been going in before turning to the Little Bighorn. So Terry ordered Custer to constantly watch to his left, so that the Indians might not slip off to the south.

After staging a very colorful and impressive review for Terry and Gibbon, George Custer led the Seventh Cavalry up the Rosebud at noon on June 22. Custer picked up extra Crow scouts for Colt, which Chris really hadn't wanted, and extra supplies for battle. Pack mules carried extra ammunition, as well as rations and forage for fifteen days. In sharp contrast to the smart appearance of the cavalry, the wagon and pack train was being led by inexperienced, green civilian contractors. General Crook labeled it "disreputable," in fact.

The military commanders were probably most

upset with the fact that Custer had refused to take Brisbin's four troops of the Second Cavalry, or the Gatling gun platoon, both of which had been offered to him. Custer had declined Terry's offer of the Gatlings because they would have hampered his mobility. Custer declined General Terry's offer of additional troops, saying, "They will not enable me to defeat any enemy that the Seventh Cavalry could not handle alone."

Late on June 24, the Seventh Cavalry reached the point where the Indian trail diverged to the west. General Terry's plan called for continuing up the Rosebud. Instead, Son of the Morning Star turned west on the trail, to the divide between the Rosebud and Little Bighorn.

His mind idled over his lingering sobriquet. It wasn't really fair to refer to him as Long Hair any longer. Libbie had had a horrible nightmare before he'd left Fort Lincoln in May. She had seen a war-painted Sioux brave in the dream, and he was yelling while holding up the bloody scalp of Custer's long blond curls. Because the dream was so real to Libbie, Custer had had his locks shorn before leaving on the campaign. He carried them in his tunic pocket.

On June 24, Custer made his men execute a night march of ten miles, in addition to the day's thirty-mile forced march. This brought his regiment, exhausted, unmotivated, and scattered out, to within ten miles of the summit of the divide.

At that same moment, Chris Colt rode on War Bonnet, with four beat-up Cheyenne dog soldiers walking in front of the big paint, ropes around their necks. They were in the circle of Oglala buffalo-hide lodges, and many warriors now surrounded him.

In the distance, Chris saw Crazy Horse emerging from a lodge. The Lakotah hero took several steps forward, but suddenly hands grabbed Chris and jerked him roughly from his saddle. His gun and knife were pulled from his holster, and numerous people started to pummel him. This all happened so quickly, and it was so violent, that Colt hardly had time to react, but it also now made him furious.

One trick that Chris Colt knew, and employed quite often in fights, was to make an opponent angry, because a "mad man fights like a fool." Unfortunately, because of the suddenness and viciousness of the attack on him, he himself now fought like a fool. Colt came off the ground kicking and punching everyone and everything in sight, which even included a camp dog that got in the way of one of his kicks. Unfortunately for the Lakotah attacking Chris, they hadn't grown up learning much in the way of boxing skills, only grappling and wrestling techniques. This, however, was a situation where Chris Colt's fists were doing damage to anyone who came within range of them, and numerous young braves ended up on their backs with black eyes, split lips, and bloody noses. Two braves jumped up with blood-curdling war cries, knives in their hands, ready to spill his intestines onto the bank of the Little Big Horn.

Colt didn't care. He was beyond caring right now, and just wanted more combat. He wanted his boots to kick more legs and groins, wanted his fists to make more contact with more cheekbones and jaws. Let them bring knives.

He screamed in Sioux at the two warriors, "Come on, cowards! Come on and fight me! Let's make the journey together! I'll shove those knives up your asses!"

The two warriors started to lunge and Colt dropped to the ground, kicking one in the knee-cap just as a gun was fired into the air. Everyone stopped but Colt. Bleeding from the nose and lips and the corner of his left eye, he jumped up and hit the first knife man with a right cross, then went in swinging on the one he had kicked with his left, sending both men flying into the crowd unconscious. Except for Colt, that was the only movement by anyone. They all just stared in wonder at this Lakotah-like *wasicun*.

Colt screamed, "Come on! You wanted me! Come here and get me!"

He grabbed another brave and hit him with an uppercut to the gut, and a second rifle shot boomed. Now Colt stopped, sides heaving, teeth bared in a long, low snarl. Like a cornered timber wolf, his head went from side to side with almost a savage leer on his face.

Crazy Horse walked through the parting crowd. He carried a Winchester carbine in his right hand. Seeing Chris and looking around, he broke into a grin. He nodded approvingly at Colt. Then Chris looked around at all the wounded braves on the ground and was completely amazed at himself. Four braves were knocked out cold, unmoving. Five more lay on the ground, moaning and nursing various wounds. One more was on his hands and knees vomiting, while holding his midsection. Crazy Horse pointed at the braves lying around and pointed at Colt, saying something in his tongue to the gathered onlookers, but

Chris couldn't pick out the words. He did get the gist of it, however, as the Oglalas laughed heartily along with Crazy Horse. Chris Colt joined in with them.

The two warriors faced each other and grabbed forearms in a firm handshake. There was a mutual respect and understanding in the way they looked into each other's eyes.

Just then a young warrior came riding into the Oglala camp circle, yelling in the native tongue of the Lakotah, "The pony soldiers are coming up the valley! They are coming towards the camp! It is a good day to die!"

Some of the scouts had gone out from Custer's column with a small patrol of soldiers. Later the soldiers discovered that one of them had dropped a box containing hardtack somewhere on what the Lakotah called the Lodgepole Trail, where the numerous travois made ruts in the ground from dragging lodgepoles and the other camp supplies into the broad, sweeping valley.

The patrol, discovering that they had dropped the box, quickly went back toward the spot where they had given up their scouting and turned around.

At the same time a ten-year-old Hunkpapa boy named Deeds, and his slightly older brother, Brown Back, were sent to the same area to fetch their grandfather's ponies, who had wandered up the divide. Both boys were nephews of the famous chief Sitting Bull. On the way to the horses they ran into an Oglala youth, also after his family's ponies which had wandered. His name was Drags-The-Rope, and he trailed Brown Back, who was slightly behind his little brother.

Deeds had gotten far enough ahead of the two other youths that he decided to sit down and wait for them, while he investigated the little wooden box he had found on the trail. The lad opened the box and started to eat the hardtack within.

At that time, the patrol rounded the bend and spotted the boy. Brown Back went wild trying to signal his brother, but Deeds' back was turned to the soldiers. He heard their footsteps and turned around just in time to be caught full in the chest by a soldier's rifle bullet. The shot killed him instantly.

The soldiers started to charge toward Brown Back, who ducked behind a bush in horror, staring at his dead brother's body. They had just held a funeral service for their grandmother the night before, and Sitting Bull said her death was the sign of a great event happening, probably the fulfillment of his Ghost Dance vision of many enemy soldiers falling into the camp.

Drags-The-Rope ran up from behind and grabbed Brown Back. He pulled him into the thick brush.

He yelled, "Come on, brother, we must warn the camp! You cannot help your brother. He has made the journey! Follow me!"

With Drags-The-Rope leading the way, the two boys made it through the thick brush, down a foliage-choked ravine that headed back toward the giant encampment. They were the first to give the alarm.

When Crazy Horse heard the alarm from the crier, as he rode through the village circle, his smile disappeared. He looked at Colt and he lifted his carbine, aiming it at Chris's midsection. Colt stared at the Oglala warrior.

Speaking in the Oglala language, Crazy Horse said, "You have a wolf in your heart and fire in your veins! The *wasicun* soldiers now come to burn our homes and kill us and our wives and children. They want to drive us onto reservations, as if we were camp dogs under their whips. You say you are loyal to them, but though their blood runs in your veins, our blood runs in your heart. If I do not hold you now, you and I will have to face each other in battle, my brother. You will try to save the pony soldiers, but I want to defeat them. They must learn that we are not camp dogs. We are warriors."

Crazy Horse nodded, and several braves seized Chris by his arms and legs. His hands were tied tightly behind his back with rawhide thongs. Colt stuck out his chin defiantly, and Crazy Horse thought he saw in Colt the same spirit he had seen in Colt's woman.

Chris knew that it would be fruitless even to attempt argument. His primary goal was to find Shirley, so he had to find out about her first. Then he would do what he had to do to escape, free her, and go back to fight alongside Custer, the man he hated and could never respect as he respected Crazy Horse.

"Crazy Horse," Chris said, "I must ask you."

Crazy Horse nodded at the men holding Chris, and they pulled him back.

Crazy Horse said, "We will talk later, Wamble Uncha."

Chris said, "Wait! We must talk!"

Crazy Horse was already gone, his mind on more important matters. Besides, he knew that

Colt would ask to join his fellow warriors to make the great fight against the Lakotah and their allies, but Crazy Horse would keep Colt from being slaughtered. He also knew that his *wasicun* brother would ask about the fate of the beautiful woman with the hair that came from the sun. That was not as important a matter as going into battle against your enemy, and her fate could be discussed later over a pipe.

Crazy Horse prepared for battle astride his horse, which he sprinkled liberally with fine dust. As was his custom, he also sprinkled some on himself. The warrior painted the red lightning zigzag down his face. Winchester in hand, he took his dark gray horse east, out of the camp. A group of warriors preceded him, and even more followed him.

The alarm was going up in all the camp circles, and Colt could hear the sounds of confusion and excitement, but above all of enthusiasm. These Lakotah and their Chyela and Arapaho cousins were ready to fight the long-knives. They were fed up,. and were not running anywhere except directly at the U.S. Cavalry.

At dawn, after Colt's escape, and led by Curly and Goes Ahead, some of the Crow scouts had found a major vantage point. From a mountaintop to the west called "the Crow's Nest," the scouts were able to make out the Sioux village about fifteen miles in the distance. From the Crow's Nest, Lonesome Charley Reynolds, a civilian scout, and the other scouts looked at the giant encampment through field glasses and wrote down a message to Custer that the camp definitely had been found, and was occupied. He

gave the message to one of the young Arikara
scouts with him, and told him to run his horse
back to the column and give the "talking paper"
to the General. Even the scouts called Custer
"General."

When Custer was given the news by the young
Arikara Red Star, he was with his Arikara and
Crow scouts, the scout Girard, and his brother
Captain Tom Custer. When he read the message,
he mounted his big red thoroughbred, Vic, and
led the group out with the other scouts.

Custer spoke to Bloody Knife and Bob-Tailed
Bull. "If we beat the Sioux, I will become the
President of the United States—the Grandfather. If you Arikaras do as I tell you and kill
enough Sioux for me and capture many ponies,
I will take care of you all when I come into
power."

When Custer had reached the Crow's Nest, he
sent Tom back to the main column to bring them
forward, while the Boy General got off of Vic
and walked up the foot path to the peak of the
promontory to see the camp for himself. When
he arrived, he looked out at the line of bluffs
that Lonesome Charley pointed to, but Custer
claimed that nothing was there. Reynolds handed
him the field glasses and asked him to look again,
and keep an eye out for columns of smoke and
dust clouds. Custer finally spotted what could
have been dust clouds and what could have been
some tendrils of smoke.

He told everyone there that they would attack
the village after dark, because the Sioux didn't
know he was there. Several of the scouts got into
an argument with him, saying that they could
not possibly be this close to the Sioux without

them knowing that the soldiers were there. Custer got very angry, arguing with several people and reminding them who was in command.

After a while Tom Custer returned, left his horse down below, and climbed the footpath to the Crow's Nest.

"Tom," Long Hair demanded, "what are you doing here?"

"General," his moody brother replied, "one of our packers packed a box of hardtack too loose, and it shook off a mule. Captain Yates discovered it, so he sent Sergeant Curtis and two men from F Troop back to find it. A Sioux boy was sitting on the box when they got there, so they shot him. Then they saw two other boys take off through the brush and get away. We sent Herendeen back up there to check it out."

Custer said, "I cannot believe they even have scouts behind us, following us."

Hairy Moccasin was up on the lookout rock and signaled for Mitch Bouyer to come quick. He made a slashing gesture across his throat, meaning that he had spotted the cutthroat Lakotahs. Seeing this sign, Lonesome Charley Reynolds opened up the medicine bag he always carried and gave away all his personal belongings to the scouts around him, who were his friends.

Mitch Bouyer turned around and looked at Custer and the scouts. "Lakotah," he whispered.

Custer asked Girard, "What is Reynolds doing?"

The color drained from the scout's face and he said, "He's givin' all his belongings to his friends, 'cause he figures he ain't gonna be alive by the end of the day, General. Ya know, General, last week, when we found where the Dako-

tahs, the Sioux, had their sundance ceremony?
Them boys found three red rocks with tobacco
offerin's near them. They also found a ground
painting, with a bunch of pony hoof marks and
a bunch of horse shoe prints. That represents
the Sioux and the cavalry. There was a bunch
of figures of dead men, laying with their heads
towards the Sioux and feet towards the horseshoe signs. That means the Sioux expect a great
victory, and will kill us all. The scouts all believe that the Dakotahs have strong medicine,
real strong."

"What do *you* believe?" Custer asked, a concerned look on his face.

"I believe yer gonna get killed today, General,
along with some or all of us, if you don't respect
the strength of the Dakotah—you know, the
Sioux."

Custer stared at Girard a minute, then laughed
nervously, saying, "Nonsense! They'll run from
us and hide. They always do."

He ran up the little path to the promontory
where Mitch was. The scout-turned-interpreter
pointed to a cloud dust in the distance.

He said, "General, eet ees only about five or
six braves. Send a unit now, and get zem quick
before zey warn zee village!"

Custer glared at Bouyer and said, "You stick
to the scouting and I'll handle the command of
my unit."

Absolutely convinced now that the Sioux had
discovered him, and spurred by visions of Indians running out the north end of the valley before Gibbon could block them, Custer made his
fateful decision to move at once to the attack.

The Son of the Morning Star returned to the

column and led the men at a fast pace toward the location they felt might be the encampment. Topping the summit at noon, Custer sent three troops, one hundred and twenty-five men, under senior Captain Frederick W. Benteen, on a scout, or reconnaissance-in-force, to the south. As the exact position of the village was not known, this movement reflected Custer's continuing apprehension that the Indians might get away to the south.

Custer assigned another three troops to Major Reno, and retained five under his personal command, then left one in the rear to escort the pack train. Reno's command and Custer's command followed the Indian trail down the creek valley toward the Little Bighorn.

Ahead of them, a column of dust rose from behind a line of bluffs that hid the Little Bighorn River from Custer's view. The dust cloud was being made by a party of about forty Sioux warriors, the rear guard of a small camp moving to join the parent village. These forty braves were finally spotted by lead elements of Custer's and Reno's columns. To Custer's way of thinking, the dust clouds and the retreating warriors signified escaping Sioux, making "another cowardly escape and refusal to meet with and engage the Seventh Cavalry forces."

Custer ordered Reno to overtake the forty retreating hostiles and attack them full-out. Custer promised to back Reno up with his own force in case he got into trouble. What Custer didn't know, however, was that the giant encampment was just over the next rise, just across the Little Bighorn River.

*   *   *

The night before, while Christopher Columbus Colt was being arrested and shackled, Sitting Bull was on his way to the hills across from the Hunkpapa circle, which was well over one half-mile across, the largest of the camp circles. He took a medicine pipe with him and smoked it, performing the *hanblake oloan*, the ceremony and Lakotah prayer asking the Great Mystery for "advance knowledge."

Again Sitting Bull saw the vision he had seen in his sundance ceremony vision; the sight of many enemy Indians and earless white soldiers falling into the Lakotah camp, bloody and dead. Just a week earlier, Crazy Horse had led some Oglalas against Gray Fox (General Crook) in a big fight on the Rosebud River, and he had soundly defeated the general and his troops. Sitting Bull thought about it and knew that this was not, however, the giant victory he had envisioned.

Even so, when Crazy Horse defeated Crook on the Rosebud, a magnificent event took place, which the Chyela would recall for years to come. A tall Cheyenne chief, Comes-In-Sight, noted for his courage and fighting ability, charged into the fray to count coups on a group of Crow scouts and Crook. His horse was shot out from under him, and neither Crazy Horse's Oglalas nor their Cheyenne brothers could rush out to save him, such was the volume of gunfire being rained upon him. Then the Crow scouts decided to charge the lone Chyela, ride him down and count coups on him. He faced them and taunted them as they charged, while the helpless Sioux and Cheyenne watched from a hillside.

His sister, Buffalo Calf Road Woman was not

prepared to let her brother die that easily. She jumped on a pony and charged out toward the advancing warriors. She rode right through their midst, swooping down on her brother under a hail of deadly gunfire and arrows. He swung up behind her on the war pony and they darted out of there under the Crow fire and to the cheers of the Lakotah and Chyela warriors, including Crazy Horse, who witnessed this event and could not believe the courage of the woman. The fight on the Rosebud against the Gray Fox was called, from that day forward, *"Kse e sewo istaniwe ititane,"* meaning "Where the Young Girl Saved Her Brother's Life."

The next morning, when the grandmother of Deeds died, Sitting Bull knew that a great event was about to take place. Although a few scouts and Crazy Horse knew that Custer was approaching them, the scouts had not seen the expected long curly blond locks of Long Hair when they spotted the pony soldiers.

Sitting Bull knew that Crook was over twenty miles away, so he assumed that the approaching soldiers were being led by some other commander, but he and most of the other leaders had no idea that it was the well-known and hated Long Hair.

Custer had changed into his leather fringed jacket with polished brass buttons, and he had had an orderly give Vic a rubdown. Beneath the fancy jacket, he wore a bright red sash he normally reserved for parades.

Custer didn't know about the previous day's dispatch sent to Fort Lincoln from the man on the little gray mule next to him. The man, a middle-aged Bismarck newspaperman, by the name of Kellogg, was chronicling Custer's exploits at Custer's own request. The Indian scouts called this rumpled man, who carried only a black leather satchel, Man-Who-Makes-The-Paper-Talk.

Many of them were singing their death songs that day, and part of the reason for this was that Girard had read the dispatch and shared it with the Crows and Arikaras.

The dispatch Kellogg sent back read: "We leave the Rosebud tomorrow, and by the time this reaches you we will have met and fought the red devils, with what results remains to be seen. I go with Custer and will be at the death."

When Benteen was sent off to the south, he had no scouts sent with him. He had been told by Custer that his primary purpose was to block any "red niggers" from escaping out the other end of the valley of the Little Big Horn. That, of course, was Gibbons' job, according to General Terry's plan of attack.

White-Man-Runs-Him, a Crow scout, was chosen by Custer to lead the main column to the giant encampment. Ironically, earlier in the day, Custer had dressed the same man down, belittling him in front of all the other scouts.

Reno's command started to pursue the group of stragglers that Custer had sent him after. These warriors, who were rear guard for the newest village, turned out to be Bad Face Sioux. Reno followed them to the west along Ash Creek, which runs into the Little Big Horn. (The Little Big Horn itself runs from north-northwest to south-southeast.)

* * *

When the scouts had reported to Custer at the Crow's Nest that the Seventh was surrounded by Sioux, they did so because of pony tracks discovered behind the main body. In truth, the tracks were not made by scouts checking out Custer's force. The night before, Little Wolf, an old-man chief of the Northern Cheyenne, had been on his way with his small tribe to join forces with Sitting Bull. He had seven lodges with thirty-some people, and only fifteen of them were fighting men. When he discovered Custer's force marching through the night, he hid his people and let the column of soldiers pass. Then he followed them, figuring that they outnumbered his men by a gigantic proportion but that maybe Little Wolf could help at some point, as a blocking or diversionary force, if Custer dared to attack the great camp. When scouts found tracks from Little Wolf's band, they thought that Sioux were all around them, scouting the force.

Reno kept on after the group that had been spotted. Then, after fording the Little Bighorn and advancing two miles down the valley, he charged the southeast end of the village, where the Hunkpapa tribal circle provided flank security. What Reno was totally unprepared for, however, was the resistance that they met when they attacked the giant encampment. When all the Sioux swarmed to confront him, he stopped the charge short of its objective, dismounted his battalion, and spread them out in a thin skirmish line. Within minutes he was outflanked on his left and receiving a withering volume of fire from the front, so he withdrew to the shelter of a cottonwood grove on his right. Tangled brush in the timber inhibited command and control; soon his force was scattered. On top of that, Lakotah warriors wanting to count coups and earn battle honors invaded the trees and brush and infiltrated the position.

Seeing that his command was about to be wiped out, Reno mounted his men and led them in a dash for better positions on the bluffs across the river. Mounted Lakotah braves mingled right into the ranks of the fleeing troopers and took an even heavier toll on Reno's troops, especially at the river crossing, before the remnants of the command gained the top of the steep bluffs on the right bank of the river. Reno's advance, battle, and retreat began at around three in the afternoon and lasted about forty-five minutes.

He lost, in killed, wounded, and missing, almost half his command, including four officers and the scout Lonesome Charley Reynolds.

Reno had expected Custer's support from the rear, as Long Hair had promised. Instead, Custer veered to the north and rode parallel to the Little Big Horn River, behind the bluffs and toward the northeastern end of the village. At one point, Custer and his headquarters group rode to the top of the bluffs and for the first time saw the immense encampment. Custer dismounted and stared. Each major tribal circle was a half-mile across, with some circles, like the Hunkpapas', containing over three thousand people. The vast pony herd was incredible, too. There were thousands of horses, and stealing them, Custer hoped, would break the backs of the Sioux and Cheyenne.

Custer called a number of his Crow and Arikara scouts up and pointed out the giant pony herd, telling them that they had to go down and steal all the ponies for him.

Ironically, when Reno's command was routed, one of the men killed in the timber with Reno was named First Lieutenant Donald McIntosh, and he was the commanding officer of G Company of the Reno Battalion. The thing that was so unusual about McIntosh was his American name, adopted when he had moved to the United States from Canada, where he was born and raised. McIntosh didn't have the look of the Scottish or the Irish. He was a full-blooded Mohawk Indian, and he had started to question what he was doing there only just before his death.

One of the interpreters that Chris Colt had met before and liked was Isaiah Dorman. He had lived with the Lakotah for a year or so, and spoke their tongue, so he had gotten a job with the Seventh Cavalry as an interpreter. Isaiah was black, and the Sioux called him "the black white man." In the timber, Dorman had been shot through the chest and was dying from the gaping wound.

An old Hunkpapa woman came out to the battlefield to start collecting battle trophies, and discovered him lying in the woods.

She pointed an old muzzle-loading rifle at his head, and was about to pull the trigger when he spoke in her tongue, saying, "Don't shoot me, Auntie! I'll be dead soon enough anyway!"

She said, "You're a sneaking cur! Why did you bring the soldiers here?"

Dorman said, "I only wanted to see this western country once more before I died."

Several Hunkpapa warriors rode up to strip his body and count coups. Dorman asked them not to, to let him die in peace.

Sitting Bull himself then rode up and recognized Dorman from his times with the Sioux.

Sitting Bull said, "Don't kill that man! He is *On Azinpi*. He used to be a friend of our people."

"Sitting Bull," Dorman said weakly. "It is good to see you, old friend. Can I have water?"

Sitting Bull dismounted from his pony, and pulled from his parfleche his own polished buffalo horn drinking cup, and got Dorman water from the stream. Isaiah Dorman drank from Sitting Bull's drinking horn while the chief of all the Lakotah held him up.

Dorman looked around at the beautiful country and up into Sitting Bull's eyes, saying, "Sitting Bull, this is a good day to die."

Sitting Bull smiled. "This is a good day to die."

Isaiah Dorman died. Sitting Bull mounted up on his black horse and headed back, telling the camp police to round up villagers and return them to their lodges.

The chief knew, however, that this had to be a diversionary attack, and the main attack would still be coming. He told everyone to be on the alert for more attacks.

Chris Colt struggled hard against his bonds. Still tied, he had been in a tepee since Crazy Horse had had him captured. He could hear much firing down the valley, and knew that Custer must be attacking the camp. The fighting lasted for forty-five minutes, and near the end of it he heard warriors and criers riding into the

Oglala circle, describing the battle and the victory. Colt could tell that it hadn't been Custer, so it must have been Reno's or Benteen's battalion. Finally he heard about the death of "the black white man," and he knew it was Isaiah Dorman, who had been assigned to Major Reno as an interpreter.

Chris felt guilty. He should be out there. He should be trying his best to stop Custer from attacking, for no doubt the fool's attack would follow shortly. He kept straining against the rawhide, and the thongs seemed to be loosening just a little. He must get out and get to Custer.

Sitting Bull ran into his nephew One Bull, covered with blood, and told him to get his wounds treated. One Bull replied proudly that he was wearing the blood of others and had no wounds at all. Relieved, Sitting Bull ordered him to go back and protect the encampment. One Bull set off for the area around Medicine Tail Coulee.

Custer had come back out onto the ridge line, and watched Reno's attack until the battalion had to pull back in the timber. Custer got down off his horse and knelt down in front of the column and prayed. He then made some hero speeches to his scouts and troopers. Next he got his scouts and led the column along the ridge line. He kept looking across the valley at the encampment, but it was mostly obscured by cottonwoods and little ridges.

Finally Custer got to a point where he could make out rows of tepees beyond the tops of the cottonwoods. Beyond those, he saw part of one of the village circles and a couple of hundred lodges. There was no movement, as most of the Indians were either out on the battlefield or in their lodges.

One Bull, riding along with Sitting Bull, spotted Custer and his column up on the high ridge line across the river.

One Bull spoke. "More soldiers, Sitting Bull. Come, let us go fight them, too."

"No, nephew," Sitting Bull said. "Stay here and help protect the village. Everyone wants to ride out to fight, but some men must stay and protect our homes and families. There may be more soldiers today who will come and attack our women and children."

On the ridge line, Custer grinned and slapped his thigh, while looking at the seemingly deserted village.

"We've got them!" the Boy General cried. "We've caught them napping!"

Turning and waving his hat at the rest of the troops, he yelled, "Custer's luck, boys! We've got them! We'll finish them off, then go home to our station! Come on!"

It was three o'clock then, and the troopers all gave a cheer.

Many of the warriors who had routed Reno's column saw Custer's excited soldiers and moved in that direction to attack.

Son of the Morning Star looked below, where Reno was just advancing to the attack. Sweeping his hat in encouragement, Custer rejoined his command. He led his troops down into Medicine Tail Coulee, which ran down to the river.

Custer summoned his bugler, John Martin, saying, "Orderly, I want you to take a message to Captain Benteen. Ride as fast as you can and tell him to hurry. Tell him it's a giant village and I want him to be quick, and to bring the ammunition packs with him. Wait, I'll write it down."

Custer wrote it down and said, "Ride as fast as you can by the same trail we came. If it's safe, return and join us, but if not, stay with Benteen."

As the bugler John Martin rode away, he turned and waved at the troopers, and many of them waved back. He was the last white man known to have seen George Armstrong Custer alive, but that was because nobody knew about Chris Colt.

Chapter 6

>>>>>>>>>>>>>>>>>>

A Blaze of Glory

Custer went down from the big ride he was on and entered Medicine Tail Coulee. He would attack the giant village by crossing the Little Big Horn at a ford where the ravine ran into the pebble-bottomed river. At that spot the waterway was about forty yards wide, but only knee-deep on the horses. Custer had witnessed several warriors crossing the river there, so he figured it would be a strategically sound place to attack, while Reno was hitting the other end of the village.

Just then, the point spotted five Sioux who had been hiding in Medicine Tail Coulee. The warriors rode in several circles, yelling and waving blankets in the air, then fled at a dead run down the coulee toward the river.

Mitch Bouyer turned to Curley, the youngest Crow scout, and handed him his field glasses.

Mitch said, "Curley, you are the youngest. You should live. Go to those bluffs yonder and watch. Those five Sioux are tricking Custer into chasing them. There will be thousands of Sioux waiting to kill us. You watch a while, and if the Sioux are besting us, you ride as fast as you can and tell No-Hip-Bone [General Terry] that we have all been killed. Now go!"

Mitch Bouyer and some of the Crow scouts rode up to Custer's side, and the lieutenant colonel turned to them and said, "You have all done your job well. You are not to fight in this battle. Go back and save your lives."

Mitch Bouyer related this to the Crows, and they started to ride back toward the pack train, but stopped when Mitch remained where he was. Hairy Moccasin and Goes Ahead told Mitch he must go with them and join his Crow wife, Magpie Outside, back at the fort. They were cut off by a voice from across the river, in the trees.

"The Lakotah call someone?" Goes Ahead, in sign language.

Bouyer tapped himself and listened as the voice said, "*Wica-nonpa!* Two Bodies! Go back, or you die!"

Bouyer said, "The Sioux have not forgotten me. They tell me to go back, but I cannot."

He waved at the scouts, wheeled his horse, and took off down the coulee to rejoin Custer at his side.

Over seven hundred warriors had charged off to fight against Reno, and they were not yet back. Only four men capable of fighting remained in the camp of the Cheyenne: Bobtail Horse, Roan Bear, White Cow Bull (the only Oglala), and Calf. Bobtail Horse looked across the river and saw the blue-clad soldiers charging at full gallop down Medicine Tail Coulee across the river, headed for the all-but-deserted Chyela (Cheyenne) camp.

For the umpteenth time that day, Bobtail

Horse shouted the alarm, *"Nutskaveho!"*, which meant, "White soldiers are coming!"

White Shield, another Chyela, had been fishing upstream, and he saw his four fellow villagers and the soldiers at the same time. Dropping his fish, he rode out of the river and disappeared into the trees with his bow and quiver-full of arrows. The other four rode in and out among the trees, firing and yelling, trying to make the noise of a thousand warriors.

So four Cheyenne warriors and one Oglala Sioux held off the two hundred and fifteen troopers of Custer's command at the ford. Custer just halted on the side of the river and waited, possibly expecting an ambush by the thousands of braves who were hidden in the trees.

Finally, Custer turned and gave the command for the column to go ahead. He led out, with Vic prancing and dancing in the knee-deep river at the ford. The Crows, who had left when Custer told them to, stopped on a bluff to watch. They saw hundreds of mounted Lakotah and Chyela charging toward Custer through the cottonwoods along the river. A soldier near Custer toppled backward out of the saddle, but Mitch Bouyer and Custer both kept firing at the four village defenders, Custer with an octagonal-barreled Remington sporting rifle and twin English self-cocking Bulldog pistols.

At the same time as Custer started the charge across the river, Chris Colt ran through the Cheyenne village toward the ford. He saw Custer across the river and he waved his arms frantically, both wrists bleeding badly from the tight rawhide bonds he'd worked loose. Custer seemed to see Chris Colt waving his arms, but just then

White Cow Bull's rifle belched smoke, as did two other guns from the four defenders. The lead man crossing the Little Big Horn River, the one with the fringed buckskin jacket and the red sash around his waist, the one on the spirited, prancing, big red horse, that man flew backward out of the saddle, a big bloody spot on the middle of his chest.

Suddenly the charge stopped, and Mitch Bouyer and several soldiers jumped down into the water and grabbed Custer to keep him from going under. He wasn't dead, but close to it. The soldiers got him up on a horse and turned around and retreated while White Cow Bull, Bobtail Horse, Roan Bear, Calf, and White Shield jumped up and down in celebration.

Crazy Horse, followed by several young warriors, charged across the river, whooping and hollering. This puzzled the camp defenders, but the great man didn't even look at them as he streaked past. They turned and saw Crazy Horse running straight at the *wasicun* who had been a prisoner in the Oglala camp.

When Crazy Horse was upon Chris Colt, the two men gave out loud yells as Crazy Horse dived headfirst from his horse's back and crashed into Chris Colt, both men rolling over and over. They both jumped up in fighting stances, shaking their heads from the collision. Chris's left eye had started to swell, as had Crazy Horse's, where they had slammed their faces into each other during the Oglala war hero's dive. Crazy Horse nodded to men behind Colt, and a group of warriors ran up behind him and seized his wrists and legs, knocking him to the ground. He was tied, once again, with rawhide thongs, and several guards were ordered to stand there and watch him with guns.

Colt and Crazy Horse stared at each other for a minute, a pleading look on Chris's face. Crazy Horse, followed by hundreds of Sioux and Cheyenne alike, took off after Custer's column. Up to this point, because Libbie had made her "Auntie" cut his hair short, the Indians still did not know that the man they were fighting was Long Hair Custer himself.

The warriors kept arriving in droves from the Reno fight and charging after the fleeing cavalry. The troopers led their horses as they dismounted and, on foot, tried to make their way up a grassy knoll above Medicine Tail Coulee. They wanted to form a defensive perimeter and make a stand there. But it was like being attacked by a swarm of angry bees: the more they ran and the more they tried to fight back, the more Sioux and Cheyenne came on the scene to attack them.

One of the bravest warriors in the fight was actually a Ute Indian named Yellow Nose. He had been captured by the northern Cheyenne down in Colorado when he was four years old and had grown up Cheyenne. He was the first brave to ride in and capture one of the cavalry company guidons. He even touched one of the cavalry soldiers with it as he rode away, counting coup on the man while a great cry went up among the assembled warriors.

Custer was not a factor at all, and sometime during the battle, near death, he turned one of his English Bulldog pistols to his right temple and pulled the trigger. Tom Custer's company took charge of Long Hair's body, slinging it across the colonel's own saddle.

Captain Myles Keogh took command of the rest of the Custer command and led the men up the north edge of the ridge line, fighting inch by inch for more ground and hoping to form a defensive perimeter on the higher ground.

By this time Curley was already gone on his horse, heading after No-Hip-Bone to tell him of Custer's death.

Chris Colt could only watch the distant battle, as helpless as he'd ever been. A tear formed in Colt's eye as he watched the entire Custer command being demolished.

Crow King led Hunkpapas and Blackfeet up Medicine Tail Coulee to surround the troops from the east. Gall, leading more Hunkpapas, as well as Minniconjous and Sans Arcs, rode up out of the coulee and kept attacking the rear of the soldiers. Comes-In-Sight and Brave Wolf led a large group of northern Cheyenne along the left flank of the retreating soldiers.

The bullets and arrows flew at an astounding rate, and numerous warriors started to charge in and out of the troopers' ranks, winning battle honors. The battle was so one-sided that many Indians were able to return to the village to get fresh horses and more arrows and bullets.

Near the end of this part of the command, an entire group of troopers' horses got away from the dying soldiers and bolted up the hill at one time. Some of the Indians thought that the troopers were trying to run away, so they charged and brought down even more soldiers.

Suddenly a whole group of foot soldiers, in sheer hysteria, charged down the hill toward the river at the Lakotah assembled there. The troopers screamed and fired blindly, but all were cut down by withering Sioux fire.

At last, several leading warriors yelled, *"Hoka-hey! Hokahey!"*

This was the signal for the assembled warriors to charge, and charge they did, eagle-bone whistles screaming over the gunfire. The horde of Sioux swept over the few remaining troopers, and they all went down in a hail of gunfire.

Custer, along with most of his command, was dead. Barely believing their good fortune, braves went from soldier to soldier to collect scalps and battle honors. The severely wounded were quickly dispatched with head shots, then scalped. The L, I, F, and C companies were not in the group that went down. Keogh had kept most of the command in some sort of formation as they advanced up a hogback, but now one thousand more Brules and Oglalas were coming up from the river, where they had served as a blocking force. Chris saw Crazy Horse lead the thousand from the river, up a ravine, to emerge at the end of the hogback where the soldiers stood.

Two Moon led another large force of Cheyennes up over the other uphill side and struck the fleeing troopers there, so that now the balance of Custer's command was surrounded on all sides, unable to get away or to fight through in any direction. Most of the Indians now dismounted and started to pick off soldiers with carefully aimed shots. Some of them sneaked in closer and closer to the soldiers, using every bush and gully they could for cover. Some still charged in, counting coups and getting battle honors, but most hung back and picked the rest of Custer's command apart bit by bit.

One of the things that happened in the midst of the battle was similar to what had happened in the Rosebud fight. A very pretty young Oglala woman named Walking Blanket Woman had lost her brother in the Rosebud fight and decided to avenge his death. She dressed herself in full battle regalia and war paint, just like a brave, and charged into the midst of the battle carrying her brother's battle staff. The whole time Walking Blanket Woman fought, she sang in the Oglala language, "Brothers, now your friend has come! Brave up! Brave up! Would you see me taken captive?"

Rain-In-The-Face saw and heard her song and yelled to everyone within earshot, "Behold! A brave young woman rides among us! Let no warrior hide behind her!"

Some of the braves who won battle honors that day were talked about for a long time to come. Not the least was Sitting Bull's eldest nephew, White Bull. He rode up to many cavalry troopers and struck them with a club, then yanked them from their horses. He was considered by all the Sioux and Cheyenne to be the bravest warrior in the entire battle, even besting Crazy Horse.

On one of White Bull's courageous charges at the remaining troopers, a bullet toppled his pony. The brave ran forward and got into a hand-to-hand fight with the trooper he had been charging. The trooper grabbed White Bull's rifle, but the brave struck him across the face with his quirt and made him let go. Finally the soldier grabbed White Bull by the hair, yanked him forward, and bit the warrior's nose, trying to bite it off. White Bull screamed for help and two warriors came to help, but finally White Bull broke free and butt-stroked the soldier in the face with his rifle.

Chris Colt saw this particular incident, and saw White Bull charging all over the battlefield that day, Crazy Horse as well. As a warrior he admired them both, but as a white man he was literally sick to his stomach.

White Bull and a Cheyenne were side-by-side in a ravine by the hill, shooting at the ten soldiers there, and the troopers finally got up and charged White Bull's position. White Bull shot one of the two leaders of the charge, who was already severely wounded, and the Cheyenne shot the other. The other eight kept charging, which forced White Bull and the Cheyenne up over the edge of the ravine. But up above, White Bull stumbled and fell down. He had been hit by a ricocheting bullet, which numbed his leg and made it swell but never broke the skin.

Chris was still being subdued by several warriors who kept him tied to a sapling and guarded him, as well.

The attack went on, with soldiers trying to mount up and break away. So terrorized were the troopers that, near the end of the battle, some of the soldiers started to shoot at each other. Finally there were only four left in that group, and they all mounted up and made a mad dash for freedom. Three were overtaken easily and killed, but the fourth, Lieutenant Harrington of C Company, had a fast-moving horse. He outran the pursuing Cheyenne and made his way to and along the river.

They chased him for a distance and finally caught up with him. Instead of killing him, however, they rode up alongside and lashed his horse's rump with their quirts and bows. Several times they fired at him but missed. Finally Harrington pulled out his gun. Instead of shooting at them, he stuck the barrel beneath his chin and pulled the trigger.

The last survivors of Custer's command were from C and F company, and they tried to make their stand on the hillside. There they were to be cut down by long-range fire, their bodies falling onto those of their own dead buddies as they died off one by one.

The very last one to go down was Sergeant Butler of L Company. He had been severely wounded earlier in the fight, but now stood up to face the thousands of warriors and fire in every direction, apparently wanting to die fighting. A number of warriors, genuinely respectful of this brave pony soldier, rushed forward, eager to count coups on an enemy so worthy. He repelled every attack with well-placed shots, and many warriors gathered around to watch, marveling at his courage. Several warriors mounted up, and had just started to make a charge when the sergeant was struck down by a long-range shot into his chest.

In the great battle's aftermath, old men and young boys who'd only watched the fight rode down and killed off the soldiers who were critically wounded but still alive. Women came out from the encampment to strip and mutilate bodies, while warriors and young boys took scalps.

As the final troopers died, Captain Myles

Keogh seemed to rise from the dead. Braves were going from soldier to soldier shooting the troopers in the foreheads with their own pistols. As they approached the body of Captain Keogh, he suddenly sat up and leaned on one elbow. He was dazed and disoriented.

Now, pistol in hand, the captain looked around wildly from Indian to Indian. A Lakotah warrior finally ran forward, yanked the pistol from the commander's hand, and shot Keogh in the forehead with it. A number of Cheyennes then ran forward and stabbed and clubbed the captain's body over and over again. According to all the Indians who were there, he was the very last man of Custer's command seen alive.

In the big camp, Chris Colt wept openly.

Rain-In-The-Face found the body of Captain Tom Custer and, true to his vow to someday cut out the Medal of Honor winner's heart and eat it, he knelt down and cut the man's heart out of his chest. While others watched, Rain-In-The-Face mounted up and rode down to the camp, presumably to eat the heart.

Many of the warriors now remembered Reno's command, which was still fortifying its position on a bluff further down the river. They left for that location. Others, battle-weary, returned to the camp, while still others remained on the battlefield, collecting "trophies." Custer's body was not touched or mutilated, for he had committed suicide and thereby dishonored himself.

The only comment Sitting Bull later would make about the devastating defeat his forces exacted on the Seventh Cavalry was, "They compelled us to fight them." Now he went out to meet with his people and count the friendly casualties. Altogether, with the Custer and Reno fights, only thirty-two warriors had been killed. The families of the thirty-two slain warriors met together to mourn, and Sitting Bull joined them.

He spoke solemnly. "My heart is sad for our fallen warriors—and for those white soldiers who fell before us. This night we shall mourn alike for our own dead and for those brave white men lying up there."

During and after Custer's fall, the Lakotah and Chyela kept a small force to hold the Reno battalion under fire at the bluff where they had entrenched themselves. Benteen's battalion finally made it to Reno's location and reinforced him, although all of Benteen's men were exhausted from riding through badlands all day. They had not seen one Sioux or Cheyenne.

Benteen took over the spiritual leadership of Reno's demoralized unit as well as his own, after several of the officers, including Reno, got into a big argument about following Custer's trail and reinforcing him. Reno was furious. Custer had been supposed to follow him and back him up, but he hadn't done so.

It was at that time that the Custer attack started and the soldiers heard all the gunfire.

Captain Weir, commander of D Company in Benteen's battalion, said, "Custer!"

Then his executive officer, Lieutenant Edgerly, said, "We ought to go down there!"

Weir said, "If Major Reno won't take the command, are you willing to go with D Company alone?"

Edgerly said, "I am."

Captain Weir, impressed by the lieutenant's

courage and determination, walked over to Major
Reno's command post to get permission to reinforce Custer. There, Weir and Major Reno got
into a very heated argument, and Weir finally
strode away. As Edgerly and the company
watched, he mounted his horse, summoned his
orderly, and rode off in the direction of Custer's
position. Edgerly started the company and followed the CO.

At five o'clock, Captain McDougall arrived at
Reno's position with the pack train. Reno now
had over twenty-four thousand additional rounds
in his ammunition packs, so he sent off after
Benteen's Company D to reinforce them. Benteen led the battalions while Reno brought up
the rear, transporting the considerable wounded.

When they had been out less than half an
hour from Reno's Hill, they were joined by the
three Crow scouts whom Custer had sent off
from Medicine Tail—Coulee, Goes Ahead,
White-Man-Runs-Him, and Hairy Moccasin.
Benteen ordered them to stay with his
command.

Before six o'clock, Benteen caught up with
Captain Weir and D Company. Benteen and the
men stopped along the river on the high bluffs,
where they were engaged by hundreds of warriors who had fought on Battle Ridge. Benteen
was willing to fight, but Reno called for an immediate retreat. The entire column slowly
fought its way back to Reno's Hill. The ridge
where they had stopped became known after
that as Weir's Peak.

White Bull, unable to walk because of his
wounded ankle, and a friend, Bad Soup, rode

back to Battle Ridge, so that White Bull could find the leggings and saddle he had stripped from himself and his horse, in mid-battle, for speed and freedom of movement. He found them, and had Bad Soup help him resaddle while he put on his leggings. As he looked at the naked, mutilated corpses, he found one with powder burns at his temple. He remembered that wounded man with a hole in the left side of his chest who had shot at him twice during the battle. The man had a leather jacket with brass buttons and long fringe, so White Bull took it for himself. After all, the man might not have committed suicide. Perhaps he had been shot in the temple by a warrior dispatching all the soldiers at the end of the battle.

White Bull reached into the pocket of the jacket and pulled out several locks of long blond hair. He showed them to Bad Soup. They stared at the corpse, realizing now that this was Long Hair Custer.

Not long after, Monahseetah, a Cheyenne woman, accompanied by her aunt Mahwissa and her little son Yellow Bird, went to Battle Ridge. They went up to one mutilated corpse and saw a brave hacking off the man's finger. The man had not been scalped, because his hair was cut so short.

Monahseetah screamed, *"Ohohyaa!"*

It meant "Creeping Panther," and was the nickname given this man years ago, by her brother Black Kettle. He had been given the name in a council meeting between the Chyela and the *wasicun* soldiers. She remembered, too, when this same soldier-chief had killed her brother Black Kettle and many of the Southern

Cheyenne on the Washita River so many years before. She also remembered when this soldier chief had taken her in his bed and planted his seed in her. That seed had become little Yellow Bird, her son, who stood next to her right now.

Monahseetah bent over the corpse with an awl in her hand and poked the awl into each of his ears.

She said, "So that Long Hair, the Creeping Panther, will hear better in the Spirit Land. He must not have heard our chiefs when they warned him that if he broke his peace-promise with them the everywhere Spirit would surely cause him to be killed."

Before the sunset, the Sioux and Cheyenne conducted hasty burials of their fallen dead and prepared to move the giant camp. Many people came to see the magnificent red horse with white stockings that belonged to a Santee Lakotah named Walks-Under-The-Ground. It had been tied by the reins to the wrist of General Custer. The horse was prancing and full of spirit, and a sight for all the people to behold.

Chris Colt had endured seeing all this, and the entire command of Custer's battalion being wiped out. He heard the stories as men came into the Oglala camp, to which he had been returned after the Custer fight. Finally, Crazy Horse rode in and confronted Chris Colt. Chris looked to his right and saw a group of warriors walking around the camp carrying nine guidons and in the front, Custer's own flag. He fought to hold back the tears.

"Many of your people fought and died as true warriors," Crazy Horse said.

He reached out with his bone-handled knife

and cut through Chris's bonds. Colt rubbed his wrists, trying to renew the circulation.

Crazy Horse laughed. "I have cut your bonds, Colt, but there are still soldiers up on those bluffs, and you will not try to go to them or you will be shot. Sitting Bull said to let them go where the Father Sun shows when he wakes up. They are still afraid, and so they hide in holes up there, but they can go home if they do not come here. Will you give your word you will not try to go to them?"

Chris said, "Will you give your word you will not try to kill them?"

"If they do not try to attack us."

Colt knew that this had to be Reno, Benteen, and the rest of the unit. Chris pictured Reno in command. He chuckled to himself, then said, "They will not attack. I give my word."

Crazy Horse summoned Colt's paint and the two rode out of the village together. Deeply sad, Chris rode next to Crazy Horse across the ford. It was getting close to sunset now, and Chris knew where they were going.

Colt said, "Did any of Long Hair's people live?"

Crazy Horse said, "No. They have died."

Chris said, "Crazy Horse, I have something important to ask you."

Crazy Horse grinned, but kept looking ahead. "We will speak of her later."

Suddenly Chris was ecstatic. "She's alive?"

The Oglala legend said, "Yes, and her arms are there and her legs are there and her head is there, too. I *think* her head is there."

Crazy Horse started to laugh at his joke, and

as solemn as the occasion was, Chris could not help but laugh too.

The two men rode up Medicine Tail Coulee and started to see bodies in the bottoms. Chris had to mask his emotions from the noble warrior at his side as they went up onto Battle Ridge. Colt looked all around and saw heads and arms and legs. He found the scalped naked bodies of Custer's command lying all over the hill, and inside he wept. What a waste, he thought, and all for the vanity of one man who wanted to be President.

Crazy Horse bragged to Colt about his own exploits, and pointed out where he had fought different people and made different charges. He told a number of things about the battle. Chris was not put off by Crazy Horse's boasting, as that was the way of the Plains tribesmen. After battle, men were expected to brag about their bravado, but they were not allowed to embellish or to lie about their deeds.

They walked their horses around the battlefield and Chris spotted Custer's body. He got down off his horse and inspected the wounds. Colt looked around the battlefield and then dropped to one knee to pray for the souls of all the fallen warriors, red and white, not letting Crazy Horse see the tears that welled up in his eyes.

After that Chris swung up onto the paint's back, and they started back.

Crazy Horse said, "I have seen this before. This is how your people speak to Wakan Tanka, the Great Mystery."

"Your people do the same thing," Chris said.

They rode back toward the camp, and Chris

could see that the village was being packed up
and people were preparing to move.

"You are smart to move," Colt finally said.
"The Grandfather in Washington will send
many *wasicun* against your people now. Long
Hair was a hero among my people. The talking
paper made him so."

"He was not a coward," said Crazy Horse.

Chris paused. "No, he was not, but he was not
a real hero either. He wanted to earn eagle feathers without the knowledge that goes with them."

Crazy Horse smiled, then the smile disappeared and he went on, "When they come after
my people now, they will not think they are coming after camp dogs."

Chris thought of the carnage behind him and
said, "No, they will sure not do that ever again."

It was dark when they crossed the ford and
entered the village. Chris kept hearing occasional shots down the river, and gave Crazy
Horse questioning looks.

Crazy Horse said, "Your people do not fight
the same way we do. They dig holes in the
ground and hide. We have men by the bluffs who
shoot them from far away to keep them from
coming toward us. We want them to go back
where they came from."

When they reached the Oglala camp circle,
Crazy Horse turned. "Come with me, my
brother," he said quietly.

They rode to the burial and mourning ceremony going on at the Hunkpapa circle. Crazy
Horse explained that he wanted to meet with the
loved ones of his fallen comrades. Many of the
Indians present eyed Chris with a suspicious

eye, but most knew who he was and the story of his friendship with Crazy Horse.

While at the ceremony, a great cry went up among the people, "The white men are coming! The white men are coming!"

"You told me they would not attack!" cried Crazy Horse.

"And you just told me that your people were sniping at them," said Colt, equally surprised, "so they wouldn't come this way but go back to Fort Lincoln."

Women and children started to scream and many braves ran toward their lodges to get weapons, as a horde of blue-uniformed soldiers swept down on the south end of the village. Suddenly, a great wave of laughter went up from those nearest to the soldiers. Crazy Horse and Chris were both surprised until they, too, saw that the "soldiers" were in fact teenaged Lakotah warriors, wearing uniforms taken from the dead bodies of the soldiers.

Everyone who had been standing around the giant bonfires now laughed, but it was nervous laughter. Chris could tell that, despite the great victory, there was a knowledge throughout the encampment that the days of the Sioux and Cheyenne as a free people would soon be ended.

Chris and Crazy Horse rode up to three old men seated around a fire smoking a pipe. They dismounted and sat down with the other men, who offered Chris the pipe. He presented it to the four winds, then smoked and passed it to Crazy Horse.

The man who stood out as the leader said, "You are Wamble Uncha."

Chris said, "And you are Sitting Bull, mighty

Sachem of the Hunkpapa. Surely, Wakan Tanka has smiled on you and your people today, although my heart is sad for my people and those you lost."

Sitting Bull said, "It is so. The white Grandfather will be angry. Soldiers as many as the sparks from this fire will come."

"Yes," said Colt.

Sitting Bull tapped his chest over his heart. "My little brother, Crazy Horse, told me that in here you are Lakotah."

Chris touched his heart. "My skin is *wasicun*, but my heart wears two colors, white and red."

Sitting Bull said, "Someday soon, my people will have to learn to have the same two colors in their hearts, or they will die."

"Sitting Bull is wise indeed."

Sitting Bull stood, and so the others did.

Sitting Bull walked away saying, "Soon, many white-eyes will come to see where Long Hair made the spirit journey on the banks of the Greasy Grass. It is almost time to go from this place."

Crazy Horse signed to Colt to accompany him, and they returned to the Oglala tribal sector. As they rode through the circle of Crazy Horse's village, Chris saw the tepee where he had been held prisoner. Right next to it was another lodge, with two sentries in front of it. Chris assumed it was the tepee of Crazy Horse.

The Oglala swung his leg over his horse's neck and slid off the right side, which was the way with the Indian. "Come," he said when Chris had dismounted.

Crazy Horse led him between the two tepees, and he scratched on the side of the door to let the person within know they were entering. Chris followed Crazy Horse inside and saw an Indian woman with her back to him. She was fixing food over a kettle and wore a dark elkskin dress with bone-hair pipes hanging from pieces of fringe on it. The woman had an excellent figure. Crazy Horse moved to the side and Chris saw that she had beautiful shiny auburn hair.

Chris said, "Shirley?"

The woman froze, afraid to turn. She was scared that if it was who she hoped it was, he would suddenly disappear.

Shirley Ebert turned around and looked at Chris, tears spilling down her cheeks and a big toothy smile on her face. She started to sob, even while smiling.

"Oh, Chris!" she cried, and they threw themselves into each other's arms.

They kissed each other all over each other's face and necks, then kissed for a long time and pressed themselves hard against each other's bodies, both hoping it would keep them from being separated. They paused and looked into each other's eyes. They heard a yawn, and both chuckled as they saw Crazy Horse acting out a counterfeit yawn.

He spoke in Lakotah. "Tomorrow, we move camp. I am sleepy, though. I must sleep. I will see you in the morning. You must find a place to sleep."

Chris didn't speak, just gave Crazy Horse a knowing look, and both men almost broke into grins. Shirley couldn't speak Lakotah, but she could tell what was going on between the men. She grinned too.

"Are you hurt anywhere?" Chris asked.

She poured him a bowl of stew. He suddenly realized how starved he really was. She poured herself a bowl as well.

Finally she said, "Will Sawyer raped me every night while he had me. Crazy Horse's men killed his friends. One had been a scout for you."

Chris hid the killing rage inside him. "Dirty Bear. I found the tracks, and read what happened."

Shirley said, "Yes. I told Crazy Horse that I was your woman, and he protected me. I have been a prisoner, but they have treated me with respect. Sawyer was allowed to leave with his life, because he had come to barter. Crazy Horse would not even listen to the secrets about Custer that scout wanted to trade."

Chris smiled and thought that there was something very good and strong about her. Shirley hadn't mentioned Crazy Horse leading her by a rope around her neck. She understood and respected the differences in their cultures, and she didn't want Chris to get angry with his friend.

She said, "He is very wise. Simple common-sense wisdom."

"You know I will go after Sawyer and kill him," Chris said.

"Good," Shirley said, as her eyes welled up with tears.

Colt pulled her to him. "I love you. You are safe now."

She untied the thongs on the side of her elk-hide dress and pulled it over her head. They melted into each other's arms.

The following morning, late, Crazy Horse returned. He scratched on the tepee and entered when Chris asked him in.

Speaking again in Lakotah, he said, "We must go, my brother."

"No, Crazy Horse," Chris said. "I have to take Shirley back to Fort Lincoln. I will go to the unit hiding on the bluffs and return with them."

"No, you cannot."

"Why?"

Crazy Horse looked directly at Colt. "Not enough time. We talk later over a smoke."

Chris had gained enough respect and trust in Crazy Horse to know that he must know what he was talking about.

"Crazy Horse says we have to go now," Chris told Shirley. "We have to travel with the Lakotah for a while."

Shirley smiled. "Wherever you go."

Two women showed up five minutes later and started to take the bison-hide covering off the side of the lodge. Shirley didn't wait for directions. She just started helping them strike the tepee and pack up its contents.

Chris rode with Crazy Horse to the Hunkpapa circle. All the tepees were loaded onto travois, and the entire circle was ready to travel. Chris saw that some of the tribal circles had already departed. The Hunkpapas would bring up the rear, the position of honor.

Crazy Horse and Chris dismounted and walked to Sitting Bull.

Sitting Bull looked dour. "The whites on the bluff have lost more men to our warriors today. I have told our men to let them go home. We have killed enough, and to kill more will make the white Grandfather even angrier."

He pointed upriver and said, "This morning our scouts found more soldiers up the valley.

Many do not ride horses, and come this way. We must go. Tonight we will camp for a little while with no lodges, then tomorrow when we camp we can hold our victory dance."

"I have told my brother Colt to go with us, with his woman," Crazy Horse said.

Sitting Bull said, "You speak true."

Chris waited, as he knew that the Lakotah respected patience, especially in conversation.

Sitting Bull looked at Colt and said, "You and your woman must never tell your people that you were in our camp when Long Hair made his spirit journey. Your people know that you are Lakotah in your heart. Some will think you betrayed your own people."

Chris gave Sitting Bull a funny look, and the old medicine man went on. "Nobody lives from Long Hair's warriors. If you live and have no wounds, they will ask why. You must never speak of it."

Chris nodded. "Sitting Bull and my brother Crazy Horse are very wise. So it shall be."

"You and your woman should travel with us until there is no danger of another fight," Sitting Bull said. "It is time to go."

Crazy Horse and Chris mounted up and rode away. Crazy Horse stopped at the pony herd, selected a bay mare, and put a bridle on it. He led it to Crazy Horse's lodge and then gave the reins to Shirley. She mounted up Indian-style, stopping Chris with a glance when he began to dismount to help her up.

The Oglala war hero didn't miss this, and was impressed. Their ways are different than ours, he thought to himself, but she is a good woman. He looked at her on the horse and thought what she would be like under a buffalo robe with him. He stopped, remembering that a friend does not think such things about his friend's woman.

They rode off into the wilderness in the midst of a great exodus of over fifteen thousand people. Some Cheyenne had been buried under piles of rocks in hidden draws and ravines, and the dead Lakotah had been left in their finest ceremonial dress in burial tepees. Benteen and Reno's forces were left alone to take care of themselves. Gibbon's force had bivouacked twelve miles away, and were slowly coming up the valley now. Sitting Bull had instructed the point elements to set a course for the Shining Mountains (Big Horns).

Chris and Shirley would ride with the Lakotah and remain with them until the morning after their big victory dance. Colt would then take her back to Fort Abraham Lincoln. He would also have to deal with Benteen and Reno as regards his arrest by Custer and his subsequent escape.

When all that had been cleared up, Chris Colt would still have a mission to accomplish. To him, it was the most important mission of his life. He was going giant-hunting. Colt was going to hunt down and kill the man who had kidnapped and raped the woman he loved—his most important scout ever. The chief of scouts would track down and kill Will Sawyer.

Chapter 7

>>>>>>>>>>>>>>>>

The Hunt

Chris and Shirley stayed in their appointed tepee, near the mouth of Lodge Grass Creek, during the victory celebration. Chris held her in his arms while she cried herself to sleep. Two hundred and forty-seven of Custer's, Reno's, and Benteen's men had been killed and sixty-five more wounded, on the Little Big Horn. It was difficult for Chris and Shirley to see anything beyond the sadness.

It was almost daybreak on June 27. Chris and Crazy Horse shook hands in the Plains custom of grabbing each other's forearm. They stared into each other's eyes with a knowing look that only two close friends could share.

As they shook, Shirley saw the little scar on Crazy Horse's hand where he and Chris had cut themselves, letting their blood run together as one. Shirley looked at Crazy Horse and wanted to give him a hug, but she knew that his customs were much different than hers. Besides that, she had seen the way he had looked at her a number of times, when he hadn't realized she was aware of it. It was a way that she would never mention to Chris, but she felt a hug might send the wrong signal to Chris's friend and blood-brother.

She said simply, "Thank you, Crazy Horse. Good-bye."

He smiled at her and said, "Lakotah no have words, 'thank you.' Feel in here. That is good thing."

He touched his chest.

Chris grabbed her by the waist and swung her up on the bay mare, then swung up into the saddle on War Bonnet. He and Crazy Horse gave each other a last look and then, sitting proud and erect and looking straight ahead, he and Shirley began to walk through the thousands of Lakotah and Chyela preparing the camp to be moved again. The two *wasicun* pointed their horses toward Fort Abraham Lincoln.

Before they left the village there was a shout behind them, and they wheeled around. White Bull, elder nephew of Sitting Bull and hero of the battle, galloped a black-and-white Ovaro paint pony up to them. He was wearing the fringed buckskin jacket of George Armstrong Custer. It made Chris sad all over again to see it.

White Bull pulled up in front of them with a sliding stop and said in the Oglala dialect, "Wamble Uncha, you are a warrior."

Chris smiled and said in Lakotah, "White Bull, you are indeed a warrior, too."

The two men turned their ponies around and walked away from each other proudly.

Shirley asked, "What did he say, Chris?"

Colt responded, "He was letting me know that some of our two peoples can get along together."

She looked puzzled but simply said, "Oh."

* * *

Back at Fort Abraham Lincoln, a very strange thing had happened. On June 25, 1876, the very same day Custer and his men were killed, some of the Crow scouts came into the post and spoke with the Army troopers. Elizabeth Bacon Custer and several other wives were inside one of the buildings and overheard the scouts and troopers talking as they listened at the window.

One of the Crow scouts said, "Today at Little Big Horn, Son of the Morning Star and all his men killed in big battle with Lakotah."

Hearing this, Libbie Custer screamed and ran from the building.

Nobody knew just how the Crows had known that Custer and his command had been wiped out on the very day it had happened, but a number of so-called "squaw men" at the fort and trappers said that it was simple. They said that the Crows sent messages back all the way from the Little Big Horn by smoke signal.

Chris and Shirley took their time returning to Bismarck, as Chris wanted to be very careful that Will Sawyer didn't get word of their approach. When they arrived, the word spread like wildfire. Chris became a celebrity around Bismarck and Fort Lincoln, as Shirley told a story of how she had been kidnapped and sold to the Indians, with Chris risking his life to sneak into a big Indian camp and free her from her captors.

She further covered Chris with her tale by saying that when Custer had found out about her capture Chris had wanted to go after her and rescue her, but Custer had wanted Chris to help him. She said that Custer and Colt had a horrible argument, and Custer even had Chris arrested but later relented, because he couldn't bear the thought of some defenseless woman being held by Indians.

There would be no trial, no arguments about Chris Colt and his actions. He was a hero in the eyes of soldiers and civilians alike. The more the story was told the more "savages" he had engaged in hand-to-hand combat, the more stealthy he had been in sneaking into the Indian camp. Some people even said he had fought with Crazy Horse for her, the man who had given him his beautiful mount.

When the news spread around about the Battle of the Little Big Horn it began to be called "the Custer Massacre," and some were calling it "Custer's Last Stand." Reno was blamed for not reinforcing Custer. When the officers who found the men of the command saw that Custer's body had not been mutilated like the others—a sure sign he had committed suicide—they hushed it up. Finally a formal board of inquiry cleared Reno, and Custer became a bigger and bigger hero.

Colt just bided his time and waited for some kind of word as to the whereabouts of Will Sawyer. A man who stood over seven feet tall would be very hard for people to miss, even in a crowd.

Colt received a dispatch in the fall of 1876, a few months after his return to Fort Lincoln. By this time, news of his single-handed rescue of Shirley Ebert had spread all over the country, especially at the frontier forts. He read the dispatch and set the paper down on his bunk to stare out the window. On an impulse, he went to the stable and saddled up War Bonnet, still adorned with red coup stripes, red handprints, and eagle feathers. He mounted the big horse and headed out away from the fort and away from people. He had some thinking to do.

That evening, Colt walked into the Frontier Café and ate dinner with Shirley. He seemed distant, and she knew something was wrong.

He waited until the dinner traffic had cleared out and said, "Can we talk privately?"

She immediately got up and put the closed sign on the door.

Shirley got them both pieces of apple pie and cups of coffee and sat down.

Chris said, "You know that I love you, Shirley. More than I can ever express."

She smiled, and tears welled up in her eyes.

He went on, "I got a dispatch today. General Howard, they call him 'Bible-reading Howard,' anticipates problems with Chief Joseph and the Pierced-Noses, the Nez Percé. He wants me to come out and be his chief of scouts. He feels that he is going to have to force the Nez Percé to move to a reservation."

Shirley said, "Where is this?"

Chris said, "West of the Snake River in Oregon, Wallowa Valley. Can you leave the restaurant?"

She now had tears dripping down her cheeks.

"I knew this day would come, Chris," said Shirley. "No, I can't, any more than I can try to make you change, Chris. You are a man of the wild. You are one of the heroes that this wild country needs to tame it. The cavalry needs you, and the Indians need you to do what you can to protect them both from each other. I will always be here for you, for I can never love anyone the way I love you, but you are like an eagle. I cannot keep you or hold you here, because you would die like a caged eagle. Chris Colt, I need you and love you, but this country is much bigger than I, and it needs you even more. Leave in the morning for Oregon and come back to me when you can. When you come back and leave again, I will cry again, but I will still wait for you."

Chris said, "Shirley Ebert, you are the most incredible woman I have ever known. I will always love you, and I will be back."

Shirley said, "Only one promise?"

"What?"

She said, "You can *love* other women, but promise you will never *fall in love* with another woman."

Chris smiled and said, "That would be impossible, to fall in love with another. Not the way I love you."

Shirley cried herself to sleep that night. She awakened with a start. The sun was out, and the birds were singing outside her window. The floral smell had awakened her. Her restaurant and adjoining house had been locked, but her room was filled with vases, glasses, and pitchers filled with autumn flowers. Twigs with leaves from various trees adorned the vases, with ferns and evergreen boughs.

On the pillow next to her there was a note and a feather. It was the tail feather of a bald eagle. She held the feather in her hand and read the note. It read:

My Darling Shirl,
This was given me by my brother Crazy Horse. Keep it, and think of me when you see it. I know

I have important work to do, but I will always come back to you. I am yours forever.

I love you,
Your most humble servant,
Christopher Columbus Colt

When Chris left Bismarck before daybreak, he laughed to, and at, himself. The stories about him had started to circulate even before his arrival at Fort Lincoln, just a half-year earlier, but now they had assumed legendary proportions. Americans wanted heroes, so Colonel Custer was lionized everywhere, even though all who had really known him had regarded him as a complete jerk. Chris was another who had become a hero in the saloon conversations, and although he didn't know it, he was also being made a legend in the lodges of his red brothers. He laughed to himself, because the big, tough, western frontier hero was now riding his horse down the road running west out of Bismarck, tears spilling down his cheeks for the woman he was leaving behind. Colt wondered what the hero-makers would say if they were to see him now.

Days later, as Colt stopped in Virginia City at the end of the Bozeman Trail, he got word. He had gone into a saloon to wash away days of dust and get the latest news, as saloons on the frontier were almost as good for this as newspapers were back east, maybe better. Some miners were in a conversation about a giant of a mountain man called Buffalo Reeves. Colt bought the miners a drink and invited them to sit at a table with him.

They sat down and he said, "This Buffalo Reeves you're talking about. How big is he?"

One of the miners said, "Oh, hell, at least

seven, mebbe seven and a half foot, and big; you know, *big*, like a buffaler."

Colt said, "Where does he trap?"

The other said, "Yellowstone country."

Chris was out the door before the miners could finish their drinks.

It was three days later when the giant, buffalo-coated Will Sawyer, alias Buffalo Reeves, heard a noise and turned. He sat on a log drinking a steaming hot cup of coffee, after having just finished checking his morning trap line.

The setting was quite eerie, as he had made his cooking fire right next to a giant pool of bubbling hot mud and clay. In the background, steam poured from several geysers and rose from the pool of boiling mud. There was so much steam and smoke in the area, on this early fall morning, that it almost obscured the view.

Sawyer's long, scraggly beard and long hair almost hid his face from view. His eyes strained to see what was making the noise he kept hearing, but he couldn't spot anything. What the hell, he thought, ain't nobody or nothin' around that can take me with gun or fist. Suddenly, he thought of Chris Colt and got a sick feeling in the pit of his stomach. He often thought about Colt, because the man had beaten him with his fists. He hated Colt, and he always wondered if he would show up someday. But now that Sawyer was a full-time trapper, he figured he could shoot Colt from ambush if the scout ever did come, and nobody would ever know.

"Sawyer." The voice was almost a whisper.

Colt's voice startled Will so badly he jumped, spilled his coffee, lost his balance, and fell backwards off his log. Getting up, he wiped coffee off his buffalo coat and looked at the man he hated so.

A geyser spouting steam behind him, Chris Colt sat perfectly still on his magnificent paint horse. Colt's half-grin and his calmness shocked Sawyer even more. Just the sight of the ruggedly handsome scout scared him. Dressed half-Indian, half-white, mounted on the paint with the eagle feathers in the mane and tail, three red stripes around each upper foreleg and red handprints on each hip, Colt was the epitome of confidence—all that was savage and rough about the West.

Well, the moment had come. Will Sawyer could finally put his fear and humiliation behind him. Colt might have gotten lucky against him in a fight, but nobody could outgun him. Sawyer took off his buffalo coat and tossed it aside. He got in a gunfighter's crouch and his lips curled back in a snarl.

In a deep, booming voice, he laughed nervously and said, "Ya mighta got lucky and whipped me in that fight, Colt, but I'm gonna shoot so meny holes in ya the miners can use ya fer a sluice box."

He laughed heartily at his own joke and went on, "I shore liked stickin' it to yer ole lady, Colt. She was *nice*. Oh, by the way, even iffin ya git lucky, my pardner Red Williams is aimin' a Sharps at yer back right now. He's in them rocks yonder."

They both heard a horse walking up toward Colt, and a figure on horseback suddenly started to show through the steam. He walked right up to Colt.

Will Sawyer just stared and said, "Crazy Horse."

The tall Oglala warrior looked at Colt and tossed a Sharps Buffalo gun toward Sawyer. He reached down next to his breechcloth, pulled out a bloody, red-haired scalp, and held it up for Sawyer to see. Crazy Horse turned his horse and slowly walked back into the clouds of steam, out of sight.

"Don't matter, Colt!" Sawyer yelled. "I don't need no help killin' ya! None, ya heah?"

Will Sawyer's hand streaked down for his right-hand gun, and Chris Colt's came up in one smooth motion. The gun bucked in his hand and Sawyer's gun flashed at the same time. Sawyer's bullet, however, hit the dirt harmlessly, like a miniature cannon shell exploding. Colt flipped his leg over the neck of his horse and dropped down to the ground. He walked forward, ejecting the empty shell from his six-shooter while giving Sawyer another grin. Will Sawyer tried desperately to raise his gun up, but he kept staring down at the growing stain of red that was in the middle of his chest. He had gotten his gun almost all the way up when he saw Colt taking careful aim at him.

I think I can take him, he thought. I can take him.

Then Colt fired, and Will Sawyer felt a boulder smash into his chest, then another, and another. He was falling backward. He didn't want to do that. He threw his hands back to protect himself. They hit boiling mud. It burned. He was under the surface. It was burning like fire. Sawyer wondered if he was in Hell, then he didn't wonder anymore.

Colt said, "If you're going to shoot a man, shoot; don't talk."

Crazy Horse rode up next to Chris while Colt walked forward, reloading, and looked at the giant bubbling pool of boiling mud. Bubbles came up where Sawyer had fallen in. Colt walked over to Will's buffalo coat and picked it up. He handed it, and Red's Sharps, to Crazy Horse.

Colt said, "It will be a cold winter, my brother."

Crazy Horse looked at the bubbling pool of mud and said, "Not for the one you called Sawyer."

Both men looked at the boiling liquid and started to laugh.

Colt said, "How long have you followed me?"

"Long enough," Crazy Horse answered.

In Bismarck, North Dakota, a beautiful young lady with "hair truly from Father Sun" looked out the window of the Frontier Café. It was autumn, but the sun was bright and the day was going to be warm and happy. It was an Indian summer. She knew that somewhere her love was doing important work, one day closer to returning home to her.

The following is from Volume Two in the
Chief of Scouts trilogy—*Horse Soldiers*,
forthcoming from Signet books in
December 1993.

Coming down out of the Grand Teton Range
near the Yellowstone, Colt followed the many
tracks of unshod horses. It turned out to be a
stolen herd of Appaloosas—part of the famous
herd of mountain horses owned by Chief
Joseph's band of Nez Percé.

Tracking the herd and its five rustlers, he also
discovered that the rustlers were being pursued
by two young Nez Percé brothers. When Chris
caught up with all of them, the rustlers were
killing the youngest of the two boys.

Colt had a gunfight with the men, killing two
and saving the life of the other boy—a brave little twelve-year-old.

The boy told Colt that the herd had indeed
been stolen from Chief Joseph while he and his
brother had been guarding the horses. Feeling
responsible for the loss of the valuable mountain
horses, the elder Indian boy had trailed the rustlers, and his ten-year-old brother had followed
him.

Chris Colt was on his way to become Chief of
Scouts for General O. O. Howard in a campaign
against Chief Joseph. He decides to take the sur-

viving three outlaws to the nearest town to face justice, then deliver the herd and the boy safely to Chief Joseph before reporting to the "one-armed general."

"What is your name, boy?" Colt asked.

The boy said, "I am called in your language Ezekiel." He then added, "In my language my name means Boy Who Bites The Badger."

Chris said, "You speak English good. Learn from missionaries?"

"Yes. Catholic," Ezekiel replied.

"Okay, Ezekiel," Chris went on, "how about grabbing their ropes off their saddles and we'll fix these gents up."

The surviving men were not in a mood to argue, or to even chance blinking their eyes. Colt had made believers of the men.

"What is your nation?" Colt asked, already knowing the answer.

Ezekiel replied, "I am Nez Percé with the band of Hin-Ma-Too-Yah-Lat-Kekht."

A rustler asked, "Who the hell is that?"

Chris laughed. He didn't speak the tongue of the Pierced Noses, but he knew the name.

He replied, "Thunder-Traveling-to-Loftier-Mountain-Heights."

The man said, "What the hay?"

Colt laughed and said, "White people know him as Chief Joseph."

Chris looked down at Ezekiel, who had gathered the ropes, and said, "I am on my way to where your band lives."

Ezekiel said, "You go to work for the blue-coat father who has one arm."

Colt grinned and said, "How do you know I'm going to work for General Howard?"

Ezekiel laughed, "You said your name is Colt. All know the name of the great scout Colt. Joseph said you are like the strawberry that has been covered with snow."

Colt, surprised that Joseph had heard of him, asked, "Why did he say that?"

"He said that because you are white on the outside but red on the inside."

Chris laughed and climbed down from his horse. It stood still after Colt dropped the reins on the ground. Chris Colt had trained his horse, War Bonnet, to the ground rein shortly after he got him from Crazy Horse. He simply buried a log under ground and had a piece of rope with a snap coming up from the log. He would ride the horse up to that spot and get off, dropping the reins on the ground. Then he would quickly hook the rope to the chin strap at the bottom of the horse's bridle. When the horse tried to tug at the line, he was unable to budge. It didn't take War Bonnet long to learn to avoid the bite from the headstall in the skin of his poll. He would stand perfectly still until his master came to him, gathered up his reins, and mounted.

Within ten minutes, Colt had tied each of the men backward in his own horse's saddle. Bound around the arms with numerous loops, each man had his feet tied into the stirrups with the rope run under the horse's chest.

The Mexican protested, "I will bleed to death, Señor! Please?"

Colt laughed and said, "No, I believe you're going to die of hemp fever. You quit bleeding several minutes ago."

The white one said, "Hemp fever! You're gonna lynch us?"

Colt said, "No, but I'm sure the law will."

The black rustler said, "For what? Killin' Injuns?"

"No, I didn't even ask Ezekiel here," Colt said. "But you stole this herd of Appaloosas from the Nez Percé. If you want, I'll take you to Chief Joseph instead of the nearest law."

The white one said, "I'll take my chances with the law, Mister Colt."

"Fine," Chris said. "I'm sure they'll be happy with you characters doing what you can to start a war with the Nez Percé."

The black one said, "What if your horse bolts while we're tied like this, or our horse falls?"

"Then you might die. Should have thought of that before riding the owl-hoot trail, mister. Honest men might not make much money, but they usually don't have to worry about being tied backward on their horse, either."

Ezekiel spoke. "My brother, Little Red Crow, and I guard the herd. These men take. We follow. I must take ponies back."

Chris gave the youngster an appraising glance. "You followed these crooks all these hundreds of miles. Did the camp know you followed them?"

"Yes," Ezekiel said, "I told them that it was my job to do. My brother followed."

"We will make camp in this place. There is water, shelter, firewood, and graze," Chris said. "Then we will make your brother ready for his Spirit Journey."

Ezekiel choked back a sob and replied, "It is a good thing."

Colt then untied the three men and let them

bury their partners. He also let the black one bandage the ear of the Mexican. Chris went through their saddlebags, taking what ammunition he needed and what food he wanted. The three men were tied in sitting positions to trees and a campfire was built. Colt wrapped the men with their blankets.

The white one said, "Mister Colt, are we to sleep this way?"

"Yep."

The black one asked, "Are we gonna git fed?"

"Nope."

The Mexican started to say something, but when Chris turned his head to listen, the man shut up quickly, thinking about his aching, partially amputated ear.

Colt fixed a dinner of beans, coffee, bacon, and biscuits. Afterward, he allowed the boy and himself a cigarette. He didn't smoke much, preferring cigars when he did, but occasionally the scout would roll a cigarette and enjoy it. With the Indians, tobacco was a real luxury, used in spiritual ceremonies or to relax.

The next day, they departed right after daybreak, leaving behind them a small valley containing the bodies of two greedy men and one small boy. The slate gray cliffs shot straight up toward the heavens like sentinels standing guard over the burial sites.

Chris reflected on that as they left the site. He thought about the many piles of bones he had seen over the years, in the desert, out on the prairie, and up in the mountains. So many men—like himself—had left home at a young age and wandered toward the horizon where they saw the sun set every night. Colt wondered how many of those lost souls had wandered into a Comanche hunting party that didn't care for white-skinned intruders, how many had been struck by lightning out on the wide flat prairie, or how many had tumbled off a cliff into some lonesome gulch. The scout pictured families sitting at home for years, wondering about the fate of a sister or brother with wanderlust, one who hadn't answered any letters for a long time. He wondered if he might become one of those unnamed skeletons someday. Chris Colt asked himself how many people would miss him if he disappeared.

They pushed farther down the canyon, minds set on the far-off Snake River. Colt studied the young Nez Percé lad out of the corner of his eye. The boy sat his Appaloosa proudly, eyes straight ahead, and back very erect. His young copper body matched the rhythm of the spotted horse's movements, at one with the pony.

The boy noticed Chris looking his way and gave the big scout a quizzical look.

Colt chuckled. "Quite an equestrian aren't you, young man?"

"Huh?" the little warrior asked.

"Never mind."

Around noon, they came down out of the rough rocks and passed into a large gorge choked with hardwood trees and evergreens. Several ice-cold streams cascaded down the canyon walls and cut swaths through the forested gorge.

Chris Colt loved the smell and sound as they rode through the stately pines and firs. He heard Ezekiel chuckling and Colt turned his head toward him.

The young warrior said, "I see it on your face,

Colt. You are like the Nez Percé. You hear Brother Wind singing a song in the big trees and you like his words. There, hear it? That way, the *wapiti* calls far off. He wants to fight another, for he is truly a powerful warrior. Up there, listen to it, Great Scout, do you hear it?"

"A red-tailed hawk."

"He cries out to the rabbits down here," Ezekiel said. " 'Watch out! I am up here, and I am looking for you.' "

"How do you know that he is not saying, 'Please don't attack me, rabbits! I want to land down there, but I am afraid of you.' "

Ezekiel laughed loudly and said, "He would never say that. For he is the hunter, and they are the prey. That would be like the great Wamble Uncha telling these bad white-eyes that he is afraid of them and wants them to leave him alone."

The three men looked over at the boy, then the man. All three of them shook their heads, as if they had planned it like a synchronized movement.

Colt said, "Do you smell the bear, Little One?"

"Yes, his smell is on the wind which runs into our faces," Ezekiel replied.

Colt reined his horse and those of the other three. The boy stopped next to him and looked at Colt's eyes scanning, as a Nez Percé warrior would do. His gaze panned the ground in front of them, going from left to right, then rose a few yards farther and moved back to the left. He then looked even farther, his eyes moving left to right again, checking every little piece of foliage and terrain, looking for a telltale patch of fur. The herd acted very nervous.

"Señor," the Mexican bandit whispered, "what is it you look for you? Is it Indios?"

"Better hope not," Colt replied quietly without looking. "Now keep quiet."

His nostrils flared out slightly as he sniffed the air. To Ezekiel, he looked like a mighty bear himself, testing the wind.

The scout said, "He is between us and the ponies. See how they're moving forward fast now? They are beyond the smell and just want to get away. If he makes a charge, you take the horses and these critters, and I'll get between you and the bear and shoot him. No matter what, keep going."

Colt thought back to his first grizzly bear. He had been out with his father-in-law on a scout looking for a bison herd. On the way back to the camp circle they stopped in a stand of cottonwoods next to a creek. The two men were pent up in a tree for two hours by a very angry sow grizzly who had wandered along the creek bed with her two cubs. They would have shot her, but didn't since she had cubs.

Colt respected all the Indian nations because they lived with nature, not against it. Every tribe of warriors practiced conservation methods. In the early days, some tribes would arrange piles of stones into a giant funnel, then chase a herd of buffalo into it and run them over a cliff at the end. That was wasteful, but was about the only way they could harvest their meat then. After bows and other more sophisticated weapons were developed, they started taking individual animals. White men, on the other hand, were starting to line up on trains and shoot bison after bison from passing railroad cars. Such a demand developed for buffalo hides that buffalo hunters would kill thousands of buffalo. Then they wasted the meat, taking only the skins.

Chris felt the animal's presence, and it scared the heck out of him. It had to be close, but he couldn't see any sign of it. That scared him more.

Suddenly, with a tremendous roar and a rush, a giant silver-tip grizzly came from the thicket on the uphill side of the trail. This monster stood over eight feet tall on its hindlegs and weighed well over a ton and a half.

A grizzly, on level ground, could outrun a race-horse in a short distance, and this big bear was no exception. He closed the distance from the thicket in seconds and Colt barely had time to spin and fire from the hip, his bullet taking the bruin in the front left shoulder with little or no effect.

The bear slammed against the rib cage of War Bonnet, his teeth snapping, and a roar emanating from deep in his chest that reverberated through the canyon like the sound of a mighty avalanche. Colt flew sideways and the horse rolled once and bolted toward the herd and fleeing rustlers. The bear stopped and stood on its hindlegs, nose testing the wind, while he swung his watermelon-sized head from side to side.

Ezekiel hesitated and Colt yelled, "Go! Save the horses!"

The bear dropped to all fours and faced his small opponent again, and Chris raised his pistol, aiming at the bear's face. The bruin charged and Chris fired, the bullet glancing off the bear's skull, creating a crease along its head. The bear slammed into Colt and only the pistol saved Chris from the mighty teeth and jaws, as the bear bit down on the gun, mangling it.

The grizzly took a quick swipe at a sapling and

the tree splintered in half. Colt pulled his horn-handled bowie knife from the beaded sheath on his left hip and switched it to his right hand, facing the shaggy killer. The bear stared at Colt through his little pig-eyes, while big heavy breaths poured out from between spike-sized teeth.

Colt felt no fear. Yes, the bear weighed hundreds of pounds more than Colt and stood two feet taller. He could pick up boulders, and with his mighty forelegs he'd excavate an entire hillside just to dig out a tasty marmot. The scout, however, was a true warrior, and he was now staring death in the face. He was conditioned not to feel fear until the combat was over. Much like many of the cavalry troopers he scouted for and American Indian warriors he fought against, he would feel great fear when the danger had passed, but right now his head was clear. His nerves were steady. Adrenaline coursed through his body and he was prepared to match his wits and strength against this superior foe. He knew the odds, but he felt that he could not be defeated.

With a roar like Satan unchained, the bear charged. Colt stood his ground and the big furry body slammed into Chris with tremendous force, but Colt fell backward and let the big body pass over him, striking upward with full power and thrusting the big bowie behind the left front leg and into the buggy-sized chest.

With an agility that seemed incredible for its size, the grizzly jumped in the air with a loud roar and twisted its body at the same time, biting at the knife which was buried to the hilt behind the joint. He rolled beyond Chris Colt who lay unconscious on the ground, his head having slammed into a flat rock when the bear crashed into him.

Chantapeta, Chris Colt's late wife, wore a soft buckskin dress as she tiptoed into the tepee and wakened him with a large apple pie. Colt smiled and looked at the steam coming off the apple pie and thought about how good it would taste. Then he frowned while lying on his buffalo blanket. How could a Lakotah woman make an apple pie in a pie pan in the middle of a Minniconjou village? He couldn't figure it out, and it made his head hurt. He looked from the pie to her and she changed into the woman he now loved, Shirley Ebert. Long, naturally curly, auburn hair hanging down well below her shoulders, she had a smile that looked like it had been stolen off the face of a cherub. Chris felt better now, as he knew that Shirley's pies were the best anywhere. He was no longer puzzled, so he could just curl up on his buffalo robe and let his mind slip into the comfortable blackness again.

War Bonnet rode across the plains and Chris admired the long flowing white mane and tail, the eagle feathers floating out with the wind, muscles and sinews working across his black-and-white body. Head swinging proudly, the big horse jumped over a clump of mesquite and playfully kicked his hindlegs in midair. He slowed down as he got closer, and he started walking toward his master. The intelligent steed sniffed Colt's face, and Chris wondered how he had gotten on his back so suddenly. When he was watching his horse galloping toward him, he had been standing up straight and now he was on his back. He closed his eyes to sleep, but War

Bonnet stuck his nose under Chris's torso and prodded him, trying to lift him off the ground.

Colt opened his eyes and sat up straight. His head swam and he looked up at his horse. War Bonnet stood over him, and he was in a tree-covered gorge with steep mountain sides. The back of his head ached.

The grizzly bear! Colt reached quickly for his pistol and found his holster empty. His hand went for his bowie knife and it was gone too. Colt felt the back of his head and there was a lump there. He looked behind him and saw the rock he had hit it on.

Memory started flooding into Chris's mind. He had been attacked by a big cinnamon-colored bear, with silver-tipped guard hairs on its neck and shoulders. Colt had shot it twice and stabbed it with his bowie knife. He looked around and saw the bear lying about ten feet away. Colt made himself get to his feet, head pounding, and he ran to War Bonnet, vaulting onto the paint's back. He rode the horse about ten feet and spun him around. The bear didn't move.

Chris rode slowly forward and dismounted about twenty feet from the bruin. He picked up a large rock and mounted again. Colt threw the rock at the big animal and hit its side with a loud thump. The bear didn't move.

It suddenly dawned on Chris that his horse had come back to him and tried to lift him up with his nose. That's what had awakened him from his state of unconsciousness. War Bonnet pranced and snorted nervously as Chris rode him closer to the grizzly. He dismounted and moved slowly forward until he saw the handle of his knife sticking out of the bear's chest, just below the left front leg. The bear was dead.

By the year 2000, 2 out of 3 Americans could be illiterate.

It's true.

Today, 75 million adults...about one American in three, can't read adequately. And by the year 2000, U.S. News & World Report envisions an America with a literacy rate of only 30%.

Before that America comes to be, you can stop it...by joining the fight against illiteracy today.

Call the Coalition for Literacy at toll-free **1-800-228-8813** and volunteer.

Volunteer Against Illiteracy. The only degree you need is a degree of caring.